"C'mon, Kyle, there's no need for you to go."

Molly's chatty, no-one-could-doubt-that-we're-just-buddies attitude was beginning to get on his nerves. Sure, it was the safest strategy—but she was starting to carry it too far.

"I doubt your brother or your parents would like us spending this much time together in a motel room."

"Don't be silly. Daddy and Shane wouldn't care. After all, you're—"

If she called him "like family" one more time, he was liable to do something incredibly stupid. Like shut her up with his own mouth....

D0030876

Dear Reader,

Well, if there were ever a month that screamed for a good love story—make that six!—February would be it. So here are our Valentine's Day gifts to you from Silhouette Special Edition. Let's start with *The Road to Reunion* by Gina Wilkins, next up in her FAMILY FOUND series. When the beautiful daughter of the couple who raised him tries to get a taciturn cowboy to come home for a family reunion, Kyle Reeves is determined to turn her down. But try getting Molly Walker to take no for an answer! In Marie Ferrarella's *Husbands and Other Strangers,* a woman in a boating accident finds her head injury left her with no permanent effects—except for the fact that she can't seem to recall her husband. In the next installment of our FAMILY BUSINESS continuity, *The Boss and Miss Baxter* by Wendy Warren, an unemployed single mother is offered a job—not to mention a place to live for her and her children—with the grumpy, if gorgeous, man who fired her!

"Who's Your Daddy?" is a question that takes on new meaning when a young woman learns that a rock star is her biological father, that her mother is really in love with his brother—and that she herself can't resist her new father's protégé. Read all about it in *It Runs in the Family* by Patricia Kay, the second in her CALLIE'S CORNER CAFÉ miniseries. *Vermont Valentine,* the conclusion to Kristin Hardy's HOLIDAY HEARTS miniseries, tells the story of the last single Trask brother, Jacob—he's been alone for thirty-six years. But that's about to change, courtesy of the beautiful scientist now doing research on his property. And in Teresa Hill's *A Little Bit Engaged,* a woman who's been a bride-to-be for five years yet never saw fit to actually set a wedding date finds true love where she least expects it—with a pastor.

So keep warm, stay romantic, and we'll see you next month....

Gail Chasan
Senior Editor

Please address questions and book requests to:
Silhouette Reader Service
U.S.: 3010 Walden Ave., P.O. Box 1325, Buffalo, NY 14269
Canadian: P.O. Box 609, Fort Erie, Ont. L2A 5X3

THE ROAD TO REUNION

GINA WILKINS

Silhouette®

SPECIAL EDITION®

Published by Silhouette Books

America's Publisher of Contemporary Romance

If you purchased this book without a cover you should be aware that this book is stolen property. It was reported as "unsold and destroyed" to the publisher, and neither the author nor the publisher has received any payment for this "stripped book."

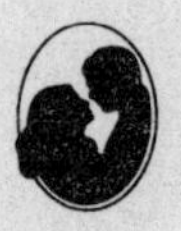

SILHOUETTE BOOKS

ISBN 0-373-24735-4

THE ROAD TO REUNION

Copyright © 2006 by Gina Wilkins

All rights reserved. Except for use in any review, the reproduction or utilization of this work in whole or in part in any form by any electronic, mechanical or other means, now known or hereafter invented, including xerography, photocopying and recording, or in any information storage or retrieval system, is forbidden without the written permission of the editorial office, Silhouette Books, 233 Broadway, New York, NY 10279 U.S.A.

All characters in this book have no existence outside the imagination of the author and have no relation whatsoever to anyone bearing the same name or names. They are not even distantly inspired by any individual known or unknown to the author, and all incidents are pure invention.

This edition published by arrangement with Harlequin Books S.A.

® and TM are trademarks of Harlequin Books S.A., used under license. Trademarks indicated with ® are registered in the United States Patent and Trademark Office, the Canadian Trade Marks Office and in other countries.

Visit Silhouette Books at www.eHarlequin.com

Printed in U.S.A.

Books by Gina Wilkins

Silhouette Special Edition

The Father Next Door #1082
It Could Happen to You #1119
Valentine Baby #1153
†*Her Very Own Family* #1243
†*That First Special Kiss* #1269
Surprise Partners #1318
***The Stranger in Room 205* #1399
***Bachelor Cop Finally Caught?* #1413
***Dateline Matrimony* #1424
The Groom's Stand-In #1460
The Best Man's Plan #1479
**The Family Plan* #1525
**Conflict of Interest* #1531
**Faith, Hope and Family* #1538
Make-Believe Mistletoe #1583
Countdown to Baby #1592
The Homecoming #1652
Adding to the Family #1712
The Borrowed Ring #1717
The Road to Reunion #1735

†Family Found: Sons & Daughters
**Hot Off the Press
§Family Found
‡The Family Way
*The McClouds of Mississippi

Previously published as Gina Ferris

Silhouette Special Edition

Healing Sympathy #496
Lady Beware #549
In from the Rain #677
Prodigal Father #711
§*Full of Grace* #793
§*Hardworking Man* #806
§*Fair and Wise* #819
§*Far To Go* #862
§*Loving and Giving* #879
Babies on Board #913

Previously published as Gina Ferris Wilkins

Silhouette Special Edition

‡*A Man for Mom* #955
‡*A Match for Celia* #967
‡*A Home for Adam* #980
‡*Cody's Fiancée* #1006

Silhouette Books

Mother's Day Collection 1995
Three Mothers and a Cradle
"Beginnings"

World's Most Eligible Bachelors
Doctor in Disguise

Logan's Legacy
The Secret Heir

Family Found
§*Wealth Beyond Riches*

GINA WILKINS

is a bestselling and award-winning author who has written more than seventy books for Harlequin and Silhouette. Ms. Wilkins has appeared on the Waldenbooks, B. Dalton and *USA TODAY* bestseller lists. She is a three-time recipient of the Maggie Award for Excellence, sponsored by Georgia Romance Writers, and has won several awards from the reviewers of *Romantic Times BOOKclub.*

It's Jared and Cassie Walker's
twenty-fifth wedding anniversary
and you are cordially invited to
the biggest bash in Texas!

After decades of caring and support
for their friends and family,
we want to honor these two lovebirds.
So, come one, come all to celebrate on the
Walker Ranch, Saturday, October 15!

RSVP with Molly and Shane Walker

Prologue

"Molly, give it up. Kyle isn't coming."

Molly Walker crossed her arms and glared at her half brother. "I want to try one more time to convince him."

Shane swept his Stetson off his head and wiped his dripping forehead with a bandana he had pulled from the back pocket of his well-worn jeans. Even at the end of September, it was still blistering hot in central Texas, and he had been working all day on the ranch he owned with their father, Jared Walker. Molly had caught him just as he was putting away the last of his gear for the day. She knew he was eager to join his wife, Kelly, and their two young daughters for dinner, but he was patient, as always, with his younger sister.

"You've sent two representatives to talk to him since we located him in late July. He sent them both back to you with a very clear message that he wants to be left alone. I know taking hints isn't one of your strong points, Molly, but even you can get that message."

"I'm just not sure he understands exactly what I'm trying to do for Mom and Dad. Having all their former foster boys together for a surprise silver anniversary party would mean so much to them. I know there are a few who can't make it, but we've got nearly everyone. Kyle's presence would make the party almost perfect."

"Not if he doesn't want to be here."

"Why wouldn't he? I know he was wounded overseas, but all the reports are that he seems to be almost fully recovered now, so that shouldn't be a problem. He was close to Mom and Dad, especially Mom. They were very fond of him. They went to his high school graduation. Mom sent cookies when he went to boot camp, for Pete's sake. He was a member of our family."

"No, honey. He just lived with us for a couple of years when he was a kid. Things change. Kyle changed. Maybe it was the war, or maybe just the passage of time, but he stopped calling, answering letters, making any attempt to stay in touch. Mom was disappointed, but she knew she had to let him go. Just as you have to do now."

She felt her lower lip start to protrude, and she made a deliberate effort to draw it back in. She would be twenty-four in just over a month. It wasn't particularly becoming for a twenty-four-year-old woman to pout. "I can't believe Kyle never wants to see us again. I just want to ask him one more time."

"So write him a letter."

"I'm not sure a letter would work. But he admired you, Shane. Maybe if you—"

"I can't go to East Tennessee to browbeat Kyle right now." He spoke gently, but firmly, his tanned face set into implacable lines that made him look very much like their father. "Dad and Cassie are leaving Friday for that cruise, and they'll be gone for three weeks. I've got more than I can handle here."

She sighed and nodded reluctantly. Shane would be extremely busy with Jared and Cassie gone for that long. It had been hard enough to talk Jared into taking his first long vacation with his wife. Only the knowledge that Shane would be here to keep the ranch running had made him finally agree.

"Send Kyle a letter, Molly." Shane squeezed her shoulder. "Tell him how much it would mean to you—and to Mom and Dad. But if he still chooses not to come, you're going to have to accept his decision. Don't let it ruin your pleasure in the party. You've already done so much. Dad and Cassie are going to be so surprised, and so pleased to see everyone you've found all together."

Molly wished she could be content with what she had accomplished in the past few months. But she couldn't get past the feeling that something was still unfinished. Something she was obviously going to have to handle personally—though she knew better than to express that sentiment to her overprotective and notoriously bossy older brother.

Chapter One

"Sixteen…ow…seventeen…damn it…eighteen…*hell.*"

The weights clattered against the concrete floor when Kyle Reeves dropped his legs and let the bar fall. He had increased the resistance today and the pain was too intense to go any further. The result was that he was now in a very bad mood—not that there was anything new about that. This particular bad mood had lasted eight months, three weeks and four days—give or take a couple of hours.

A clap of thunder rattled the windows, followed by another ominous rumbling that seemed to echo his disposition. Rain had started to fall, not very heavily yet, but steadily. It was supposed to storm this evening, and storms were always dramatic in the mountains. He rather enjoyed them.

Pushing himself off the weight bench, he limped

across the stark, white-walled room and stepped into a short hallway with oak plank floors and unadorned walls, also painted white. His cabin in the Tennessee Smoky Mountains wasn't large—two bedrooms, one of which served as his exercise room, one bath, a small living room and an eat-in kitchen. The furnishings were minimal, the decor Spartan, luxuries nonexistent.

The place needed some work—a few boards on the front porch had rotted, and cold air poured through numerous cracks around doors and windows—but the roof didn't leak, and the view from the redwood deck attached to the back of the house was spectacular. And best of all, as far as Kyle was concerned, there were no neighbors within sight.

Reaching the kitchen, he picked up a bottle of prescription pain pills, glanced at it, then tossed it back onto the butcher-block countertop. He shook two ibuprofen into his palm instead, popped them into his mouth and washed them down with a few swallows of bottled water.

He pushed a hand through his sweaty brown hair, leaving it standing in spikes. He caught a glimpse of his reflection in the shiny door of the refrigerator when he put away the water. In addition to his messy hair, he had a four-day beard growth, which didn't quite conceal the scar that ran down his left jawline. His sweat-stained gray T-shirt was paired with black knit shorts that bagged on his too-thin frame. No socks, but he wore a good pair of athletic shoes because he needed the support. He looked like hell—but since there was no one around to see him, he didn't really care.

As if in response to that thought, someone knocked on his front door.

His eyebrows shot up in surprise. He was hardly expecting company, and he doubted that his only real friend in the area, Mack McDooley, would have ventured up the mountain in an approaching storm on this Thursday afternoon. He was even more surprised that he hadn't heard a car engine, but he blamed that on the noise of the worsening weather.

The knocking came again. Sighing heavily, he limped into the living room and jerked open the door without bothering to see who was on the other side. "What?"

He'd have been hard-pressed to guess who looked more surprised at that moment. His visitor, in response to his curt greeting, or himself, at his first sight of the woman on his doorstep.

Even in the deepening darkness of the rainy afternoon, he could tell that she was stunning. Masses of red hair, dotted with moisture, tumbled past her shoulders to the middle of her back. Dark lashes surrounded large green eyes emphasized by smudgy eyeliner. Her perfect nose was decorated with a smattering of golden freckles, and her mouth was full and glossy. She was of average height, with a slender figure packaged in a snug green pullover and dark jeans that made her legs look a mile long.

He couldn't imagine what a woman like this was doing on his doorstep. "Are you lost?"

She eyed him speculatively before responding, and he had the uncomfortable suspicion that she didn't miss one detail of his grubby appearance. Not that he cared, of course. She would be on her way as soon as he gave her directions to wherever she was supposed to be.

But she shook her head, causing gold highlights to glimmer in her hair. "I'm not lost—at least, I don't think I am. I mean…are you Kyle Reeves?"

Hearing his name spoken in a distinctly Texan accent drew his frown even deeper. "Look, I've tried to be polite with you people, but you're carrying it too far. Tell Shane and Molly that it was nice of them to think of me, but I won't be attending their reunion thing. Make it clear this time that I won't be changing my mind—and I don't want to have to repeat the message again."

Though he'd spoken tersely, he could have been a lot less polite about it—and he was fully prepared to be, if she started getting pushy, regardless of her killer eyes and delectable mouth. It was only his lingering fondness for the Walker family and his reluctance to hurt little Molly's feelings that kept his temper in check—though he couldn't guarantee he could control it much longer.

Enough was enough.

Planting her hands on her hips, the woman cocked her head to study him more closely. Something about that gesture looked vaguely familiar to him, but before he could pin it down, she spoke again. "Do you mind if I come in for a few minutes? I didn't expect it to be so chilly here, and to be honest, I'm sort of cold."

Her three-quarter-sleeve shirt and jeans would probably have been plenty warm enough back in Dallas in early October, but on a rainy day at this altitude, a light jacket would have been appropriate. Still… "You don't need to come in. Go back to Texas where it's warm, and give Shane and Molly my regrets. It's that simple."

Lightning lit the purple sky behind her, flashing behind the distant mountains and making her damp hair seem to come alive for just a moment. And then the sky dimmed, leaving her in shadows again. "All I want is five minutes of your time. Surely you can spare that much, Mr. Reeves."

If he were really as hard-hearted as he was trying to be, he wouldn't be in the least affected by the slight tremor in her voice. He didn't know whether it was caused by cold or nerves, but it got to him. He wavered a few moments more, then mentally cursed himself for being a fool and stepped out of the doorway.

"You've got five minutes. Say your piece, but you might as well know I won't be changing my mind. At the end of your spiel, I'll expect you to leave and make sure that no one else bothers me about this."

"Thank you."

He noticed her taking in every detail of his living room, which was neat, if a bit dusty, and equipped with only the most basic of furniture, other than his treasured big-screen TV. A big fireplace dominated one wall, but he hadn't started any fires yet this season, so it was dark and empty behind the functional black screen.

The place probably looked stark and primitive to this hothouse flower. Good. Maybe she wouldn't be tempted to stay beyond her allotted time.

Though he didn't invite her to sit, she settled onto the battered, secondhand, brown leather couch, anyway. Much too conscious of her gaze on him, he made an effort to control his limp as he moved to the nearest of two brown-and-tan plaid recliners and sank into it.

"Let me save you a little time. You want to extend an invitation for me to attend a surprise anniversary party for Jared and Cassie Walker next week. All their former foster boys are invited. Shane and Molly are putting the whole thing together and little Molly will be very disappointed if I don't make an appearance. Has that pretty well summed up what you were planning to say?"

She laid one arm across the back of the couch, looking as comfortable as if she were a regular visitor to his home. "You've stated it pretty well."

"I've heard the pitch a couple of times before."

"I know."

"Molly and Shane are persistent, I'll give them that. I've never been so aggressively 'invited' to a party before."

"You were special to the family, and they've missed you. It would mean a great deal to them for you to be there."

"The Walkers have had a whole string of foster boys at the ranch. They won't miss one at their reunion."

"Everyone will have a good time even if you don't come," she conceded. "But it will be even better if you're there."

"I'm sorry, that isn't possible."

She studied his face a moment, then sighed lightly. "Then you're right. We should leave you alone."

Finally. He nodded curtly. "I appreciate it."

"Is there a message you would like to send to the family—other than to leave you alone?"

He found himself looking at her mouth. If she was particularly chagrined that she hadn't coaxed a commitment out of him, she wasn't letting it show. Her luscious lips curved into a slight smile as she gazed at him through those thick, dark lashes. A jolt of awareness shot through him, reminding him of the first moment when he had seen her and had been body-slammed by unexpected attraction.

He mentally shook his head and tried to concentrate on something other than how much time had passed since he'd been with a woman. "A message? I guess you can tell them happy anniversary for me. And you can tell Molly I'm sorry she went to so much trouble on my behalf."

One slender eyebrow arched in question. Her smile widened. "Why don't you tell her yourself?"

"I don't—" He eyed her expression. "Oh hell. Surely you're not—"

"You never asked my name," she reminded him. "Have I really changed so much?"

He felt himself sink more deeply into his chair. An uncharacteristic warmth flowed up his neck and onto his face. Kyle wasn't often embarrassed—and he was even more rarely taken completely by surprise—but she had just accomplished both. "You're Molly?"

She ran her fingers through her curtain of hair, never taking her gaze off him. "I believe you called me 'little Molly' earlier. Did you think time had stopped since you left the ranch almost a dozen years ago, Kyle?"

"How old are you?"

She seemed more amused than offended by the question. "I'll be twenty-four in a few weeks."

Twenty-four. He shook his head slowly in disbelief. Maybe he *had* thought time had stopped. On the rare occasion when he had pictured Molly, he'd remembered a freckle-faced carrottop with gaps in her teeth and dirt on her face. She had been a bundle of energy, chattering a mile a minute, tagging at her father's heels whenever he would let her—which was often, since Jared had been able to deny little to his only daughter.

Having no experience with gregarious little girls, Kyle had been rather intimidated by her then. He willingly admitted that she terrified him now. Talk about trouble in a nicely wrapped package....

"You're twenty-nine," she murmured. "You were almost seventeen when you came to us. You stayed a couple of months after your eighteenth birthday to finish high school, and then you left for boot camp. I was twelve when you went away. I was heartbroken, you know. It always broke my heart when anyone left us."

"I remember you cried your eyes out when the kid before me left not long after I got there. His name was Daniel, wasn't it?"

"Daniel Castillo—though he uses the last name Andreas now." Her smile turned radiant. "He's back in the family now. He recently married my cousin B.J."

"No kidding." He tried to focus on the conversation rather than the way her smile pushed tiny dimples into the corner of her mouth. "I remember her. Her name was Brittany, but she wanted everyone to use her initials, instead."

"Everyone pretty much does now—except her mother, who still insists on calling her Brittany."

"So she married Daniel."

Molly nodded. "It was a whirlwind courtship, and I think it's fantastic. They're perfect together—they always were, even when they were teenagers."

Kyle suddenly scowled, wondering what the hell he was doing sitting here listening to family gossip from Molly Walker—no longer "little" Molly Walker. If they kept this up, he would find himself all duded up for a silver anniversary party he'd had no intention of attending.

He shifted in his chair, and pain shot through his left leg and up into his back. The feeling was so familiar, he was able to hide his reactions from Molly—or at least, he thought he had, though her sharp green eyes had suddenly narrowed speculatively.

"Your five minutes are over," he reminded her, his bad mood returning with a vengeance.

* * *

Molly thought she had done a pretty credible job of hiding her shock at Kyle's appearance. She couldn't help comparing the man in front of her to the photograph that sat in a place of honor in her parents' living room, along with photos of the other foster sons Jared and Cassie had nurtured during their marriage.

Kyle's portrait had been taken at his high school graduation. Wearing a black cap and gown, a gold tassel dangling at one side of his tanned face, he had looked young and healthy. His thick brown hair had been freshly cut, and his amber-brown eyes gleamed with satisfaction. During her teen years, even as her memories of Kyle faded, Molly had found herself studying that photograph occasionally, wondering about Kyle, thinking that of all the nice-looking boys who had passed through her family home, his face had intrigued her the most.

Had she not known who he was when he had opened his door to her this afternoon, she might never have recognized him as the same person in the photograph. He was almost painfully thin, and he walked with a pronounced limp. The tan had been replaced by a rather scruffy pallor. His day-old beard did little to conceal the uneven scar that now marred his left cheek along the jawline. His hair was disheveled, and needed a good shampooing and styling.

For just a few moments he had seemed to relax a little with her, and she'd hoped that he was becoming more open to the possibility of attending the party. But then she had seen him flinch, as if in pain, and his expression had abruptly closed.

"I had hoped you would extend that five-minute deadline a bit once you figured out who I am," she admitted with a wry smile.

He didn't smile back at her. "I'm not trying to be rude, but you really should go before—"

A shatteringly loud clap of thunder drowned out his words, followed by a deluge of rain that hammered on the roof and rattled the windows.

"—before the storm gets worse," Kyle finished with a sigh.

Molly stood and walked to the window, rather surprised by the violence of the downpour. "Wow. It's a real gully-washer out there, isn't it?"

"To say the least. This is what remains of the tropical storm that hit the coast of South Carolina a couple of days ago. Haven't you been listening to the weather forecasts?"

She turned away from the window. "Actually, no. The radio is broken in my car, so I listened to CDs during the drive."

Though she wouldn't have thought it possible, his frown deepened. "You didn't drive here from Dallas?"

"Well—yes, I did," she admitted. "It's about a sixteen-hour drive, so I left at noon yesterday, spent the night in Memphis, then started out again this morning."

"Alone?"

She shrugged. "It was a pleasant drive. The weather's been nice, at least until I reached Gatlinburg, and I don't often have a chance to spend time by myself just to think and listen to my favorite music. And the scenery in this area is breathtaking."

"I can't believe your parents allowed you to make a drive like that by yourself."

Now it was her turn to frown. "First, I'm almost twenty-four years old, and I no longer have to ask my parents' permission to leave home for a few days. Second, I wouldn't have asked them, anyway, because I'm planning a surprise party for them and I don't want them to know I'm here. And finally, they left almost two weeks ago for a three-week Mediterranean cruise to celebrate their anniversary."

"Your brother didn't have a problem with you coming here?"

She cleared her throat, resisting an impulse to shuffle her feet like a kid caught in a fib. "I don't have to answer to Shane, either—but he thinks I'm spending a few days shopping in Houston with a friend from college."

"So he *wouldn't* approve."

"He didn't want me to pester you about coming to the party after you'd already declined a couple of times. And, no, he probably wouldn't like the idea of me driving so far by myself—but Shane tends to be overprotective."

"He always was when it came to you—and he didn't hold a candle to your father. I have a feeling Jared would pop a vein if he knew what you've done."

Molly was getting seriously defensive now. She had been trying for the past few years to convince her family that she was no longer a little girl to be indulged and watched over, but a competent young woman who could make her own decisions. She certainly hadn't expected to have that same battle with Kyle Reeves.

"I'll worry about my family's reactions," she informed him a bit curtly. "Obviously, I thought it was worth the effort for the chance to talk to you about the party."

"I'm sorry you wasted the trip. If you had accepted the answer I sent back by way of your representatives, you would have saved yourself a lot of trouble."

"I don't take no for an answer very easily."

His mouth quirked in what might have been the merest hint of a smile, though there seemed to be little humor in it. "From what I remember, you never did."

She waited through another rumble of thunder, which seemed to echo her annoyance that he still thought of her as the little girl he had known more than eleven years ago. "My parents were very fond of you, Kyle. Your senior picture still sits in the living room, and Mom mentions you every so often with such wistfulness in her voice. It would mean a lot to them if you would come to their party."

"I'm really just not a party kind of guy."

She didn't doubt that, especially now that she had seen the isolated cabin where he lived without even a telephone to connect him to the outside world. "I can understand that you might not like large groups of people—even though this will be a casual, no-pressure party where everyone will be welcome and should be comfortable. I think you might even have a good time there, if you would let yourself. But if you can't make it to the party, at least think about coming to visit Mom and Dad sometime, will you? It's important to them to know that their boys turned out all right."

An odd expression briefly crossed his face, as if it had startled him to be referred to as one of "their boys." He masked it swiftly as he stood and crossed to the window to look out at the worsening storm. She thought he walked with extra care, perhaps trying to control his limp.

For several long minutes, neither of them spoke, so that the storm seemed even louder inside the quiet room. It was obvious that she hadn't gotten through to Kyle at all; he had made it clear that he wanted to be left alone to brood about whatever had happened to him. She was beginning to feel guilty for having come at all, invading the privacy he seemed to value so greatly, ignoring the messages he had already sent.

She could almost hear her brother saying, "I told you so." She was sure she *would* hear those words as soon as she returned to the ranch and told him what she had done. "Maybe I'd better be going. It doesn't look as though the rain is going to let up anytime soon."

"I'm afraid you can't leave just yet." He looked glum as he made the announcement in a resigned voice. "You don't know how dangerous these roads can be in storms like this. Rain falling this hard and this heavily overfills the creeks that run next to the roads, causing them to wash over the pavement. The rushing water can sweep you right off the mountain if you don't know what you're doing—or even if you do, in some cases."

Molly looked at the window again, which was being pounded by windswept rain so hard it looked as if it were falling horizontally. She couldn't even see her car now. "Do you think it will last long?"

His silence was an answer in itself. She bit her lip and wondered how long she was going to be stuck here with a man who wished she were anywhere else.

Chapter Two

Resisting an impulse to curse, Kyle pushed away from the window. "I've been working out and I'm sweaty. I'll take a shower and then we'll decide what to do."

He didn't give Molly a chance to respond. Making an effort to control his limp, he crossed the room toward the hallway. Maybe he'd feel more in control of this situation once he had showered and taken a few minutes to recover from the surprise of finding little Molly Walker all grown up on his doorstep.

It was just his luck that she had arrived right in the middle of a storm. As much as he wished he could send her on her way, he couldn't allow her to head out in this weather. The steep, winding roads around here were tricky enough, but the risk of flash flooding was very real under these circumstances. He wished she hadn't come, but since she had, it looked as though he was going to have to play reluctant host for a few hours.

At least, he hoped that was all it would take until the roads were safe again. Unfortunately, it was late afternoon, and wet asphalt in the dark wouldn't exactly be ideal traveling conditions, either.

Though he was well aware that he was procrastinating, he took his time showering, shaving and dressing in a clean gray T-shirt and comfortably faded jeans. He even ran a comb through his wet hair—not because it mattered particularly how he looked, he assured himself. But being caught off guard had put him at a disadvantage earlier, and he wanted to regain the upper hand in this situation as quickly as possible.

Finally reassured that he looked presentable, he headed back down the hallway. He was having little success controlling his limp now. He had probably overdone the workout that afternoon. Had Molly not been here, he might have pulled out his cane for the rest of the evening, just to give the leg a rest. Needless to say, her presence meant that wasn't going to happen.

Molly wasn't in the living room. Since he knew she wasn't in the back of the cabin, that left only the kitchen. But the kitchen, too, was unoccupied and he felt his stomach tighten with nerves. If she had tried to leave, driving down the mountain in this storm…

The back door was ajar. Muttering a curse, he moved toward it, jerked it open and stepped outside. Protected from the downpour by the overhang that shaded half the deck, Molly stood with her arms crossed, watching the rain sweeping over the cloud-draped mountains. Dark, heavy clouds hid the afternoon sun, turning the landscape into a gray, impressionist scene that seemed to fascinate her.

"It's so beautiful," she said, though he hadn't realized until then that she'd heard him step out beside her.

He was tempted to agree with her. But because he was all too aware that he wouldn't have been talking about the scenery, he scowled and motioned toward the door. "Go back inside. You're so cold your lips are blue."

He wasn't exaggerating much. He could see the goose bumps on her arms, and the tip of her nose was pinkened by the damp, chilly air.

She gave him a look that told him she didn't like being given orders now anymore than she had when she was a spunky kid. "I'm fine."

He shrugged. "Suit yourself."

Maybe she felt as though she had made her point. Molly was only a few steps behind him when he walked into the kitchen. Kyle set the teakettle on a burner and pulled two mugs out of a cabinet. "I don't drink caffeine, but I have several blends of herbal tea," he said, waving a hand toward the assortment of boxes arranged for easy access. "Pick what you like."

He tossed an orange spice tea bag into a mug for himself, then stood aside so Molly could make her own selection. She debated for what he considered to be an absurdly long time over the six selections available to her before finally choosing cinnamon apple. By that time, the kettle was whistling.

Kyle carried his steaming mug into the living room, leaving Molly to follow if she wanted. She did—and her next comment indicated she had been watching him more closely than he liked.

"What happened to you, Kyle? How were you injured?"

"A close encounter with a bomb in the Middle East," he answered shortly. "I don't like to talk about it."

"How long has it been?"

"Eight months." And three weeks, and four days. And counting.

"I'm sorry," she offered quietly.

He shrugged with practiced nonchalance. "Don't be. I was luckier than the three guys who were with me and didn't make it back."

It had taken him a while to come to that conclusion, and there were still days when he wondered if his friends had been the lucky ones. He had learned very soon after the attack to hide those feelings, which always drew far too much attention from the military shrinks.

"Is that why you don't want to come to the party? Because you were hurt?"

"No."

She seemed completely undaunted by his curt tone. "Because if you're worried that anyone there will think less of you or pity you or anything like that, that would just be silly."

Kyle set his mug down with a thump and glowered at his uninvited guest. "Either you like living dangerously, or you're totally oblivious when it comes to taking hints."

Molly sighed and spread her free hand, cradling her tea mug in the other. "It's the latter, I'm afraid. Shane always says it takes a two-by-four upside the head for me to recognize a hint. He jokes, of course, but he's not exaggerating by much."

"Then let me put it in short, simple words you'll be sure to understand—I don't want to talk about this."

Molly blinked at him for a moment, then absolutely floored him by smiling broadly. "You sounded just like Daddy when he's in one of his grumpy moods. Maybe he rubbed off on you more than you realize."

Kyle was rendered almost speechless by that artless observation. Grown men had been known to pale when he had spoken to them the way he'd just snarled at Molly. And she just grinned and compared him to her daddy?

He wondered grimly how much longer it would be before the rain stopped and he could send her safely on her way.

The visit with Kyle was not going as well as Molly had hoped. She supposed she had been rather arrogant in thinking she could charm him into changing his mind about attending her party. She had thought a little friendly reminiscing, accompanied by a couple of soulful looks and maybe a few winsome smiles would accomplish exactly what she wanted.

That sort of thing always worked for Shane, she thought with a slight pout.

Amazingly enough, she didn't think even Shane could get through to Kyle at this point. It was a shame, too. Molly suspected that Kyle was a lonely, unhappy man who was just too stubborn to admit he needed anyone else.

She glanced at her watch. It was just before 6:00 p.m. and still raining heavily. Deepening shadows blurred the corners of the room now as dark gray clouds obscured the skies outside. Kyle reached out to turn on a lamp on a table between the two recliners. "Are you hungry?"

She was, actually. She had stopped for a light lunch

and a stretch break at just before noon, and she hadn't had anything since. "I'm a little hungry."

He put his hands on the arms of his chair and pushed himself to his feet. "I'll see what I've got."

Maybe this was his way of apologizing for snapping at her—not that an apology was necessary, since she was the one who'd tried to push him into talking about something that he'd already said made him uncomfortable. "There's no need to go to any trouble on my behalf."

He shrugged and kept walking. "I'm hungry. I'm going to eat, anyway—you might as well have something, too."

It was hardly a gracious invitation, but considering she had arrived unannounced and uninvited on his doorstep, she considered herself fortunate that he was being even somewhat tolerant of her presence. She followed him into the kitchen. "Is there anything I can do to help?"

He opened the refrigerator door. "I can handle it."

"I'm restless, Kyle. I'd like something useful to do to take my mind off the weather."

He sighed gustily and tossed something onto the counter with a thump. "You can clean the lettuce and chop tomatoes and cucumbers for a salad. I've got a package of pasta and a jar of pesto sauce we can have with it."

"That sounds good."

With one of his characteristic shrugs, he said, "I eat a lot of prepackaged stuff. I'm not much of a cook."

"Neither am I." She stuck the lettuce under running water to wash it. "I'm sure you remember how Mom is about her kitchen. She loves to cook, and doesn't like anyone underfoot when she's busy. Since I was always happier outside with Dad and Shane anyway, I never did much cooking. A few years ago, Mom decided belatedly that I should learn how. Maybe she waited too late, but it was not a raving success. After eating a few of my meals, Dad and Shane begged me to go back out to the barns."

She was babbling—but then Shane had always accused her of seeing silence as a vacuum begging to be filled.

Kyle didn't chuckle in response to her story, nor did he pause in his dinner preparations. For a moment she wondered if he had been listening to her at all, but then he spoke. "Do you still live with your parents?"

Something about the way he asked annoyed her. She had told him she was almost twenty-four. Did he think she had accomplished nothing for herself since he'd left? Oh, right—he still thought of her as "little Molly."

"I live on the ranch at the moment. I moved back full-time after I obtained my master's degree in education last spring at Rice University in Houston. I've been tutoring the foster boys we're housing now to bring them up to grade level while I wait for a full-time teaching position to open up in the local schools. I've been told a position should become available in January, and if it does, I'll look for an apartment then."

Again, she had given him way more information than he'd asked for. Maybe she was just the tiniest bit defensive about being unemployed and still living at home at almost twenty-four. She could easily have found a teaching job in the Dallas metroplex, probably, but the small school district closer to the ranch tended to have less turnover.

Her father had talked her into coming back to the ranch, rather than moving more than an hour away to live in Dallas. He had told her he needed her assistance now that he'd begun to take in more foster boys, turning the small ranching operation into a full-time group home for at-risk teenage boys. The truth was, Jared would be perfectly happy to have her live at home indefinitely.

"Shane still lives on the ranch, too," she added when Kyle didn't comment. "He added on to his house when he and Kelly had their two girls. Now he handles most of the livestock and general maintenance chores so Dad can concentrate on the day-to-day business aspects of running a group home."

"How many boys are in residence there now?"

She was pleased that he had asked a question. Surely that meant she'd piqued his interest, right? "There are four now, but we're approved to accept up to six. It isn't officially a therapeutic foster home, since we don't take boys with serious emotional or behavioral problems, just the ones who don't seem to fit in anywhere else. I know when you were there we could only take one or two at a time, but we've made some changes. One of the barns has been converted into a dormitory, complete with a dining room and a study area with computers for homework. That's where I spend most of my time with the boys."

"Still no girls?"

"No. They've decided to focus solely on boys, since having girls there would open up a whole new set of challenges."

He grunted, and she assumed that was an assent.

"So Shane has kids of his own now, huh?" he asked after working a few more minutes in silence.

"Two girls. Annie and Lucy. They've taken my place as the little girls all the boys become big brothers to."

Fifteen years older than Molly, Shane had been a grown man when Kyle lived on the ranch. Shane had already built his house on the property and had been busy with his own life and friends—among them, Kelly Morrison, whom he had married not long after Kyle left.

"The girls have Shane—and Daddy—wrapped around their little fingers," she added with a chuckle.

"That doesn't surprise me. So did you."

"I know." She smiled unrepentantly. "I was shamelessly spoiled—and now Shane's girls are being treated the same way. It's a good thing Kelly is more like my mom when it comes to being the disciplinarian, or Annie and Lucy would be little brats."

Kyle poured the strained, hot pasta into a bowl. "I saw your dad lay down the law to you a few times."

"Let's just say I knew exactly how much I could get away with before he drew the line. He got a bit more strict with me as I got older."

"I'll bet."

Had that been a note of amusement in his voice? Encouraged, she carried the salad to the round oak table that sat at one end of the narrow kitchen. "It's funny, but when it comes to the foster boys, Dad's the disciplinarian and Mom's the one who spoils them."

"I remember that, too."

"He knows so well what it was like to be an angry teenager, separated from his family and shuffled from one foster home to another. He knows what it takes to get through that anger and give the boys hope for their futures. His record of success has been amazing."

Kyle had the table set now with plain, mismatched dishes and sturdy flatware. Without asking, he filled two glass tumblers with ice and water, setting them on the table along with the bowl of pasta and a plate of bread.

The rain was still falling heavily outside, and for some reason the sound of it hitting the windows made their simple dinner seem more intimate. Falling back on her usual habit, Molly started talking again to ward off any awkward silence.

"I've never been to this part of the country before. It's really beautiful. How did you happen to end up here?"

Concentrating on his dinner, he shrugged. "I visited the area with a buddy and I liked it. When I had to choose a place to live after I got out of the Marines, I decided to come here."

"I like your house."

"It's small," he said. "Needs some repairs. A little isolated for some people's tastes. But it was affordable and it suited me."

"I think it's great," she assured him, entirely sincere. "The view alone is priceless. As for the location, it's not so very far from Gatlinburg."

He glanced at the window and the storm that raged outside. "Sometimes it seems farther than at other times."

Like now, for example, his tone implied. With the storms making the roads so hazardous, the closest town might as well be hours away.

After they'd cleared away the dishes, Kyle looked at the window again. "It looks to me as though you have two choices. I can try to drive you back down the mountain, or you can spend the night here and leave in the morning."

She crossed her arms and frowned at him. "You neglected to mention the third choice. I can drive myself down the mountain."

"Not an option."

"Why not? If it's safe for you to drive…"

"I didn't say it was safe. It would be a reckless and foolhardy drive with me at the wheel—and I know this mountain like the back of my hand. You'd never make it down. The best solution is for you to stay here tonight—but if that's unacceptable to you, I'll drive you."

"Why would it be unacceptable to me?"

He looked decidedly uncomfortable. "I wouldn't blame you if you have reservations about spending the night in a house with someone you barely know…."

She couldn't help laughing, though she doubted he would share her amusement. "Give me a break. I'm not worried about being here with you."

His sigh seemed to hold sheer exasperation. "Do you have *no* sense of self-preservation? You set off on a crazy, solo drive halfway across the country without telling anyone, then have no qualms at all about spending the night with a total stranger in an isolated house on a mountainside?"

"Kyle, you are not a total stranger. You were a member of my family for more than a year."

"I was never a member of your family. I just lived there for a while when I had nowhere else to go."

With that, he turned on one heel and stalked into the other room. Molly took a moment to admire how fluidly he moved, despite the limp—kind of a sexy, rolling gait that made her pulse rate increase before she shook her head and started after him. "So are you telling me I *should* be worried about staying here with you?"

"No, of course not," he snapped impatiently, throwing himself into a chair. "You're perfectly safe with me."

"So, what's your point?" She planted her hands on her hips to study him.

"The point is—hell, I can't remember." Slouching in the chair, he glared at his feet.

"Okay, then." She dropped her arms. "Since I have no intention of risking either of our lives on the road, I might as well crash here until the storm's over. I'll take the couch."

"Damn straight."

She giggled, even though she knew he wasn't joking. Funny how he could annoy her at one moment and amuse her at the next. Rather like Shane—except that she didn't in any way think of Kyle as a brother.

"I have a computer in my bedroom," he said, still looking grumpy. "You can send your brother an e-mail, if you want to."

"That's not necessary. He isn't expecting to hear from me today."

He shrugged. "Whatever you think best."

Exactly what she liked to hear—that someone thought *she* knew what was best for her. "I'll call him tomorrow morning, as soon as I have a cell phone signal."

"Fine." He glanced at a clock on the wall—the only thing he'd bothered to hang on the white-painted Sheetrock. "I don't know if you're interested in football, but there's a college game starting, and I was planning to watch."

"Go ahead and watch your game. You don't have to entertain me."

"I didn't intend to," he replied, reaching for the remote to the big-screen TV in one corner of the room—the only luxury he had apparently treated himself to. A few minutes later, he was engrossed in the game, leaving Molly to wonder if he was even aware that he still had company.

She wondered if his rudeness was his odd way of reassuring her that she really was safe from any unwanted advances from him. If so, she could have told him it wasn't necessary. Maybe *her* libido had kicked into overdrive when she had watched him cross the room, but he seemed totally oblivious to her, other than as an inconvenience.

She stood and wandered toward the windows, debating whether she wanted to risk going out to her car for her bag. A painfully loud clap of thunder and a gust of wind-driven rain answered that question.

One corner of Kyle's living room held a small bookcase, overflowing with paperbacks stacked two deep on the shelves. Since he was making so little effort to play the gracious host, she figured that relieved her of some of the rules of etiquette, as well.

Without asking, she knelt to scan through the titles. Thrillers, mysteries, science fiction, a little fantasy. No real surprises there, except for the sheer number of books. Living alone here as he did, so isolated in his mountain cabin, he probably turned to his books for company.

She plucked a promising-looking novel from the selection. "D'you mind if I read this while you watch your game?"

Without glancing at her, he gave a grunt that she assumed was an assent.

She curled up on one end of the couch and opened the book. She managed to read a page and a half during the next half hour. The writing was fine, the premise interesting—but when it came to holding her attention, the story could not compete with the reality of the man in the recliner a few feet away from her. He sat without moving, his full attention seemingly focused on the game playing on the screen, proving again that she wasn't nearly as distracting to him as he was to her.

He fascinated her.

Granted, her memories of him were hazy. She had been so young when he left, and there had been several boys in her family since. He had been quiet even then, standing apart from group activities. So many of the boys had arrived rebellious and angry at the circumstances that had landed them in foster care, but Kyle had kept his emotions carefully locked away. From what Molly had been told, he'd been obedient and cooperative, though so obsessively guarded that it had taken Cassie and Jared several months to coax a genuine smile from him.

Molly remembered his smiles. Perhaps because they had been so rare, and because she had been so accustomed to winning over everyone she met, she had been thrilled the few times Kyle had actually smiled in her direction.

Whatever their challenges, Molly had considered each of the foster boys brothers. Even though she had known from the start that their stays would only be temporary, she had still grieved each time one of them moved on. Her parents had protected her from physical dangers during her childhood, but they hadn't been able to prevent the heartaches that accompanied each departure. Instead, they had shared them—and then all of them had opened their home and hearts again to the next boy who needed them.

During the past year or so, she had realized that her

childhood had set a pattern for the way she interacted with the men she'd met as an adult. She had never had a serious relationship. It seemed that anyone who initially expressed a special interest in her had ended up seeing her more as a kid sister or close pal.

Her girlfriends had accused her of manipulating the situations to ensure just that outcome. They had suggested that she was commitment-phobic, or had her standards set too high. Her response had been that she was too young to get tied down to one guy.

While that had been the truth, she suspected there had been more to her reluctance to give her heart completely to anyone. But for some reason, she had always shied away from examining her skittishness more closely.

Oddly enough, it had been easier for her to see those potential suitors as brother figures than it was to think of Kyle that way now, even though he'd once been a part of her family. She had thought of the others as nice boys. Kyle was a man battered by experience, a soldier hardened by battle. He was only a little more than five years her senior, but she was painfully aware of the vast differences between his life and her own decidedly sheltered existence.

Did he still see a little girl when he looked at her? Unfortunately, he wouldn't be the only one who did.

Though he didn't look at her, Kyle was all too aware of Molly's eyes on him during the evening. He focused fiercely on the game, though he was unable to enjoy it as much as usual.

Why did she keep staring at him? He wasn't doing anything entertaining. He certainly wasn't that interesting to look at. Was she studying his scars, wondering how he'd gotten them? Was she comparing the man she saw now to the boy she remembered?

He could have told her she might as well stop looking for similarities. As far as he was concerned, that boy had died in a fiery blast in the Middle East.

When he could stand her scrutiny no longer, he gave a silent, mental curse and shoved himself to his feet. "I'm getting something to drink. You want any—"

Before he could complete the question, he stumbled, almost taking a nosedive straight down to the floor. His bum leg had locked up while he'd been sitting so self-consciously motionless, and now it refused to cooperate, punishing his too-sudden movement with a jaw-clenching wave of pain. He knew the spasm would subside if he stood perfectly still for a few minutes, then swallowed a couple of pain pills. He'd certainly had enough experience.

Soft hands clutched his arm. "Are you all right?"

He shook her off. "I'm fine. Just a cramp. What do you want to drink?"

"Why don't you sit down and I'll get us something?"

She could almost feel the embarrassment, frustration and anger seething in the look he gave her.

She took a hasty step backward, raising both hands in a gesture of surrender. "Okay. Fine. *You* go. I'll have whatever you're having."

It took every ounce of strength he had to force his feet to move and his legs to support him as he headed for the kitchen. Pain slammed through him with every step, but he kept his head high and his shoulders squared.

Life and war had left him with very little, but he still had his pride. It refused to allow him to show any further weakness in front of Molly Walker.

Chapter Three

It was all Molly could do not to rush to help Kyle into the kitchen. As the minutes crept by after he disappeared into the other room, the urge to check on him was almost overwhelming. Only the memory of the glare he had given her kept her in her chair.

He had looked hard and sort of aggressive, and she suspected most people would have been intimidated. Maybe a little annoyed that their instinctive offer of help had been so coldly rebuffed. Molly's reaction had been just the opposite. Her heart had twisted in sympathy for him, an emotion she had known better than to let him see.

A lifetime of experience with angry and bitter young men had made her quite skilled at reading pain—physical and emotional. She had seen both when she looked into Kyle's eyes.

A good fifteen minutes passed before he returned, carrying two cans of caffeine-free cola. Most of the color had returned to his face, she noted, but his eyes were still dark. Deep lines had settled in around the corners of his mouth, as though he held his facial muscles clenched.

She wondered what it was costing him just to keep moving. She would bet that if she wasn't there, he would be flat on his back and moaning right now.

Her knowledge of the male ego kept her from voicing any of her concerns aloud. She thanked him for the soda, then pretended to read again while he walked with carefully measured steps to the recliner.

She let a few more minutes pass, and then she yawned delicately, but audibly. "Gosh, I'm getting tired. It was such a long trip here."

After a pause, Kyle said almost offhandedly, "I'll go back to my room so you can get some rest in here."

She kept any hint of satisfaction out of her voice when she replied, "I don't want you to miss your game."

He shrugged. "It's pretty one-sided, anyway."

Pleased that she had come up with a way to send him to bed without a loss of pride—and making him think it was his idea in the process—she said, "Just don't leave on my account. I can wait until you're ready to turn in."

He gave her a look that might have held a hint of suspicion, but she kept her expression as unrevealing as her voice. His shoulders seemed to relax when he nodded. "I'll get you some sheets and a blanket. You can bunk down here on the couch, and I'll read in my room until I'm ready to turn in."

A very short time later, Molly lay on the couch listening to the rain that fell more gently against the roof now. With only a very brief "good-night," Kyle had retired to his room. She hadn't heard a sound from that direction since.

She hoped he had gone to bed—and that he had taken a pain pill or two while he'd been in the kitchen earlier. She knew he had some; she had seen the prescription bottles on his counter.

She supposed she would head back to Texas first thing tomorrow. If she left early, she might make the trip in one day. She would be worn-out when she got home, but satisfied that she had done absolutely everything she could to make sure her parents' anniversary party was perfect. She wasn't content with the results of her efforts, of course, since Kyle still refused to attend—but she had given it her best shot. That was all she could do.

Shane had accused her of being obsessed with Kyle Reeves during the past few weeks, so determined to convince him to attend the party that she couldn't think straight. This impulsive trek to Kyle's home probably proved her brother right about her mental condition. But now that she had made the trip and had a definitive answer, she should be able to put it behind her.

The funny thing was, now that she had actually spent time with Kyle, she seemed to be even more obsessed with him than she had been before.

Kyle's first thought when he woke the next morning was that the pain had mercifully subsided to a more manageable—and all-too-familiar—dull ache. The sleep and medication had done their stuff, letting him get out of bed with a minimum of discomfort and grumbling.

It was only when he reached the closed bedroom

door, which he usually left open at night, that he remembered he wasn't alone in his house. Grinding out a curse, he turned back toward the dresser to pull out a pair of gray sweats. He doubted that Molly would appreciate the sight of him in his underwear first thing in the morning.

Grateful to find the bathroom empty, he showered, but didn't bother with shaving. He had just shaved the afternoon before, and he saw no need to do so again.

Dried and dressed, he moved toward the kitchen. He found himself walking with much the same quiet caution he'd used in the military when he'd been braced for a surprise attack. Maybe he would find that observation amusing later. After Molly was on her way.

He stopped in the doorway of the living room. Molly was still asleep on the couch. Her long, red hair tumbled around her face and onto the pillow he had provided for her. She had kicked off her blanket, revealing the fact that she had slept in her clothes, removing only her shoes and socks.

It couldn't have been comfortable spending the night in her shirt and jeans. He should have offered her something to change into—a big T-shirt or something. But the thought of Molly sleeping on his couch wearing nothing but one of his shirts made his entire body clench.

Maybe it was just as well that he hadn't offered.

He reminded himself of who she was, and the way she had looked the last time he'd seen her. But, damn, it was hard to visualize a little girl when Molly was lying on his couch all warm and flushed and curvy. Those full lips that could go so quickly from sexy pout to blinding smile were slightly parted in sleep, and he could imagine all too well how sweet they would taste.

She sighed and nestled into the sofa cushions, drawing one leg up into a more comfortable position. Which, of course, only made him imagine how comfortably those long legs would fit around him.

That jarring mental image made him stumble backward, a near panicky retreat. He must have made some sort of sound. Molly stirred and opened her eyes. She smiled when she saw him. "Good morning."

Between the effects of her smile and the sleepy huskiness of her voice, it was all he could do to respond without stammering. "Morning," he said curtly. "Sorry I woke you."

With a rather feline stretch that drained the last of the moisture from his mouth, she swung her bare feet to the wood floor, then quickly lifted them again with a little yelp. "Cold floor," she explained.

He scowled toward the front door. "The weather stripping is shot. I keep meaning to work on that."

She had already retrieved the chunky clogs she'd worn the day before. Sliding her feet into them, she stood, tugging her shirt down over the waistband of her jeans. "You look as though you slept well."

He was glad now that he'd taken the time to shower and comb his hair. He hadn't liked showing any weakness in front of her the night before. "Not bad. You?"

"Surprisingly well," she said cheerfully.

The rain had stopped during the night and sunlight streamed through the east-facing windows. Kyle figured she could safely be on her way at any time, since the water ran quickly down the mountain once the rains ended. Cheered by the awareness that he would soon have his house to himself again—and would be spared any more inappropriate fantasies about Molly Walker—

he decided he might as well feed her before ushering her out.

"Want some breakfast?"

She nodded eagerly. "Sounds good. Just let me freshen up and I'll help you prepare something."

"I can handle it. Take your time. There are clean towels in the bathroom cabinet if you want a shower."

Because just the passing thought of Molly in the shower was enough to make him sweat again, he turned toward the kitchen. He needed to busy his mind and his hands. Immediately.

Mesmerized by the beauty of the washed-clean mountain scenery around Kyle's cabin, Molly was tempted to linger for a while outside when she retrieved her bag from her car. The air was chilly, but so fresh and clean it was almost intoxicating. Pearl-gray clouds hung low over the mountaintops, clearly demonstrating why they were called the Smoky Mountains. Rushing water tumbled over huge boulders in the creek that ran alongside the gravel road leading away from the cabin, and a full orchestra of birds performed in the treetops.

Forcing herself back inside, she showered and dressed quickly. As she checked her reflection in the steamy mirror over his bathroom sink, she mused that she could certainly understand why Kyle had chosen this place to hide himself away and heal.

She hadn't brought many clothes with her on this hasty trip, but she was satisfied that the pumpkin colored, three-quarter-sleeve T-shirt and low-slung, bootcut jeans flattered her. Not that she was trying to impress Kyle or anything, she assured herself as she fluffed her freshly washed and dried hair and checked her makeup.

By the time she joined him in the kitchen, he had breakfast already on the table. Her tummy rumbled in response to the scent of food filling the room. He was just setting out a container of orange juice when she walked in.

Something about the way he looked, standing there with the morning sunlight washing over him, his shaggy brown hair tumbling onto his forehead, his too-thin-but-all-male body encased in a gray sweatshirt and loose jeans, made her brain shut down. Before it kicked back into gear, she heard herself blurting, "No coffee?"

She answered herself as she belatedly remembered what he had said the night before. "Oh, that's right. You don't drink coffee."

"No. But I can make you a cup of herbal tea, if you want."

"Orange juice is fine." She crossed the room and slid into the chair he indicated for her. "I'm not all that crazy about coffee, anyway. I just drink a cup in the mornings out of habit. Daddy, now, has to have his coffee—entirely too much of it. Mom finally talked him into switching to decaf after noon."

She was babbling again. And as far as she could tell, Kyle hadn't heard a word of it. He had already started eating his simple breakfast of scrambled eggs, bacon and toast.

Molly drew a deep breath to steady herself and reached for the condiments he'd set out. Her spirits rose when she saw the container of Cajun seasoning—a mixture of salt, black and red peppers and garlic.

She reached for it eagerly and sprinkled it over the fluffy scrambled eggs. "Obviously you learned a few things while you were on the ranch—like how to season eggs."

"I learned a lot more than that."

She would have liked to follow up on that mumbled response with a barrage of questions about exactly what lessons he had learned from her parents, and about the memories he had carried away with him, but she knew better. Kyle would volunteer what he wanted her to know and that, apparently, wasn't much.

"Don't push them," her mother had once said when Molly asked how Cassie managed to connect with so many emotionally withdrawn young men. "You have to treat them like wild animals, in a way. Respect their fears and suspicions, knowing they've come from experience. Show them kindness and let them come to you in their own time."

It had worked for Cassie, as she'd had amazing success with her foster sons. Yet Molly had heard that Cassie's strategy had been a bit different when it had come to another wary, emotionally guarded male. According to Molly's aunts, Cassie had gone after Jared with a relentless, single-minded determination, giving him no choice but to fall in love with her and make her his wife.

Molly studied Kyle across the table, free to do so because he was pointedly not looking at her. If—hypothetically, of course—a woman wanted to catch Kyle Reeves, which method would be more effective? The patient, wait-until-he-comes-to-you approach? Or the no-holds-barred pursuit?

"Eat your eggs before they get cold," he muttered, letting her know he was aware of her scrutiny.

"I'm eating." She forked another bite of spicy eggs into her mouth to prove her point, then swallowed them hastily so she could ask, "Just one more question?"

He sighed. "What?"

"Don't you ever get lonely up here on your pretty mountaintop?"

"I've only lived here a little more than five months. Haven't really had time to get lonely yet."

"And when you do?"

He shrugged. "*If* I do—I'll find some company. In the meantime, I'm considering what to do now that I'm out of the Marines earlier than I'd planned."

It sounded as though he had planned to retire from the military. "Do you have any other ideas yet?"

"A couple."

When it became clear that he wasn't going to expand on that, she spoke again. "Do you plan to stay here in Tennessee or will you go back to Texas eventually?"

"There's nothing for me in Texas," he said bluntly.

She tried to recall what she had been told about his past. She remembered that his mother had died when he was a teenager, and that he'd had no other family willing to take him in. She didn't know anything about his father.

She thought he'd been assigned to a couple other foster homes before he'd come to the ranch. Cassie had said that Kyle was never a behavioral challenge, just so deeply withdrawn and introverted that his social worker had thought it would do him good to be placed with the easygoing and gregarious Walker family.

"When will you—"

"I thought you said there was just one more question," he cut in before she could finish asking more about his plans for the future.

"Sorry. I'm just curious about you," she admitted.

He grabbed his breakfast dishes and stood, his chair rattling against the floor. "Trust me. I'm not that interesting."

She didn't believe that for a minute. But she knew when to back off—at least, for now—so she pushed the rest of her questions to the back of her mind and gathered her own plate and fork. "Please let me do the dishes. It's the least I can do to repay you for your hospitality."

He looked for a moment as though he was going to argue, but then he nodded shortly. "Fine. Just leave them in the drainer to dry. I'll put them away later."

He didn't stay to keep her company while she worked. A few minutes later, she heard the television come on in the other room. It sounded as though he had tuned in a cable morning news program. She wouldn't have thought he was the type to be interested in politics. Maybe he would just prefer to listen to the Senate majority leader than to deal with any more of her questions.

The kitchen was spotless when she had finished. She tossed a damp paper towel in the trash can beneath the sink, unable to find an excuse to delay any longer. She might as well be on her way. She had a long trip ahead of her today.

She had just walked into the living room where Kyle was settled into his usual chair when someone knocked on the front door. Trying to hide her curiosity, she perched on the couch while Kyle crossed the room to answer. A stocky, gray-haired man stood on the doorstep, holding a large cardboard box in his hands.

"Morning, Kyle."

Kyle didn't seem surprised by his caller's identity. "Morning, Mack."

"I told Jewel I was coming up to see if you rode out the storm okay, and she sent a couple of casseroles for you to put in your freezer."

Kyle reached for the box. "Tell her thanks for me. She knows I'll enjoy them."

"Her cooking has put a couple of pounds back on you, but not near enough," the older man observed, eying Kyle critically.

Molly frowned. Kyle had *gained* weight? Wow, how thin had he been before?

"Come in, Mack, while I set these in the kitchen." Kyle stepped out of the doorway, and Molly wondered if she was correct in thinking he did so a bit reluctantly.

"I wouldn't turn down a cup of that herbal tea you like so much. It's right chilly this morning." Mack had gotten all the way into the living room before he spotted Molly. "Well, hello."

She stood, giving him a friendly smile. "Hi."

"Molly Walker—Mack McDooley." Apparently considering the introduction complete, Kyle disappeared into the kitchen with the casseroles.

Looking in the direction in which Kyle had just disappeared, Mack chuckled wryly before turning back to Molly. "Kyle's not much for conversation."

Molly laughed softly. "No, he's not."

Waving her to the couch, Mack took the nearest recliner and crossed his right leg over his left knee, looking completely at home. He wore a gray plaid cotton shirt and neatly pressed jeans with black socks and brown suede shoes. His skin was weathered, and his eyes were as gray as his hair and brows.

Molly guessed his age to be early to midsixties—maybe a couple of years older than her own father. Also like Jared, this man looked as though he was no stranger to strenuous physical labor.

"So, have you known Kyle long?" Mack asked, using a jovially paternal tone probably meant to soften the blatant curiosity behind the question.

"Since I was a child, actually."

"Really." That had obviously taken him aback. "I didn't think Kyle had any living family members."

"Oh, we're not family—exactly." Because she wasn't sure how much Kyle told anyone about his past, she wasn't comfortable mentioning that he'd once been in foster care. "Just friends."

"I see." But he obviously did not.

Figuring one good question deserved another, Molly asked, "Are you Kyle's neighbor?"

"Not exactly. I live in Gatlinburg with my wife, Jewel. She just about fretted herself silly last night worrying about Kyle up here alone in that storm. She was half convinced a tree fell on him during the night, crushing him in his sleep."

"Jewel shouldn't worry so much," Kyle said, coming back into the room. "It isn't good for her."

Mack reached for the steaming cup of tea Kyle offered. "You know how she is. Especially when it comes to you."

Though he hadn't asked if she wanted one, Kyle had brought tea for Molly, too. He handed her the mug, then settled into his recliner. She noted that he hadn't brought tea for himself, and that he sat rather stiffly, self-conscious in his role as host—a role she would bet he didn't play very often.

She was almost squirming with curiosity now. She wouldn't have expected Kyle to make friends like this in his relatively short time living in this area. As introverted and grumpy as he tended to be, she certainly wouldn't expect him to be all-but-adopted by a local couple.

No, there was obviously more to this relationship

than a recently instigated friendship. "Your wife sounds like my aunt Layla," she said in what she hoped was a subtle attempt to learn more. "She's the official worrier in our family—and it's a very large family, so we keep her busy all the time."

She was guiltily aware that Layla would have hysterics if she knew about Molly's long, solitary drive to eastern Tennessee. Of course, Layla would have to stand in line behind Molly's parents, brother and a couple dozen other relatives to yell at her for her reckless trek. And if her aunt Lindsey found out she had driven right through Little Rock without stopping to say hello—well, that didn't bear thinking about just now. Suffice it to say that Lindsey would not be pleased.

"Yes, well, Jewel doesn't have that many people to worry about anymore," Mack said quietly, giving Kyle a look that spoke volumes, if only she knew how to read it. "Kyle, here, is one of them."

Molly glanced at Kyle, who was looking increasingly uncomfortable. "I'm sure he appreciates her concern."

Her comment made Mack's somber expression lighten. "I'm sure he does. Maybe someday he'll even admit it to himself."

"Either of you ever hear that it's rude to talk about someone as if he weren't in the room?"

Both Mack and Molly smiled in response to Kyle's grumbling—not to mention the faint flush of embarrassment on his cheeks.

Mack took pity on him. "I didn't see any damage on the drive up. Still some water on the roads, but no travel problems."

Obviously relieved by the change of topic, Kyle nodded. "Good to hear."

"Did your roof leak?"

"No. The guy you recommended did a good job."

Mack grunted in satisfaction and sipped his tea. After a moment, he turned back to Molly. "I think I hear more than a hint of Texas in your voice?"

She chuckled. "Guilty. I grew up on a ranch outside of Dallas."

Mack's brows rose. "The ranch where you lived for a while, Kyle?"

Kyle nodded, and once again Molly had to struggle to hide her surprise. So Mack knew at least a little about Kyle's past. Interesting.

"I came to invite Kyle to a party—a reunion, of sorts—at the ranch next week."

Kyle shot Molly a look of reproval even as Mack said hastily, "Well, that sounds like fun. I'm sure you'll enjoy—"

"I'm not going."

Mack shook his head in disapproval. "Why not? It would do you good to get away for a few days, see your old friends. You're getting around real well now, so—"

"I've already informed Molly that I am unable to attend," Kyle cut in stiffly. His tone made it very clear that the subject was not open to further discussion.

"Well, that's a shame," Mack replied frankly. "I bet you'd have had a good time—if you'd let yourself."

"How's the renovation on the cottage coming along?" Kyle asked, very deliberately changing the subject again. "Made any headway since last week?"

"All the rain we've had the past few days hasn't helped." Mack seemed resigned to allowing Kyle to lead the conversation. "I'm hoping the guys can get back to work by midweek."

He turned to Molly, making an effort to keep her involved in the conversation. "My wife and I own a motel in Gatlinburg and a few cabins in the mountains. We rent them to tourists in summer and during winter ski season."

"Have you lived in this area a long time?"

"We both grew up in these parts. Bought the motel thirty years ago, and picked up a few rental properties along the way. Our son—well, he was going to take it all over eventually. He loved these mountains, especially in the winter."

His use of the past tense twisted Molly's heart. "Do you have any other children?" she asked softly.

"No. We just had the one son. We were both in our thirties when Tommy came along. To say he blessed our lives would be an understatement."

He had adored his son. It was written in the sudden softness of his face, and the deep sorrow in his eyes. Molly bit her lip, unsure what to say since she knew so few details.

Mack seemed to mentally shake himself out of his bittersweet memories. He smiled toward Kyle. "It's been real good for Jewel to have Kyle here to fuss over since we lost Tommy. Kyle was Tommy's best friend in the Marines, almost like brothers. We came to think of Kyle as a member of the family when he'd come home to visit with our boy. We were sure glad he let us talk him into buying this little cabin and staying close by where we could keep an eye on him while he recuperates."

Kyle cleared his throat—hard—and pushed himself to his feet again. "I just remembered that I have a couple of Jewel's empty casserole dishes in the kitchen. Let me get them for you, and you can be on your way,

Mack. I know you'll have things to do now that the storm's over."

He limped into the kitchen without giving Mack a chance to respond.

Chapter Four

After Kyle's abrupt escape, Mack gave Molly a quizzical look that made her giggle. "Guess Kyle's ready for me to go. He's not exactly subtle with his hints."

Nodding her head in agreement, she thought ruefully that Kyle would be pushing her out the door as soon as he'd gotten rid of Mack.

Mack studied her with frank appraisal. "It's a shame you couldn't talk him into going to the party. He spends too much time up here by himself. Not that I want you to take him back to Texas permanently, of course," he added. "I'm too selfish to want to give him up—for my sake, as well as for Jewel's."

"When did you lose your son?" she asked tentatively, wondering if she already knew.

He confirmed what she had guessed. "Almost nine months now. He was in the same explosion as Kyle. It was tough for all of us," he said, lowering his voice, "but Kyle's having a difficult time dealing with the guilt of surviving when Tommy didn't make it. Jewel and I are doing our best to convince him that we don't blame him, and that he shouldn't blame himself, but...well, it's been hard."

Molly reached out impulsively across the distance between the sofa and the recliner to lay a hand on Mack's arm. "I'm so very sorry."

He blinked a couple of times, then cleared his throat, set his tea mug on the coffee table and reached into his shirt pocket. "Want to see a picture of my boy? I always carry it."

"I'd love to see it."

Even though it had been encased in plastic, the snapshot was battered from much handling. Molly's throat tightened as she studied it.

Kyle looked so much younger in the photo, though it probably hadn't been much more than a year since it had been taken. He was smiling self-consciously for the camera, but he looked happy. Healthy. He stood beside a grinning young man with windblown sandy hair and Mack's kind gray eyes. The scenery spreading behind them was local, so they must have been on one of those visits home Mack had mentioned.

Her voice was husky when she returned the photograph. "He was a very handsome man. Like his father."

"I like this young lady, Kyle," Mack said, sliding the much-treasured photo back into his pocket. "A smart man wouldn't let her get away too easily."

Kyle scowled as he entered the room, holding two clean casserole dishes. "Tell Jewel I said thanks for the food, and that I'll be down to see her in a few days.

And thanks for coming by, Mack. It's always good to see you."

Mack stood and held out his hand to Molly, who had risen when he did. "It was real nice to meet you, Miss Molly. Maybe we'll have a chance to visit again someday."

She smiled at him, liking him immensely. "Maybe we will," she said, though they both knew it was unlikely. She doubted that she would have any reason to visit Kyle again after she left today.

It made her sad to think she would never see him again—so she decided to be optimistic, instead. After all, there was still a chance—however slim—that he would change his mind about attending the party.

Kyle escorted his friend to the front door, stepping out to chat for a few more minutes on the front porch. Molly couldn't hear what they were saying, nor did she try to listen in.

Meeting Mack had made her feel a little better about Kyle, in some ways. Kyle had seemed so alone before; she was glad to know he had someone nearby who cared about him. And whom he obviously cared about in return. Despite his gruffness, he hadn't been able to completely hide his fondness for Mack McDooley.

She understood a little better now why Kyle was so grim. Not only had he been seriously injured and forced to leave his chosen career, but he'd lost his best friend at the same time. It was no wonder he was angry with life in general just now.

Yet he had chosen to settle near his friend's parents, so he hadn't been able to cut himself off entirely from other people. Obviously, it had been a beneficial arrangement for all of them.

"I like him," she said when Kyle came back inside and the sound of Mack's car engine faded into the distance.

"He's a good man," Kyle said simply. "And his wife really is a jewel."

"You were close to their son." It wasn't a question, but her tone invited him to tell her about his friend if he wanted to.

Kyle picked up the mug Mack had left on the coffee table. "He was the closest I ever came to having a brother."

She swallowed, a little surprised he'd opened up even that much to her. "I'm sorry you lost him."

He was silent for a long moment, perhaps to make sure his voice was uninflected when he said, "So am I."

Without looking at her again, he carried the mug into the kitchen.

Remembering the two smiling friends in the photograph, Molly didn't try to follow him immediately. The sizable lump in her throat made it doubtful that she'd have been able to speak steadily just then, herself.

Kyle wasn't in any hurry to return to the living room where Molly waited. Though he was usually able to hold his emotions tightly reined around other people, seeing her looking at that photograph of him and Tommy with such sadness on her face had triggered his own grief again. He'd been able to push it back down, but it had taken a massive effort. He needed a few minutes to make sure the emotional barriers were firmly back in place before he rejoined her.

Before he could decide whether enough time had passed, she came to him.

"Is there anything I can do?" she asked, standing in the doorway watching him too intently for comfort.

Though he was well aware she wasn't talking about housework, he shook his head. "I've got everything cleared away in here. But thanks, anyway."

She bit her lower lip, and he found himself aching to smooth the faint marks her teeth left. With his own lips. Which only went to show, he thought in disgust, that he wasn't nearly as much in control of himself as he had hoped. Standing here wanting to kiss Molly Walker? Apparently he had temporarily lost his mind.

He had the odd sensation that the air was slowly escaping the room, leaving it hard for him to breathe. He tugged at the neckline of his gray sweatshirt. Glancing toward the windows, he cleared his throat. "Morning's slipping away."

She looked at her watch, then nodded slowly. "I suppose I should get on the road. It's a long drive back to the ranch."

"Too far for you to be making the trip by yourself," he grumbled, genuinely concerned at the thought of her making that long drive alone. But what the hell was he supposed to do about it?

"I'll be all right. I've got a car charger for my cell phone in case the battery goes dead, and a credit card for gas and expenses. My car's in good shape, and the tires are brand-new. The only thing that doesn't work is the radio, and I've got plenty of CDs."

CDs and a credit card, and she thought she was prepared for anything. Hell.

"Call your brother as soon as you get a cell phone signal," he ordered her. "Let him keep track of your progress this time."

She nodded. "I will. Kyle—"

He braced for the question he knew was coming.

"Won't you please reconsider coming to the party? It would only be for a few hours, and it would mean a lot to my parents. It would mean a lot to me, too," she added softly, her eyes so dark with emotion they were almost emerald.

It was more difficult to say it each time, but he managed to get the words out. "No, Molly. I can't."

"You can't stay up here brooding forever. Even Mack thinks it would be good for you to get away for a few days."

Not for the first time, it occurred to him that she was either the most courageous or most foolhardy woman he'd ever met. Didn't she know that wounded strays were likely to lash out at anyone who reached out to them? If she had cornered him like this only a couple of months earlier, she'd have been lucky to escape unscathed.

Fortunately, he'd recovered somewhat since then—both physically and emotionally—so he simply gave her a cool look and said, "I know best what's good for me."

Her lips twisted into a little smile that looked very sad. "I'm sure you believe that."

She'd always had a tender heart. He remembered how easily she had cried as a child—rarely for herself, that he remembered, but usually when someone else had been hurt or upset. Now she'd apparently decided that he deserved her sympathy. He could almost feel his male ego shriveling in response to the pity he was afraid he saw in her eyes.

But, because she was Molly, he couldn't be angry with her. Anyone else, maybe—but not her. "I'll help you carry your bags, out," he offered, his tone uncharacteristically gentle.

She seemed to give herself a little shake. "I only have one. I can handle it."

He remained where he was when she turned to go collect her things. She would be on her way very shortly. And then his life could get back to normal. And he was *not* sitting up here "brooding," he assured himself with a touch of defiance. He stayed busy. He worked out, he did repairs on the house, he read and researched possible paths for his future.

He had offers—Mack was urging him rather persistently to join him in the rental business, for example. Or he could go back to school on the military's tab, studying anything that interested him.

Maybe he had gotten a raw deal, but he wasn't brooding and he didn't need her to rescue him. It was bad enough that Mack and Jewel fretted over him so much, a situation he tolerated only because he knew they needed to do so.

No, he had enough people in his life for now. Molly had plenty of others to cater to her—her parents, her brother and his family, all those aunts, uncles and cousins he remembered, the other foster boys who had probably all stayed close to the Walker family.

She probably had a boyfriend. A lover, he corrected himself, belatedly remembering her age. At least one, considering the way she looked. Hell, guys were probably lined up at her door.

It must have been a new experience for her to have to drive across two and a half states to practically beg a man to visit her.

Her green overnight bag was slung over her shoulder, and her car keys were in her hand. She was going. And the fact that his first instinct was to throw himself in front of the door to bar her way was proof that she wasn't leaving too soon.

"You'll be careful?" He tried to speak brusquely, but he wasn't sure he was entirely successful.

"I'll be careful." She moistened her lips, then held out a hand to him. "I wrote down all the numbers at the ranch and my own cell number. Our e-mail address is on here, too. Maybe you could call or drop us a line sometime—just to let us know how you're doing."

"You sent me all that information when you invited me to the party the first time." But he took the folded sheet of paper, anyway, since she had gone to the trouble of writing it all out for him.

"Just hang on to the list." She smiled faintly. "Maybe you'll decide you want to use it someday."

"Maybe I will." He supposed anything was possible. Maybe someday when he was in peak shape again, more certain of his future, better able to face his past—both recent and distant—maybe he'd get a yen to visit the ranch.

Or maybe not.

"It was good to see you again, Molly," he said awkwardly, feeling the need to send her off on a positive note. "Say hello to Shane for me—and tell your parents I wish them a happy anniversary."

"I will." She hesitated a moment, and then she moved toward him. He was startled when she gave him a quick, firm hug, her head nestling naturally into his shoulder, the overnight bag bumping his hip. "Take care of yourself, Kyle."

His arms rose reflexively to encircle her. He knew she came from a family of huggers, and that despite his arguments to the contrary, she still considered him a member of her family. Yet as hard as he struggled to think of *her* that way, his long-deprived body still reacted very strongly to having a soft, curvy, sweet-smelling woman pressed closely against it.

He released her and stepped back a bit too quickly before he embarrassed himself. The jolt of pain through his leg in response to the jerky movement helped rouse him out of the mental paralysis her unexpected hug had sent him into. "You'd better get going," he said, his voice husky, his arms itching to reach for her again. "You've got a long drive ahead."

Back to her real life, he added silently. Back to the men who were whole in body and spirit and who were probably waiting to offer her anything she wanted. Everything she deserved.

Her eyes seemed unnaturally bright when she turned away. Kyle's chest felt as though someone were still squeezing him—this time in a grip tight enough to hurt.

Molly paused for a moment at the door, her hand on the knob, and then she squared her shoulders and stepped outside without another word. The door closed firmly behind her.

Kyle let the curse that had been building inside him escape in a sibilant hiss that seemed to echo in the sudden silence inside his house. He turned abruptly toward the kitchen. Maybe a cup of tea would ease the tightness in his chest and throat. After that, he would—

A sharp crack came from outside the front door, simultaneously accompanied by a startled cry. Moving faster than he had in the past eight months, Kyle ran for the door and threw it open.

Molly lay sprawled on the front porch. Her overnight bag had tumbled to the ground, and one of her shoes lay beside it. Her right leg was twisted painfully beneath her, the foot stuck in a hole created when a rotten board had given way beneath her weight.

Her face was utterly colorless, making her white skin stand out in sharp contrast to her fiery hair. She looked up at him through a film of tears she was doing her best to hold back. "I think my leg is broken."

Molly sat on a paper-covered medical examination table, her bandaged right foot stuck out in front of her. She wore a thin cotton hospital gown over her undergarments. She doubted that her jeans would fit over the Velcro-fastened walking brace that now covered her right leg halfway up to the knee.

She was fortunate that there had been no broken bones, though her ankle was badly sprained. Her lower leg was swollen and her bare toes looked almost purple beneath the brace. She had the strangest feeling that she should be in pain. She could actually feel a distant throbbing, but it seemed almost disconnected from her body.

So did her injured foot, for that matter. She gazed at it in fascination as it appeared to float at the end of her leg. "Wow."

"What's wrong?" Kyle had been hovering nearby, watching her with a deeply concerned frown, but he moved closer when she spoke. "Are you hurting?"

"No. I just feel strange." She gave him a smile. He had such pretty eyes. "You're sweet to worry about me."

His expression turned suddenly wry. "You're floating on pain pills. Why do I get the feeling you have a low tolerance for medications?"

She heard herself giggle, though she tried to suppress it. "That's why I tried to tell everyone I didn't need any pain meds, though no one would listen. Shane says I can get high on aspirin. He says it's a good thing I've never wanted to experiment with drugs or booze, since I'd probably be a real cheap drunk."

"Sounds like you need to listen to your brother."

"I'm sure he would agree with you. Is it cold in here to you?"

"Here." He reached for the thin white blanket that lay behind her on the exam table and wrapped it around her. "Is that better?"

"Um-hmm." She snuggled into the blanket's warmth, wishing she could nestle so comfortably into Kyle's arms. She would bet he radiated heat—but she wasn't quite high enough to throw away all remnants of her common sense.

"The nurse should be back to release you soon, so we can get out of here."

He looked as though it couldn't be soon enough to suit him. Kyle seemed to have a pathological aversion to medical facilities. She suspected he had spent far too much time in them during the past nine months.

"Am I supposed to wear this gown out of here?" she asked, only marginally concerned. "I don't think I can get my jeans on over this cast thingy."

"I'm taking care of that."

Someone tapped tentatively on the door.

"Come in," Molly sang out, looking expectantly that way.

The door opened and Mack McDooley entered, along with a tiny, silver-haired woman who had to be his wife. The woman carried a bulging shopping bag in her arms.

"Mack!" Molly greeted him with genuine, if drug-enhanced, pleasure. "What are you doing here?"

"Kyle called us from a hospital pay phone. I'm sorry you were hurt. How are you doing now?"

"It's my fault," Kyle muttered grimly, before she could answer. "I knew there were rotten boards on the porch but I forgot to warn her about them."

Molly sighed gustily. "Will you stop blaming yourself? I slipped on a wet spot and my foot went through a board. It wasn't your fault, Kyle. It's wasn't anyone's fault. Just an accident."

"Molly," Mack said quickly, cutting off the argument Kyle looked prepared to make, "I'd like you to meet my wife, Jewel. Honey, this is Kyle's friend, Molly Walker."

"It's nice to meet you, Molly. Mack told me all about his visit with you this morning. He was quite taken with you." Jewel spoke in a rich, slow Southern drawl that wrapped around Molly like another warm blanket. "I'm sorry we had to meet under these circumstances. I've brought you something to wear out of the hospital."

"That was so sweet of you." What a nice lady, Molly thought, beaming at Kyle's friends. What a nice couple. Heck, *everyone* around here was nice, judging from how well she had been treated since Kyle brought her in.

"They gave her something for pain," Kyle explained quietly to the McDooleys. "She's kind of out of it."

"I am not," she protested, turning to him so quickly she would have tipped over if he hadn't steadied her. And then she ruined her indignant denial by giggling again.

"Why don't you and I step outside, Kyle, and Jewel can help Molly get dressed."

Kyle nodded in response to Mack's suggestion, though he lingered a bit longer at Molly's side. "You'll be okay?"

She rolled her eyes. "I don't need you to help me get dressed, if that's what you mean."

His slight flush amused her again. Muttering something she didn't quite catch, he stepped outside with Mack, letting the door swing shut behind them.

Molly shook her head. "The way he's carried on, you'd think I'd done major damage to myself rather than just tearing a ligament in my ankle."

Jewel set the bag on a chair and reached into it. "He's feeling bad about you being hurt at his house. It must have scared him half to death when you fell."

"I think he was more scared than I was," Molly confided, remembering how Kyle's hands had trembled when he had helped her up and assisted her to her car. She had tried to be brave, as much for his sake as for her own, but she hadn't been able to suppress the occasional gasp of pain. Each time she'd moaned, he had gone a shade paler.

The drive down the mountain to the nearest medical facility had been accomplished at breakneck speed, making her worry that neither of them would arrive in one piece. When they'd reached the hospital, Kyle had told her to remain in the car while he'd dashed inside to fetch someone with a wheelchair. He had then proceeded to snap orders at everyone who had come near her—orderlies, nurses and doctors alike—until someone had sent him out of the room while she was treated. He hadn't been allowed back in until they'd finished with her.

Jewel held up a pair of wide-legged gray fleece pants with hot pink piping and a drawstring waistband. "I figured a drawstring would help them fit better if I guessed your size wrong from Kyle's description of you. The wide legs should fit over your brace without any problems."

"They're perfect," Molly exclaimed, though she

couldn't help wondering how Kyle had described her. "They look very comfortable."

Smiling, Jewel pulled another garment out of the bag, this one a long-sleeved hot pink T-shirt that matched the piping down the sides of the pants. "I didn't know if you'd torn your blouse when you fell, so I bought the whole set. Kyle neglected to mention that you're a redhead, but fortunately, this color will look fine on you. There's another set in the bag, in navy with a lime-green shirt."

"This was so sweet of you." Molly was aware that she was overusing the word sweet, but it seemed to be fixed firmly in her medication-clouded brain. "I'll reimburse you for the clothes, of course."

"Kyle's taking care of that."

As she allowed Jewel to help her into the clothes, Molly decided that she would argue with Kyle about that later. He was already paying the medical bills, assuring her that his homeowner's insurance would cover them. He shouldn't feel that he had to buy her clothes, too.

The sporty outfit fit very well. Molly felt much better once she was fully dressed and could set the drafty hospital gown aside. A nurse came in, had her sign some papers, then bustled out again, promising to be right back with a pair of crutches.

Molly sighed. "I'm beginning to wonder if I'm ever going to get out of here."

Jewel patted her arm sympathetically. "That's the thing about hospitals. They run on their own time."

Looking down at her injured leg again, Molly groaned.

"Is your leg hurting, hon?"

"Not really. I was just thinking about what a mess I've

gotten myself into this time. I have to call my brother, and he's going to chew me out for being here at all, much less doing something stupid like spraining my ankle. I'm not sure I can drive in this brace thing, so I don't know how I'm getting back to Texas. And I've caused poor Kyle so much trouble already, nagging him to attend a party he said all along he didn't want to go to."

Jewel's hand tightened bracingly on Molly's arm. "Now, don't you be fretting about Kyle. You were right to invite him to that party, and if he knew what was best for him, he'd go. As for spraining your ankle, surely no one would blame you for that."

"You haven't met my brother."

After a quick, sharp rap of warning, Kyle came back into the room, followed closely by Mack. Kyle nodded in approval when he saw Molly's comfortable and practical outfit. "Thanks, Jewel. I know you'd come through."

"It was my pleasure." Giving Molly's arm a final, friendly pat, Jewel moved away to allow Kyle to take her place. "The nurse is bringing crutches so Molly can leave. I think you should both come to our house. It's past lunchtime and I'm sure everyone is hungry."

"*I'm* hungry!" Molly placed a hand on her stomach.

Jewel nodded as if everything were settled. "Mack and I will go get lunch started. You two follow as soon as you can get away from here."

"Looks like we have our orders," Kyle murmured when the older couple had left the room.

"They're so sweet." The medication was making Molly drowsy. She blinked heavy eyelids and leaned against Kyle's shoulder for support. After only a moment, his arm went around her.

She knew he was simply steadying her. A friendly, platonic gesture—but it felt good to be held by him, anyway.

Carrying a pair of metal crutches and pushing a wheelchair, the nurse returned. "You can ride out in this, then use the crutches when you get home."

Molly wrinkled her nose as she studied the wheelchair. "I'd rather walk out on my own, thank you."

"Get in the wheelchair," Kyle murmured. "You'll likely spend the next few weeks on those crutches. You'll be plenty ready to get rid of them as soon as you can."

The memories mirrored in his eyes showed her he knew exactly how important it was for her to assert her independence again. She wondered how long he had been on crutches. She knew he must have hated every minute that he had been incapacitated.

This, she thought with a sigh, was not at all the way she would have chosen to bond with him.

Chapter Five

The McDooleys lived in a small but comfortable house behind the office of the picturesque motel tucked into a hillside near downtown Gatlinburg. The town, itself, was a prime tourist spot, the streets crowded with restaurants, miniature golf courses, candy stores and boutiques filled with souvenirs and craft items.

A large aquarium was a main draw, along with an observation tower and a ski lift that rose from the main thoroughfare into the mountains that loomed over the town. A gondola lift carried tourists upward in another direction, disappearing into the more distant mountains.

Even in town, Molly was delighted to see the numerous streams she already associated with this area. Swollen by the rains, they rushed along the sides of the roads and flowed through the center of town beneath bridges and pedestrian walkways. Gazing up at the mountaintops, hearing the sound of splashing water always in the background, she could see why Kyle had chosen this beautiful and peaceful place for his recuperation.

She would have loved to spend an entire day exploring every cranny of the inviting town, and several more trekking through the mountains and nearby park areas. She was thoroughly disgruntled with the way her spur-of-the-moment trip had turned out.

Framed photographs of Tommy McDooley covered the walls and most of the flat surfaces of his parents' home. From infancy to military service, every stage of his life had been documented and was lovingly displayed. A few snapshots of Kyle were mixed in with his friend's. In most of them, he stood at Tommy's side, or slightly behind him. But there were a couple of shots of Kyle alone, proving that the McDooleys considered him a member of this family.

Awkwardly balanced on her crutches, Molly circled the living room, studying the photographs while Kyle hovered behind her, poised to catch her if she stumbled. Jewel was in the kitchen finishing lunch preparations, having firmly declined offers of help. Mack had excused himself for a few minutes to check on a new employee in the motel office.

Molly paused in front of a photograph of Tommy with his parents. "Tell me about Tommy. What was he like?"

"He was..." Kyle looked at the picture, a muscle working in his jaw. "He was a great guy."

It wasn't much of an answer, and he seemed to know it. But she could tell by his expression that he simply couldn't say anything more just then. There was so much pain in his eyes when he looked at his friend's photograph that it made her own fill with tears. She turned away quickly to hide them, nearly overbalancing on her crutches.

Kyle caught her elbow to steady her. "You can't move that quickly on these things," he said, his voice gruff. "You'll fall flat on your face."

"They're a pain in the…leg," she amended quickly. "But I guess I'll get used to them eventually."

"You'll never get used to them," he corrected her. "You'll just learn to use them better."

"How long did you have to use crutches after you hurt your leg?"

"Too long," he said shortly.

"Were you—"

"You really should sit down," he cut in, motioning toward the deep-cushioned, floral couch against one wall of the tidy living room. "The doctor told you to keep that foot elevated for the rest of the day. You're supposed to have an ice pack on it, too. I'll go get you one."

"I'm keeping the weight off my ankle by leaning on the crutches," she reminded him, but she moved toward the couch, anyway. To be honest, her arms were starting to get tired—and her entire body ached as a result of the jarring fall. She saw no need to mention either of those facts to Kyle; he would just start feeling guilty again.

The couch was so soft that she sank deeply into it. Kyle insisted on propping her foot on a pillow on the oak coffee table. Though she felt rather foolish, she didn't argue with him. She lay back against the cushions and nodded when he said he was going to get an ice pack.

Left alone in the silence of the living room, Molly focused on a portrait of Tommy in his dress uniform. He'd had such a nice smile.

She wished she could have met him, she mused, her eyelids getting heavy as the medications combined with the shock of the accident sapped her of any remaining energy. She would have given anything to spare Kyle the heartache she had seen in his beautiful brown eyes.

It wouldn't have been too difficult to talk Kyle into taking a pain pill, himself. He hurt all over. He'd overdone it trying to half carry Molly to her car after she'd fallen. Then, unable to sit still long enough to rest his leg, he'd paced restlessly through the hallways of the hospital while she'd been treated.

Hadn't they been a pair this afternoon, he thought with a disgruntled shake of his head as he headed back to the living room to tell Molly that lunch was ready. The lame helping the lame—he limping on his left leg, Molly on her right. He hadn't even been able to carry her to his car. Some hero.

Not that he'd ever wanted to be a hero, he reminded himself. All he'd ever aspired to was to do his job, earn his promotions while serving his country, hang out with a few good friends, enjoy the present and let the unhappy past fade into oblivion. A deadly explosion had turned those vaguely pleasant daydreams into a pile of ashes.

He had just opened his mouth to speak to Molly when he saw that she had fallen asleep on the couch. Holding the towel-covered ice pack, he stared at her, wondering if he should wake her or let her sleep. She looked so relaxed. The medications she had tried to refuse at the hospital had obviously knocked her for a loop.

"Let her sleep," Jewel said softly from behind him, looking around him toward the couch. "She's obviously tuckered out. I can heat up her lunch when she wakes up."

"Maybe she'd rather I wake her." Kyle knew he wouldn't like being in her position, sound asleep while others made decisions on her behalf. But maybe Molly wasn't as much of a control freak as he was.

"The rest will be good for her. Come on into the kitchen and have some..."

A sudden, muffled ringing interrupted her words. Kyle and Jewel both looked around in confusion for the source of the sound. Jewel found it first. She snatched up Molly's soft leather handbag, which Kyle had carried in from the car for her, and held it out to him. "I think it's her cell phone."

He glanced toward the couch. Molly hadn't stirred. Guessing the caller was her brother, and figuring Shane would worry if he couldn't reach his sister, Kyle handed Jewel the ice pack, then stepped into the hallway. He dug into the purse and pulled out the phone.

Maybe he was overstepping his bounds here, but he couldn't just let the phone keep ringing. "Hello?"

"Is this Molly Walker's phone?" a man's voice asked.

Kyle leaned against a wall of the hallway, recognizing the distinctive drawl even after so many years. "Shane?"

"Yeah. Who's this?"

He hesitated a moment before drawing a deep breath and saying, "It's Kyle Reeves, Shane."

"Kyle? Well, I'll be— It's good to hear your voice again. How are you? I heard you found yourself some trouble over in the Middle East."

"Yeah, you could say that." Kyle appreciated Shane's matter-of-fact phrasing. "But I'm doing okay. Almost back to full speed again."

He figured it wasn't much of a lie.

"Glad to hear it. Uh—you mind telling me why you're answering Molly's cell phone? Where is she, anyway?"

"She's here with me. In Tennessee."

Shane groaned loudly. "I cannot believe this. You mean she flew all the way to Tennessee just to—"

"She didn't fly, Shane. She drove."

There was an ominous silence on the other end of the line. "She *drove?*"

"Yeah. She spent Thursday night in a motel in Memphis and reached my place in the middle of a storm yesterday afternoon. The weather was too bad for her to go out again, so I talked her into bunking on my couch last night."

Braced for a brother's misgivings, Kyle was mildly surprised when Shane seemed more annoyed by Molly's long drive than by the fact that she had spent the night in a near stranger's house. "I appreciate you watching out for her. I can't believe she took off like that without telling anyone. Dad would lock her in her room for a month if he heard about this stunt."

Though he had chided her himself for what had seemed like a somewhat reckless trip for a young woman alone, Kyle found himself tempted to defend her now. Shane talked as though Molly were a teenager rather than a grown woman of almost twenty-four. If this was the way her family treated her, no wonder she'd gotten so defensive in asserting her right to make her own decisions.

Which made it even more awkward for him to have to tell Shane about the accident. "She handled the trip just fine. But there has been a, um, problem."

"What sort of problem?" Shane asked in audible trepidation.

"Molly fell through a rotten board on my porch. She's torn a ligament in her ankle. It was just a bad sprain—no broken bones or anything like that," he added hastily, thinking of the hardware that held his own shattered leg in one piece. "She has to wear a Velcro brace and use crutches for a few weeks, but she'll be fine."

"Is she in much pain?" Shane's voice was very quiet, a bit too controlled.

"She's fine. She's napping now. The medications they gave her made her drowsy."

"Damn, I didn't need this right now."

Had Shane changed so much? "It isn't as if Molly sprained her ankle just to inconvenience you," Kyle said stiffly.

He could almost hear Shane wince at the other end of the line. "I know. I didn't mean that the way it sounded. I'm sorry she was hurt—even if I'm still kind of annoyed with her for taking off on this harebrained trip in the first place. It's just that everything is pretty hectic around here, with Dad and Cassie being away and my youngest kid down with a bad cold. I guess I'll have to come get Molly—or maybe I can send one of the uncles. Or maybe our cousin—"

"I'll bring her home."

During the surprised silence that followed Kyle's blunt announcement, he had time to wonder what on earth had made him say that. He'd had no intention of offering to drive Molly back to Texas. But something about Shane's attitude irked him. He didn't like the thought of someone coming to collect Molly as if she were a runaway child. And since she couldn't drive herself...well, that left it up to him.

"You'll bring her?" Shane repeated as if he wasn't sure he'd heard correctly.

"Yeah. I'll drive her car, then fly back. It's the least I can do since she fell through my porch."

"You're sure that isn't too much trouble?"

"It's no trouble at all," Kyle lied. "We'll head out tomorrow morning if she's feeling up to it. I doubt she'll be able to make the trip in one day, so we'll probably have to stop in Memphis overnight."

He was pretty sure *he* wouldn't be able to make a drive that long without a break; his entire body would likely stiffen up if he tried. No need to mention that to Shane, of course.

"If you're sure you don't mind, that would be great," Shane said in relief. "Any other time I'd be on a plane as soon as we hang up, but the way things are now…"

"You don't have to worry about her. I'll get her home safely."

"I'm sure you will. It will be good to see you again, Kyle."

Kyle shook his head in bemusement. Shane, as Molly had, acted as though there was no question that she would be safe with him. They continued to treat him as if they knew him well, even though it had been more than ten years since they'd last seen him. They had no idea of the things he had seen and done since he'd left the ranch—no way of knowing how those experiences had changed him.

"Yeah, well, I'll keep in touch. Let you know our itinerary."

"Thanks. Tell Molly I'll talk to her later, okay?"

"Yeah." Kyle was tempted to order Shane not to yell at his sister when he did speak with her, but he supposed that was none of his business. Still, it griped him to think Molly would be chewed out for something that really wasn't her fault.

It occurred to him that he was doing a lousy job staying detached and objective with Molly, as he had tried so hard to be from the time she'd shown up at his door. And now he had committed himself to chauffeuring her all the way back to Texas—back to the ranch he'd had no intention of revisiting for now.

It looked as though he was going to have to face his past again, after all. Ready or not.

Molly was a little embarrassed to awaken on the McDooleys' couch and realize she had slept through lunch. Jewel quickly put her at ease again, assuring her that she knew what it was like to be temporarily overcome by the effects of medication.

Feeling much more clearheaded now, she reached for her crutches and hobbled into the kitchen with Jewel. "Where are Mack and Kyle?"

Motioning her into a chair at the table, Jewel helped her prop her injured foot on another chair. She then walked over to the stove, removed the lid from a large pot and scooped soup into a bowl. "Mack's taking care of a little problem in one of the motel rooms. Kyle's gone back up to his house to pack a bag."

The food Jewel had set in front of her looked delicious, and the aromas rising from it were inviting enough to make Molly's mouth water. She was suddenly starving. Picking up her spoon, she scooped up a bite of the homemade beef and vegetable soup, repeating absently, "Kyle's packing?"

"Yes." After setting a glass of iced tea and a plate of

corn bread muffins on the table for Molly, Jewel settled into another chair with a cookie and a glass of tea for herself. "He's planning to drive you back to Texas tomorrow in your car. He figured it would take a couple of days to make the drive tolerable for both of you."

She took a sip of her tea, then added, "He's bringing your bag with him when he comes back. I told him you might as well both spend the night here and then leave early in the morning after a good breakfast."

Jewel had managed to draw Molly's attention away from the food. "Kyle's driving me home tomorrow?"

Nodding patiently, Jewel smiled. "He knew you wouldn't be able to drive in that bulky brace. You have to get back home somehow, so the logical thing is for him to drive you, then fly back here. I believe your brother offered to send someone for you, but Kyle told him that wasn't necessary."

"Wait." Her head swimming, Molly set her spoon on the table. "Kyle talked to Shane?"

"Is that your brother?"

She nodded.

"Then, yes, he did. Your cell phone rang while you were asleep and Kyle answered, in case it was an important call. He told your brother what had happened, and they made the arrangements to get you back home."

Her jaw tight, Molly muttered, "Did they?"

"Now, honey, don't go getting all chippy," Jewel advised in a motherly tone. "I'm sure you're used to making all your own decisions, but in this case, it was necessary for Kyle to make the arrangements."

Actually, she *wasn't* accustomed to making her own decisions, Molly thought glumly. Which was exactly the problem. Shane was in the habit of treating her like a kid, but she hated having put herself in a position to cause Kyle to think of her as someone who needed a keeper.

Making this trip on her own might have been a teensy bit impulsive on her part, but it had felt really good to be completely on her own for a couple of days. She'd been an adult making her own way without anyone telling her how or when to do anything. Then she'd had to ruin it all by falling down during her theatrical exit from Kyle's cabin.

"What's wrong, Molly?" Jewel was studying her face with uncomfortably sharp perception. "Do you not want to make the drive with Kyle?"

"It isn't that. I like being with Kyle—it's just that—well, I've really messed things up. He didn't want to go to Texas, and my brother didn't want me to come here to badger him about it, and now both of them are going to be annoyed with me for interfering with their plans."

"You're in the habit of letting your brother tell you what to do?"

Though pride made her want to deny it, Molly sighed and nodded. "I let *everyone* tell me what to do. My brother, my parents, my aunts and uncles. Everyone."

"Why is that, do you think?"

She shrugged. "It's just as you said. Habit. My brother is fifteen years older than I am, so I was literally the baby of the family. My father's the overprotective, take-charge type. It was just easier, for the most part, to let them tell me what to do than to argue with them. Besides, I know they always have my best interests at heart. It's just—"

"It's just that you're of an age now where you'd like to be seen as a mature adult with a brain of her own."

"Exactly." Molly smiled gratefully at the older woman.

Jewel chuckled. "I have four older brothers, the eldest of whom is nearly twenty years my senior. I know all about being bossed around and overprotected."

"I guess you do. So—how do you get them to stop?"

"Stop letting them get away with it," Jewel said simply. "You listen respectfully to your father, thank him for his advice, then do what's best for you. As for your brother—you tell him to put a sock in it."

Molly laughed and picked up her spoon again. She'd had her share of arguments with Shane, but she had never used the words "put a sock in it." She was rather looking forward to doing so.

"That said," Jewel went on, "I think it's a good thing that Kyle's taking you home. He hasn't left that cabin for more than five months, except to come down to town occasionally to see us and the doctor, and pick up a few supplies. Visiting some old friends will give him something new to focus on for a little while."

"But he had already chosen not to visit those old friends," Molly reminded her. "I didn't realize quite how serious he was about his refusal until I asked him myself."

Jewel was silent for a moment, seeming to consider her next words. "In this case, I think it's Kyle who needs a little prodding for his own good. I've been worried about him lately. He spends too much time alone with his painful memories. When he isn't by himself, he's with me and Mack. He needs to spend some time with someone closer to his own age. Someone with energy and enthusiasm, who'll challenge him and argue with him and distract him, the way you have."

Molly grimaced. "Well, I've argued with him. And I

suppose I distracted him when I fell through his porch. But I'm not sure I would say it's been good for him...."

"*I* would," Jewel countered firmly. "There was more animation in Kyle's face today than I've seen in a long time. Since the last time he was here with Tommy, maybe."

Molly wasn't so sure she'd have described Kyle's mood that day as "animated." Irritated, maybe. A little frazzled by everything that had gone wrong—from her unannounced arrival in the middle of a storm to the accident that had delayed her departure.

"How long have you known Kyle?"

Jewel smiled reminiscently. "Almost six years. He and Tommy knew each other even longer than that, but it took a while for Tommy to talk Kyle into coming home with him for a visit. Mack and I liked him immediately. He was so polite. So appreciative of every little thing we did for him."

She gave a soft sigh. "He and Tommy were such good friends. Connie said it was strange that they were opposites in so many ways, and yet still so much alike in others. Tommy thought of Kyle as the brother he always wanted growing up."

"Who's Connie?"

"She was Tommy's girlfriend. He was planning to propose to her the next time he came home. Had it all planned out just how he was going to do it. But...well, it didn't work out that way. She moved to Nashville recently to start a new job and make a new life for herself."

"I'm so sorry, Jewel." Molly's eyes burned with tears she barely managed to blink back.

Jewel took a sip of her tea, her gaze unfocused, as if she were seeing into a rosier past. And then she gave herself a little shake and spoke briskly again. "After Tommy's funeral, Mack flew to Germany to be with Kyle in the hospital. To be honest, there was a time when it didn't seem as though he was going to make it. He was hurt so badly. Mack hesitated about going at first—he thought I needed him here, but I had good friends from my church and community to turn to for support, and Kyle had no one. I couldn't bear knowing that he was there alone, with no one to sit beside him and watch out for him. And I knew he must be grieving almost as deeply as we were."

She set her cup down, speaking a bit more briskly. "When Kyle was well enough, Mack asked him to consider coming here for his recuperation. Kyle was a little hesitant at first—he seemed to think it would be painful for us to have him here—but Mack convinced him that we needed him as much as we think he needed us."

Deeply touched by the story, Molly could only swallow hard and push her empty soup bowl aside. "My parents would have gone to him, if they had known. They always thought of him as one of their boys."

"It's a shame he didn't keep in touch after he moved on. He always had such fondness in his voice on the rare occasions when he talked about the ranch. I asked him once why he didn't make more of an effort to stay in touch with his foster family, and he didn't really have a good answer. He seemed to think your family had moved on with their lives and wouldn't be particularly interested in hearing from him."

"He was wrong. But I suppose it wasn't entirely his fault. Maybe Mom and Dad should have made it more clear to him that they wanted him to stay in their lives."

"It's because I've known Kyle so long and so well

that I think he needs to go with you tomorrow," Jewel said with a nod. "He's slowly making peace with his future, making decisions about what he wants to do—but I think perhaps he needs to make peace with his past, as well. He should be reminded of the good times, rather than dwelling on the unhappy memories."

"I was still pretty young when he left, but he seemed happy enough while he was there. He seemed fond of my parents, and they cared very much about him. None of us understood then why he stopped calling and writing and visiting. He wasn't the only one who failed to stay in contact after he left, but losing touch with him seemed to really bother my mother. I guess that's why I was so determined to get him to change his mind about attending the party."

"When is the party?"

"Next Saturday. A week from tomorrow."

"Mmm." Jewel pursed her lips. "I suppose it would be difficult to detain him there for that long. But at least he can visit with your parents while he's—"

Molly shook her head. "My parents won't be back until the night before the party. They're on a cruise to celebrate their anniversary. The party is going to be a surprise. They don't even know I've seen Kyle."

"Oh." Jewel sighed. "Well, maybe visiting this time will make it easier for him to come back someday. Not that I want you to keep him there permanently, of course," she added with a slightly self-conscious laugh.

Molly couldn't help but smile at Jewel's unwitting repetition of her husband's words. "I don't think that's anything you need to worry about. Kyle seems perfectly content here."

Jewel stood and began gathering dirty dishes. "Would you like a brownie? I made them yesterday."

"I'd love one. Thank you."

Jewel set a plate of brownies within Molly's reach, then asked a bit too casually, "So you enjoy being with Kyle?"

Molly frowned. "What do you mean by that?"

"Nothing," Jewel assured her with an expression that was much too innocent to be credible. "Just asking."

A door closed noisily in the front of the house, followed by the rumble of men's voices.

"Sounds like the men are back," Jewel said unnecessarily, turning toward the doorway with a smile of anticipation.

"Brownies?" Mack said, his gaze zeroing in on the plate of sweets. "Got any coffee to go with that?"

"I'll make you some." Jewel turned toward the counter, asking over her shoulder, "Herbal tea, Kyle?"

"Sounds good." He was studying Molly's face, which felt suddenly flushed for some reason she couldn't have fully explained. "You doing okay?"

"Yes, I'm fine, thank you."

He touched her shoulder as he passed her chair, toward the empty chair beside her. It was a very light touch, perhaps intended as a bracing pat to reassure her that everything was under control. There was no way he could know that fleeting contact had just stolen the breath from her lungs, leaving her shaken and flustered and trying desperately to hide it.

What, she asked herself in shock, was *that?*

Chapter Six

Molly had an odd look on her face, Kyle noted as he took his seat. Her cheeks flushed, and then faded to leave her rather pale. She seemed to be making an effort to avoid looking at him, staring down instead at the brownie she was crumbling on her plate.

"Did Jewel tell you about the arrangements I've made to get you back home?" he asked, wondering if that had something to do with her behavior.

"Yes." She looked at him then, her expression somber. "It really isn't necessary for you to drive me all the way home. I'm sure one of my uncles or cousins would fly out to drive me if Shane is too busy to do so."

"I've already told your brother I'll drive you. It's the least I can do."

"It isn't your fault that I hurt myself," she said, as she had a half-dozen times since she'd fallen.

He still had a hard time letting himself off that hook. He had known about the rotten boards and he'd neglected to inform her of them. The fact that he had been distracted—by her—was no excuse.

Paying her medical bills was the easy part of the penance he had assigned himself. Spending two days in close quarters with her, trying to think of her merely as someone for whom he was temporarily responsible—*that* was going to be the difficult task. He just hoped it didn't prove to be beyond his ability.

Having stashed her crutches in the backseat of the car, Molly balanced her weight on her uninjured leg as she turned to say goodbye to her hosts Saturday morning. She had grown very fond of both Jewel and Mack during her brief stay with them; it made her sad to think she might never see them again.

Jewel gave her a hug. "You take care of that leg," she murmured into Molly's ear. "And don't take any guff from those bossy men, you hear?"

"I won't," Molly promised with a smile that felt slightly tremulous. "Thank you so much for all you've done for me."

Jewel looked a little sad, herself, then. "It was nice to have young people in the house again."

With a hard swallow, Molly turned then to Mack. "Thank you, too, for opening your home to me."

He patted her shoulder with a rather awkward warmth. "You make Kyle drive carefully. And make him treat you nice."

She smiled. "I will. And I'll send him safely home to you."

"Do that, too," he said gruffly, patting her shoulder

again. "And come back yourself, sometime. Jewel and I will give you a tour of the area, maybe take you out to Dollywood for the day, if you like amusement parks."

"I love amusement parks." But she made no promise to return, since she couldn't foresee any reason to do so.

Kyle seemed to have had enough of the touching farewells. He opened the passenger door of Molly's car and motioned her in. "We'd better get underway," he said to the McDooleys. "See you in a couple of days."

Molly's eyes met Jewel's for a moment as they shared wry smiles, and then Molly maneuvered her way into the passenger seat, lifting her right leg in very carefully. Kyle made sure she was safely inside before closing the door with a decisive snap. She had her seat belt fastened and had wriggled into a reasonably comfortable position by the time he slid into the driver's seat.

There was an oddly hollow feeling in the pit of her stomach as she watched the McDooleys' motel disappear behind them.

"You're a very lucky guy," she said after a while, breaking the silence within the small car.

"Lucky?" Kyle seemed surprised by the word, as if he wasn't in the habit of applying it to himself.

"Oh, yes. Not only do you have a great house in a beautiful setting, you've found a family here who love you very much."

One might almost have thought Kyle was stunned by her comments. He couldn't seem to decide which part to focus on first. "You still think I have a great house?"

"Of course. It's small, but very well arranged to make the maximum use of the floor space. It needs a little work, obviously—" she motioned almost absently toward her leg "—but that's all minor stuff. Maybe I would decorate it a little more, but no amount of decorating could compete with the view from your deck."

"I would have thought you'd consider it too isolated."

"I grew up on the ranch, remember? Sure, there were always people around, but it's no closer to a town than your place is. As you pointed out, when you have the urge to be with people, you aren't that far away from them."

"Hmm."

She wasn't quite sure what to make of that sound, but she didn't press him to say more. If he wasn't in the mood for conversation, she certainly wasn't going to talk his ears off all the way back to Texas. She was perfectly content to ride in silence, if that was what he preferred.

Her resolve lasted all of fifteen quiet minutes. Squirming a little in her seat, she asked, "What kind of music do you like?"

"There's only one kind of music. Country."

You could take the boy out of Texas…

Hiding a smile, she asked, "Do you mind if I put in a CD? How about George Strait?"

Without taking his eyes off the road, Kyle shrugged. "I can listen to Strait."

She reached behind her seat and brought out her bulging CD case. She stored her CDs alphabetically by artist, so it took only a moment to locate a "best of…" collection by George Strait. Shortly afterward, his smooth voice filled the car with the opening verse of "You Look So Good in Love."

She could relax a little more now that it wasn't so quiet. She didn't have to babble to fill the silence. And it was hard to be tense when George was crooning a cowboy love song.

She made it through two songs before the compulsion to speak grew too strong to resist. "Did you know that Jewel was a nurse in Vietnam?"

"I knew."

"Mack was over there, too. In the army."

"Yes."

"Jewel told me all about it last night while you and Mack were watching the game. Even though they grew up less than thirty miles apart, they met in Vietnam. Strange, isn't it?"

"I know their history. I've learned quite a bit about them in the past six years."

"Did you know Mack still has nightmares about Vietnam? Jewel said he stopped having them for a long time, but they started again after Tommy died."

She watched Kyle's fingers tighten on the wheel. "No," he said after a moment. "I didn't know that."

"Do you and Mack ever talk about your war experiences?"

His expression hardened, though she could only see his profile. "We have other things to talk about."

"Jewel thinks it would be good for both of you. She said sometimes a man needs to talk to another man—but it's hard for Mack to initiate that sort of conversation. She knows it's hard for you, too."

For several long minutes, George Strait's voice was the only one she heard. When she finally decided Kyle wasn't going to say anything, she spoke again, "Have you ever talked to *anyone* about what happened over there?"

He sighed gustily and shot her a stern look. "This is going to be a very long trip," he warned in a near growl. "You really don't want to make me cranky when we're just getting started."

"This subject makes you cranky?"

"Very."

"Then *you* start a conversation," she challenged.

"We have to talk?"

"I'm afraid so. I thought I could resist, but I just can't."

It pleased her to see one corner of his mouth tilt with what might have been a very faint, very reluctant smile. "Then talk. About anything you want—except my experiences overseas."

She would have liked for him to tell her more about Tommy, and the time they had served together—just because it was such an integral part of who Kyle was now. But at least he had indicated his willingness—however grudging—to converse about anything else. "What do you remember most about living at the ranch?"

"Do your conversations always consist of questions?" he asked in mild exasperation.

"Mostly," she admitted readily. "How else would I find out about people?"

"Anyone ever tell you to mind your own business?"

"Other than you—not very often. Most people like talking about themselves."

"I've never been like most people."

"Which makes you even more interesting," she pointed out.

He sighed again, a long-suffering sound that made her laugh. "Lucky me," he murmured. "What was the question again?"

"The ranch?"

"Yeah, okay. What do I remember about being there?" He thought a moment, then said, "Your mom's cookies. I don't think I'd ever had a homemade cookie before I went to the ranch—not that I remembered, anyway."

It amazed her how easily he could tug at her heart without even trying. She debated briefly about asking him more about his earlier childhood, but decided she'd better not push her luck just then. "I remember Mom sending you cookies after you went away," she confided, instead. "She packed them in those tall potato chip cans. She let me help her."

"They were good. Sharing those cookies made me a few friends in my barracks."

"Tommy?"

"No." His voice roughened. "I met him later."

"Oh." Obviously still a taboo subject. "Mom still makes the best cookies in the world. Shane's girls are always begging her to make some and let them help."

She spent most of the next couple of hours chattering about life at the ranch—her parents and her brother's family, the boys currently staying with them, the extended family members she thought Kyle might recall. Kyle didn't contribute much to the conversation, but she could tell he was listening. She thought maybe he even seemed interested in what she had to say—or maybe she was simply looking for a reason to keep the mostly one-sided conversation going.

They stopped for a late lunch at a roadside chain restaurant in Central Tennessee. Molly noticed that Kyle walked very stiffly after several hours in the car. The long drive had to be uncomfortable for him, but he hadn't complained—nor would he, she knew.

A large, tourist-oriented gift shop was attached to the restaurant. Molly insisted on going through it after they ate. Though it was difficult maneuvering through the narrow aisles with her crutches, and she had no real interest in the merchandise, she could tell that it made

Kyle feel better to walk around a little. He grumbled about the unnecessary delay, but she saw him surreptitiously stretching his bad leg, flexing the knee.

She could almost see some of the tension drain from his facial muscles as the hearty meal and light exercise combined to ease the aftereffects of the morning's long drive. Pleased with herself, she bought a black coffee mug with the state of Tennessee outlined on one side in gold—her excuse for visiting the shop—then handed the bag to Kyle to carry as they headed for the parking lot.

"It felt good to be out of the car for a little while, didn't it?" she asked as she fastened herself in.

"It put us another half hour behind," he retorted, starting the engine.

"That's just more time for me to pelt you with questions," she said cheerfully.

It pleased her inordinately when he chuckled—a sound that seemed to surprise him almost as much as it did her. He grew immediately somber again, but she treasured that slight laugh. A bit too much for comfort, actually, she realized, her own smile fading.

Just over eight hours after they'd left Gatlinburg—almost halfway through the trip home—Molly noticed that Kyle's jaw was clenched and his face was pale. When he glanced her way, she saw that dusky shadows had formed beneath his eyes, making them look hollow, and that the long scar on his jaw stood out in contrast to his ashen skin.

This long car trip was too much for him, she thought guiltily. They had taken a couple of breaks, but he was still obviously uncomfortable. She really should have insisted that he allow one of her family members to come after her, rather than driving her himself. Yet he had been so adamant that it was his responsibility, and maybe she had allowed herself to be persuaded a bit too easily.

She was trying to think of a tactful way to suggest that he take a break for the evening when he said, "You've been suspiciously quiet for a long time. Is your leg hurting?"

The dull throb was still tolerable, but she seized quickly on the excuse. "It's getting sort of cramped and sore. But I can keep going as long as you can," she added bravely.

He frowned. "You don't have to try and keep up with me. If you need to rest, you should have said something."

She tried to look contrite.

"We're coming up on Memphis. We'll find a place to spend the night, then head out again early in the morning."

It would be dark soon, so she felt fully justified in nodding and saying, "I *am* getting pretty tired. Maybe we should call it a day."

Half an hour later, Kyle parked in front of a brightly lit chain motel. "I'll go in and get us a couple of rooms. Keep the car doors locked until I get back. It'll only take a couple of minutes."

"At least put my room on my credit card."

He didn't even bother to reply. He just got out of the car and closed the door.

Shaking her head, she leaned back into her seat and watched him cross the driveway and enter the glass door into the motel office. He really did have a sexy way of moving, she thought with a wistful sigh. She noticed the limp, of course, but her attention tended to focus on the purposeful swing of his arms at his side, and the way his nice, tight…

With a groan, she made herself stop thinking along that particular line. She had never let herself think that way about any of her foster brothers—had never been tempted to do so, actually. They were her brothers for the short time they'd stayed with her. The one constant about them was that, eventually, they all moved on.

It was the one sure prediction she could make about Kyle—and one she would do well to keep in mind at all times with him.

As he had promised, he was back in a very short time. He handed her a key, then started the engine and drove to the back of the building, where he parked in front of a blue door marked 116.

"I'm in one-sixteen, you're in one-seventeen," he said, opening his door. "I'll get the bags. You need help getting to your room?"

"No, I can make it." She reached for her crutches, determined to prove that she didn't need his assistance. If he could tough out this trip without complaining, then so could she.

"There's no room service, but there are a couple of fast-food restaurants nearby," he said as he dumped her bag in her room. "I'll go get us something to eat and we can crash in front of our TVs until bedtime. Unless you want to go out?"

His expression told her he would escort her to every blues bar on Beale Street if she desired, but that he really, really hoped she was too tired to even consider leaving the motel room.

"I'm much too tired to go out again," she said dutifully.

He didn't exactly sag with relief, but she got the distinct impression he had to make an effort to prevent himself from doing so. "I'll go get us some food, then. Any preferences?"

"Why don't you stay here and order pizza? If we do that, you won't have to go out again, either. And, besides," she added quickly, before he felt the need to assure her he was perfectly capable of making a food run, "I like pizza."

"So do I," he admitted. "I don't get it much at home—no one delivers to my house," he added with a slight smile.

"I don't doubt it."

They were both still standing in the center of the room, which looked like every other motel room on the planet with its two beds, blue-and-green patterned spreads and curtains, boring landscapes and obligatory bolted-to-a-dresser television set. A small, round table with two blue-upholstered chairs sat in front of the single window. Molly made her way to one of the chairs and lowered herself into it, dropping her crutches on the floor beside her. It felt good to stretch her legs out in front of her; there wasn't room to do so in her small car.

Kyle moved to the small nightstand attached to the wall between the two beds and opened the single drawer, pulling out a telephone directory. "What kind of pizza do you like?"

"There is no bad kind of pizza."

"Then I'll order one with everything."

"Sounds good."

The order placed, Kyle moved toward the door that connected their rooms. "I think I'll take a quick shower before the food gets here."

Her mouth went dry at the thought of him naked and wet, but she managed to reply airily, "Okay. I'll just chill in here."

Which was exactly what she needed to do, she scolded herself after Kyle disappeared into the other room. Chill out. Cool down. Stop carrying on like some love-struck fool over Kyle Reeves.

Having a harmless little crush on him would have been okay, maybe even sort of fun—but this wasn't feeling like a crush. The emotions that were growing stronger with every minute she spent with him seemed significantly more dangerous than a simple schoolgirl-type infatuation.

She had never had her heart broken before. She suspected she was coming entirely too close to learning about that pain firsthand. And that was one experience she would just as soon forgo.

There was only one sure way to handle this disaster-in-the-making. The same way she always kept any potentially awkward relationship safe and pleasant—by turning Kyle into a buddy. Just another in a long line of temporary brothers—emphasis on temporary.

She could do that, she assured herself. No problem—she had done it plenty of times before.

And then she heard the shower start in the other room, and her heart started to pound again.

Okay, so maybe it wouldn't be quite as easy as it had been in the past. But Molly Walker never surrendered without a fight.

His hair still damp from a long, steamy, muscle-loosening shower, Kyle walked back into Molly's room with only a quick knock to warn her he was coming in. She had moved, he noted, from the chair to one of the beds. Having piled pillows against the headboard, she leaned against them as she sat with her legs stretched in front of her.

She was dressed in the navy-and-lime athletic pants and T-shirt set. Her left foot was encased in a white sock, her right foot hidden within the bulky brace. Her red-and-gold hair tumbled around her shoulders in a casual, tousled manner, and she wore very little makeup, if any. It was hardly a seductive scene—and yet, he took one look at her and felt his throat close.

Resisting an almost overpowering impulse to join her on the bed, he moved, instead, to one of the chairs. "What's on?" he asked gruffly, nodding toward the TV.

"A James Bond marathon. *You Only Live Twice* just ended and *Die Another Day* is just starting."

"You like Bond movies?" he asked in surprise. He would have thought she'd have considered the series too violent and sexist.

"I *love* Bond movies. Shane got me hooked on them when I was a kid. I've seen them all—even the one with George Lazenby playing Bond."

"But the ultimate Bond is, of course…" He left the sentence hanging, an obvious test.

She passed it with a confident chuckle. "Sean Connery. Duh. Followed very closely by Pierce Brosnan. Though the films with Roger Moore and Timothy Dalton were good—they *were* Bond movies, after all."

Strangely enough, this casual conversation made him even more attracted to her than blatant flirtation could have. He was growing entirely too comfortable with her. Found himself enjoying her company too much, even when she completely exasperated him. He didn't want to grow too close to her—and he sure as hell didn't want to miss her when he went back to Tennessee without her.

Surely that couldn't happen after only a few days with her. Right?

He'd have to make darned certain that it didn't.

Someone tapped on the motel room door. Wallet in hand, Kyle answered, paid the smiling young man for the pizza, added a generous tip, then closed the door and set the fragrant pizza box on the table. "I saw a soft-drink machine just down the walkway from your room. What kind do you want?"

"Diet soda is fine—doesn't matter what kind."

It amused him that someone who put away food the way Molly did always drank diet beverages, but he didn't bother to comment. It took him only a few minutes to fetch a couple of sodas—diet for her, caffeine-free for himself—and then they dug into the pizza.

Sitting at opposite sides of the table, they lifted still-steaming slices to their mouths, strings of melted cheese trailing behind, thick sauce dripping over their fingers. It wasn't a gourmet meal, and their surroundings were far from elegant, but it suited Kyle much more than any fancy restaurant. The pizza was good, but he suspected it was more the company that made this meal so enjoyable.

And that realization made him grumpy all over again.

Molly didn't seem to notice. She appeared to be having a great time, chattering like a magpie, watching the movie—and licking pizza sauce off her fingers in an unselfconsciously sexy manner that made Kyle almost choke on a pepperoni slice.

He'd noticed something slightly different in Molly's manner toward him since he'd returned from his shower.

He couldn't quite put his finger on what it was—but her smiles seemed brighter and her voice breezier, more familiar in some way. She seemed to be almost studiedly casual with him, as if they'd spent many evenings sharing pizza and soft drinks in motel rooms.

Perhaps this was her way of ignoring the inherent awkwardness of the situation, he mused. By treating him like an old pal, she didn't have to acknowledge even to herself that she was in any way uncomfortable with him.

Sounded like a good plan. One he should probably utilize himself. The problem was, not only did he find it impossible to feel like a brother to her, he found it increasingly annoying when she treated him like one.

There was only one slice of pizza left when both of them were too full to eat another bite. Carrying the rest of her cola with her, Molly hopped to the bed and settled back into the nest she'd made for herself earlier. She motioned toward the empty bed with one hand. "Might as well make yourself comfortable."

He looked from her to the empty bed, then cleared his throat. "I think I'll go on into my own room. I packed a book I've been wanting to start."

"You can bring it in here. I won't disturb you while you read."

She seemed reluctant to be left alone, but he shook his head, anyway. "Just knock on the wall if you need me for anything during the night," he said, moving toward the connecting door. He tried not to think of all the things he would like her to need him for in the night.

"C'mon, Kyle, there's no need for you to go. We can hang out together for a few hours—watch the movie, maybe play some cards. I've got a deck in my bag."

Her chatty, no-one-could-doubt-that-we're-just-buddies attitude was beginning to get on his nerves. Sure, it was the safest strategy—but she was starting to carry it too far.

"I doubt that your brother or your parents would like us spending this much time together in a motel room."

She made a sound that came very close to being a "pshaw." "Don't be silly. Daddy and Shane wouldn't care. After all, you're—"

If she called him "family" one more time, he was liable to do something incredibly stupid. Like shut her up with his own mouth…

The kiss lasted quite a while. Molly looked stunned when he finally straightened. She didn't try to detain him again when he stalked through the door, closing it sharply behind him.

He cursed himself colorfully and creatively as he threw himself on one of the beds, his entire body aching from the drive and throbbing with a desire he shouldn't be feeling. He most definitely should not have done that. Kissing Molly ranked way up in the top five dumbest things he had ever done—no matter how good it had felt.

Maybe now, at least, she would stop trying to treat him like a long-lost brother. A damned platonic friend. Maybe now she would understand that he wasn't the nice guy she had made him out to be in her imagination. He'd been trying without success to make her understand that ever since she had shown up so trustingly at his door.

He'd tried snapping at her, snarling at her, rebuffing every attempt she made to reach out to him. Nothing had gotten through—but maybe now she no longer thought of him as "safe."

What would eat at him for the rest of the night—and probably for quite some time afterward—was the knowledge that Molly had made no effort to push him away when he had kissed her. That she had, in fact, kissed him back. And there had been nothing in the least sisterly about the way her lips had moved beneath his.

Chapter Seven

Molly didn't sleep much that night. When she did manage to doze, her dreams were restless and unsettling, leaving her tired and tense by the time daybreak finally arrived.

She showered, then wrapped herself in a robe and hopped to her suitcase to find something to wear. She wasn't sure she could tuck her jeans inside the splint and still strap it tightly enough to support her ankle during the long drive ahead, so she donned the hot-pink-trimmed gray pants again, pairing them with a clean white long-sleeve pullover. She braided her still-damp hair, applied enough makeup to hide the ravages of the sleepless night, then settled into a chair, waiting for Kyle to let her know when he was ready to leave.

Kyle. Just the thought of his name made her lips start to tingle like crazy again.

She still couldn't believe he had kissed her. He had simply loomed over her without warning, grabbed her chin in his hand and crushed his mouth down on hers before she could finish whatever it was she had been saying at the time. Her world had tilted on its axis—and she had a strong feeling that it would never go back to the way it had been before.

No one had ever made her feel like that with just a kiss before. And what worried her most was the fear that no one else ever would.

She had been waiting for almost twenty-four years to find a man she couldn't turn into an honorary brother. And wasn't it ironic that the first man who fit that description would most certainly be leaving on the first plane out of Texas?

She didn't delude herself for a moment that Kyle was falling for her. That there was any chance he would stay in her life, rather than drop her off at the ranch and run back to his secluded cabin. He had his friends, the McDooleys, and they seemed to provide all the companionship he wanted or needed. Maybe he would be amenable to the occasional sexual liaison—he wasn't a monk, after all—but nothing more. And certainly not with her.

Which meant it was up to her to protect herself from getting hurt. Plan A hadn't worked out. No matter how hard she tried, she wasn't going to be able to turn Kyle into a brother figure.

So it was time for Plan B. Carefully maintained distance. Polite, but detached. Completely uninvolved in his life. No more personal questions, no more friendly touches, no more pressuring him to share his feelings with her. If she occasionally noticed how pretty his eyes were, or how broad his shoulders, or how tight his…

Well, if she happened to notice any of his physical attributes, she would simply appreciate the view and remind herself that Kyle was only another guy who was in her life for just a brief stay.

He rapped on the door connecting their rooms, and her stomach clenched. She could do this, she promised herself. She wouldn't be able to pretend the kiss had never happened, but she would make it clear that she neither expected—nor wanted—it to happen again.

"How's the leg?" he asked by way of greeting when she hobbled across the floor to open the door.

"It's fine."

There was no way to read his expression, which was absolutely emotionless. His voice was cordial enough when he inquired, "Did you sleep well?"

"Like a baby," she lied through her teeth. "You?"

"Yeah. Great. Ready to get on the road?"

"Definitely."

He nodded. "We'll grab some breakfast at a drive-through window to save time."

He was really in a hurry to dump her and get back home, she thought with a pang. "That will be fine."

It was going to be a very long day.

Even considering the occasional outbreaks of orange barrels forcing highway traffic into one lane for construction purposes, they made good time after entering Arkansas. They stopped every couple of hours for breaks, but Molly didn't try to talk Kyle into any more shopping or sightseeing delays. He thought she seemed as impatient to reach the ranch as he was.

She had been uncharacteristically subdued during the first half of the day, seemingly content to listen to the music playing from the CD player and to watch the scenery passing by her window. It was a beautiful, crisp October Sunday morning. Traffic was light and the moron-driver factor was lower than usual.

Kyle might have been in a fairly decent mood had he not still been so angry with himself for losing control—even so briefly—the night before. He prided himself as a man who always remained in control, and the fact that he had given in to irritation and impulse, especially with Molly, really shook him.

He had lain awake last night, much too aware of Molly lying on the other side of a thin wall. Remembering much too vividly how good her lips had felt. Worrying that she, too, was lying awake and reliving the moment. And wondering why she hadn't even tried to push him away.

Slanting her a sideways look, he noted that her fingers were interlaced in her lap, and that she was sitting unnaturally still. Normally she would have been bouncing in her seat, tapping in time to the music, chattering a mile a minute about whatever popped into her head, flashing him those smiles that seemed to bring the sunlight right into the car with them.

He realized that she hadn't really smiled at him all morning. And he missed those smiles entirely too much.

Was she afraid of him now? He tried to read her profile, searching for any sign that he intimidated her in a way he had not before.

"Molly?"

She turned to look at him. "Yes?"

No, he decided. She wasn't afraid. Maybe a little wary—as if she weren't quite sure what he might do next. Maybe still a little bemused by the unexpected kiss. But not afraid, he decided in satisfaction. "Nothing."

"Oh." She looked out the window for a moment, then turned to him with a rush of words. "Why did you kiss me?"

He tightened his hands around the steering wheel to keep the car from swerving. He should have expected something like this from her. He should probably be surprised that it had taken her so long. "It would probably be best if you just forget about that."

"I've been trying to," she admitted. "But I still want to know why."

"Call it an impulse. An ill-advised one."

She thought about that for a moment, then said, "You looked annoyed when you kissed me."

She was going to analyze this to death, he thought with a scowl. "You were annoying me at the time."

"So you kissed me? I'm sorry, Kyle, but that doesn't really make sense."

He heard the low growl of frustration escape him before he said through clenched teeth, "You're starting to annoy me again."

"Does that make you want to kiss me again?" she shot back, fearless as always.

Yes. The unspoken reply seemed to hang in the air between them. Kyle wondered if Molly was as aware of it as he was.

Maybe she was. She subsided into her seat again, riding quietly for the next few miles. Even though he kept his own gaze focused fiercely on the road ahead, he could feel her looking at him. Studying him. Trying, most likely, to understand him.

Good luck with that, he could have told her. He didn't even understand himself right now.

* * *

Okay, Molly thought. That was it. No more questions. Questions only led to answers she didn't necessarily want to hear.

Kyle considered their kiss an ill-advised impulse? Not very flattering.

But he hadn't said no when she'd asked if he wanted to kiss her again.

No more questions, she promised herself. She would just continue to sit quietly, listen to the music, watch the passing scenery….

"Kyle?"

"Yeah?"

"If we don't mention the kiss, is it okay if we talk about something else?"

"Talk about whatever you want," he said in surrender. "Just give me the right to decline to comment if I choose."

"Permission granted," she said with a smile and a wave of relief. Maybe if they were talking—it didn't matter about what—she would be able to finally stop thinking about the kiss. Maybe.

"So, what do you want to know this time?" he asked in that same resigned tone. "My blood type? My bank balance?"

She couldn't help but laugh. "Did you actually make a joke?"

"No. Just an educated guess."

"Well, as a matter of fact, I don't care about your blood type or your bank balance. I was just going to ask if you have any family left in Texas."

"No."

"No aunts, uncles? Cousins?"

"Not as far as I know."

She couldn't even imagine having no relatives. "Were your parents orphans?"

"If my father ever had any family, they ran him off long before I came along. He had a talent for getting thrown out of all the best places—jobs, apartments, marriages."

There was no anger in his voice that she could hear. Only a cool dispassion that didn't quite mask a lifetime of disappointment.

"What about your mother?"

"Let's just say she never baked me cookies."

There was the anger. Whatever his mother had done to him, he still hadn't forgiven her.

"When's the last time you were on a horse?" she asked, making a quick decision to guide the conversation into less treacherous territory.

He looked a bit startled, but relieved. "Almost three years ago, I guess."

Something in his answer told her there might be a story involved. "Tell me about it."

After only a momentary hesitation, he did. "Several of the guys in my unit were invited to a party at a ranch near Camp Pendleton, where we were waiting to be deployed to Iraq. One of the other guests was a pretty brunette Tommy wanted to, um, get to know better. He had never been on a horse in his life, so he asked me for a few pointers that would help him impress her. I gave him a few."

Delighted by the nuances of his tale, Molly followed along easily. "And what were the results of your advice?"

Kyle grinned, making him look—just for a moment—young and amused. "The horse went left, and Tom went right. He hit the dirt face-first."

Molly laughed. "That was so bad of you. Did it ruin his chances with the brunette?"

Kyle chuckled and shook his head. "She felt so sorry for him that she spent the entire night personally tending to his scrapes and bruises. He always had that kind of luck with the ladies."

"That was before he started dating Connie, I take it."

An odd expression crossed Kyle's face. "Uh, no. They were dating then, I guess. But it wasn't as if they were married or anything," he added, defensive on his late friend's behalf.

"I see." So Tommy hadn't been quite the saint he'd been made out to be. Interesting.

"Look, he wasn't perfect. But he was a great guy. And he'd have been a good husband to Connie. Once the vows had been exchanged, he would have lived up to them."

She reached out to rest a hand lightly on his arm. "I'm not judging your friend, Kyle. I'm sure I would have liked him."

He seemed appeased. "You would have. Everyone did."

Without moving her hand, she said quietly, "I've never lost anyone who was really close to me like that. My family has been extremely fortunate that we're all still together, even after a couple of close calls. It must have been a nightmare for you."

"Yeah," he said after a moment. "It was."

And was still, she mused. Kyle was a long way from coming to grips with the loss of his friend.

But this wasn't a counseling session. She drew her hand from his arm and asked lightly, "So, tell me the truth, Kyle. Were you as lucky with the ladies as your friend?"

He snorted. "Hardly. I never had Tom's knack for flirting. Put me in a social situation and my tongue glues itself to the top of my mouth. Maybe you remember that I've always been like that."

"Mmm. Some women are drawn to the silent, brooding type," she teased lightly—and thought that it apparently applied to herself. Especially when it came to Kyle.

Looking mildly embarrassed, he growled, "Time to change the subject again."

"So I take it you didn't fall off your horse?"

"No. I remembered just enough of what your father told me to stay in the saddle."

"Do you think you could still rope a calf if you tried?"

He grunted. "Only if the calf walked up and offered to put his feet in the lasso for me."

She giggled.

With a shrug, Kyle said, "It was painfully obvious when I lived on the ranch that I had no real talent as a cowhand."

"So you went into the military."

He nodded. "Your dad told me about his stint in the navy. It sounded like a good deal, so I went to sign up, though I chose the Marines rather than the navy."

"Did you like it?"

He gave her a look that made her feel foolish for asking, but he replied evenly, "It suited me at the time."

Embarrassed about asking such a blatantly insensitive question—even though it was partially his fault for being so hard to converse with—she moved on. "You said you were considering several options for your future. What do you think you'll do next?"

He shrugged and turned his attention back to his driving. "Maybe I'll take Mack up on his offer to go into property management with him. I'm not too good at the dealing-with-people part, but I've always been pretty good at making repairs."

She wondered if that was what he really wanted to do, or if he felt obligated to step into the place Tommy would have taken had he survived. Jewel and Mack had obviously accepted him as a surrogate son, trying to fill the hole their own son's death had left in their lives, and Kyle was probably grateful for the assistance they had given him since he'd been injured.

She was trying to think of a relatively tactful way to ask that question when Kyle turned the tables on her. "I think it's my turn to ask you questions."

Though she was a bit surprised, she replied, "Sure. Go ahead."

"Doesn't it cramp your social life to live with your parents at your age?"

Social life? She almost laughed. The closest she had come to a social life in the past year had been the family barbecues the Walkers threw every chance they got. "Since I'm not seeing anyone in particular right now, it isn't really an issue."

"And that's okay with you?"

"For now it is. I told you I'm planning to find a place of my own as soon as a teaching position opens up at one of the elementary schools within a thirty-mile radius of the ranch."

"I'm sure there are teaching positions in the bigger cities. Dallas. Houston. San Antonio. Austin."

Of the cities he had named, Dallas was the closest to the ranch. Yet at the time she had earned her degree, even an hour had seemed too far away. She had been so glad to be back among her family, safe in the close and loving circles in which she had been raised.

She had justified her return by telling herself they needed her there, but she'd known even then that she had needed them more. "I guess I'm just a homebody. Like Shane, I've seen no need to live far from the ranch."

"Are you going to imitate your brother and build a house on the other side of your parents?"

She was making an effort not to get defensive. Kyle was just taking a little revenge on her, pelting her with personal questions in retaliation for her doing the same to him. "I don't think that's a very practical option. But I'm sure I can find something in the vicinity."

"When you grow up," he murmured.

"Now you're just being a jerk," she informed him with a toss of her head.

He laughed. The deep, rich sound sent a rush of heat through every inch of her body. It was a good thing, she thought rather dazedly, that he didn't do that very often, or she would be a quivering puddle on the floorboard by the time they reached the ranch.

Molly didn't suggest stopping in Little Rock to visit her aunt and uncle. Though Lindsey would be annoyed, Molly doubted that Kyle was in the mood for a sociable visit with her relatives. He was ready to get her safely delivered to the ranch so he could quickly get back home, she assumed.

They made it as far as Hope, Arkansas—almost halfway between Memphis and Dallas—before something went wrong with the car.

"Are you *kidding* me?" Kyle exploded in frustration

when the engine made a funny popping sound, then died. He tugged frantically at the steering wheel, guiding the rapidly slowing vehicle safely to the side of the freeway, avoiding being hit from behind.

"What's wrong?"

"Damn engine just quit." He turned the key, resulting in nothing but further frustration.

"You can't start it again?"

"Do you hear it running?" He reached beneath the dash to release the hood lock, glanced in his side-view mirror to check traffic, then opened the driver's door and got out of the car.

Molly watched through the windshield as he opened the hood, obscuring himself from her view for a few minutes. She knew absolutely nothing about car engines, but maybe Kyle knew enough to fix whatever had gone wrong. Could be a loose wire or something, she thought optimistically. Maybe all he would have to do would be to jiggle something or tap on something or…

He dropped back into the driver's seat with a disgusted expression that put an end to that hope. "I can't fix it."

"I don't understand. I never have trouble with my car. I have the oil changed every three thousand miles, I use good quality gasoline, I watch all the dials and gauges. I know it has sort of high mileage, but the only thing broken is the radio."

"A broken radio doesn't keep it from running."

Biting her lip, she studied him as he stared out the windshield, drumming his fingers on the steering wheel. "Do you think it's really bad?"

"I don't know. It looks like we're going to have to call a tow truck and have it taken to someone who can answer that."

She reached up to rub her temples, feeling dazed by this latest misadventure. It was almost as if someone didn't want her to get back to the ranch. "Kyle, I'm—"

He cut her off with a slash of his hand. "We'll handle it," he said.

She sighed and dug in her purse for her cell phone.

They wouldn't be reaching the ranch that evening. They wouldn't even see the Texas state line. It took more than an hour to have the car towed to a garage that was open on a Sunday afternoon, and then nearly another hour of boredom in a grubby waiting room to find out that the situation was as bad as Kyle had feared.

The timing chain on Molly's aging little import had broken, and the garage didn't have a replacement on hand. It would be late the next day before they could get on the road again.

Her expression stricken, Molly straightened the stack of year-old magazines she had been reading to pass the time while Kyle paced and stared impatiently out the single, wavy-paned window. "I'm so sorry," she said. "Everything keeps going wrong."

"It isn't your fault," Kyle admitted a bit grudgingly. As much as he might have wanted to place blame for the mishaps of the past few days, he had to concede that Molly hadn't intentionally hurt her leg, nor had she been able to predict the car trouble. It wasn't fair of him to take his frustration out on her. "You'd better call your brother and tell him we've been delayed again."

He couldn't help thinking of how the five-hour drive remaining to the ranch seemed so very far at the moment. Had he been the superstitious type, he'd have wondered if the fates were conspiring to keep them from getting there—after doing everything possible to get him started on this journey he'd had no intention of taking.

Without moving, Molly sat looking at her cell phone for so long that he finally asked, "What's the problem?"

She sighed. "I'm giving myself a mental pep talk before calling Shane."

"Why is that necessary?"

Wrinkling her nose, she explained, "He's going to chew me out again, and I'm bracing myself for it."

"Why would he chew you out? This is no more your fault than spraining your ankle was. Your car has been well maintained, but there's no way to prevent an occasional mechanical problem. It's just bad luck that it happened near a small town on a Sunday afternoon."

Though she looked grateful for his reassurance, she seemed no more eager to call her brother. "Shane will point out—rightfully so—that I never should have been on the road today in the first place. Had I gracefully accepted your answers about the party and resisted the impulse to drive to Tennessee to nag you, I wouldn't have sprained my ankle and I wouldn't have put you to all this trouble and expense. And don't even think about paying one penny of these car repairs or our motel rooms for tonight. These charges go on my credit card."

"I'll pay my own motel bill. As for everything else, it's really none of your brother's business, is it?"

She made a rueful face. "You really don't remember Shane very well at all, do you?"

"I take it you and he don't get along very well."

Her eyes widened almost comically. "Shane and I get along great! He's always been my best friend in the world, in addition to being my big brother."

Never having had a sibling, Kyle was confused. "But you said he yells at you all the time and that he bosses you around."

"Well, yeah. But that's just Shane. And he doesn't really yell at me. He just worries too much sometimes. He was fifteen when I was born, you know. He's kind of overprotective. Almost like a second father."

"He still thinks of you as a little girl who needs his advice and protection."

"Yes," she conceded with a sigh. "I've been trying to change that, but it's taking time. He says when he's seventy-five and I'm sixty, he'll still think of me as his baby sister."

"Mr. Reeves?" A barrel-chested mechanic in grease-stained work clothes stood in the doorway of the waiting room. "Your loaner car is here. I'm sure you and your wife will be more comfortable in one of the local motels than here in this room."

Kyle didn't bother to correct the guy about his marital status. "Thanks. Maybe you can give me directions to the nearest decent motel?"

"There are a couple of chains just off the freeway. And several restaurants and fast-food places nearby. You shouldn't have any trouble getting around. I'll call the cell number you gave me as soon as your car's ready tomorrow."

Kyle nodded. "The earlier you can get to it, the better. We have a long drive still ahead of us."

"I'll do my best."

"Thanks, Bill." Kyle handed Molly her crutches, then slung the straps of her overnight bag and his own over his shoulders. He couldn't help wondering what Bill-the-mechanic was thinking as he watched Molly hobbling across the room with Kyle limping along behind her. Probably that they made an odd pair—and he would be right about that.

As Bill had assured them, they found a motel without any problem. Once again, Kyle rented two rooms, putting one on Molly's credit card, as she demanded.

He didn't think another cozy dinner in her room was a good idea—especially since he was still aching from the kiss they had shared. Instead, he gave her time to call her brother and prop her foot up with an ice bag for a while. He tried to talk her into taking something for pain, since he could tell she was uncomfortable, but she refused to take anything more than an over-the-counter anti-inflammatory. He supposed that would have to do—and he couldn't blame her, since he hated pain pills himself.

After they'd both rested and freshened up, he took her to a casual steak house he had spotted on the way to the motel. Molly ordered fried shrimp and French fries, while Kyle selected a thick-cut steak with a baked potato. They were both hungry after the long drive and a very light lunch, so they ate without speaking for a while.

Kyle kept expecting Molly to get the conversation going again, but when she didn't, he finally asked, "How did your talk with Shane go? Was it as bad as you feared?"

She dipped a fry into a puddle of ketchup, stirring it around without enthusiasm. "No, it was okay. He was sort of resigned this time, I guess. He told me to be careful and to call him tomorrow when we get underway again."

Kyle studied her face, trying to read her expression.

She sounded kind of down, but she wouldn't look at him, so he couldn't see her eyes. Maybe she was just tired. Or still sore from her injury. Or maybe her brother had been less understanding than she had let on.

It really ticked him off to think of Shane yelling at her—for any reason, justified or not. Kyle was guiltily aware that *he* had snapped at her a few times when he shouldn't have, but he thought he might just take a swing at anyone else who treated her with anything less than respect. Even her brother.

The inappropriately possessive and protective nature of that thought made his scowl deepen.

"What's wrong?"

He smoothed his expression and met her eyes. "How would you like to go to a movie or something after dinner?"

"A movie?"

It had been an impulsive offer, but now that he thought about it, it sounded like a pretty good plan. Sitting in a movie theater wouldn't be too taxing for her, yet it would be much safer than spending too much time alone together at a motel. "Sure. Why not? It isn't as if we have anything better to do."

Actually, he could think of several more interesting ways to pass the time, but the movie definitely sounded like the wisest option. "I'm sure there's a theater around here somewhere. I'll ask the hostess on our way out."

"Yeah, okay." Molly seemed intrigued enough to smile again—which made him feel absurdly smug. "It's a date."

No, he almost refuted immediately, frowning again. It wasn't a date. That word implied an end to the evening that wasn't even a possibility. Seeing a movie together was just something to do to kill a couple of hours before going to bed—in their separate rooms, of course. It was definitely not a date.

He decided to let her statement go unanswered before he steered them onto a conversational path that was much too precarious.

Chapter Eight

It wasn't a date, Molly reminded herself more than once during the evening. Even though it sort of felt like a date, sitting in a darkened theater next to Kyle, sharing a bucket of popcorn, their hands colliding occasionally, knees almost touching.

The movie they had selected was hardly a romantic "date flick." Instead, they saw a noisy, frenetic action film, complete with bullets flying, bad guys and heroes, fast cars and faster women. Just her type of movie.

She had needed this diversion. For two hours, she was able to forget about her leg, her car, the big party that was coming up entirely too soon, the fact that her brother was exasperated with her and that Kyle was probably thoroughly sick of her. She didn't think of the kiss they had shared more than two or three times during that two-hour interlude—which was much less frequently than she had replayed it during the rest of the day.

Unfortunately, it all returned to her when the lights came back up at the end of the film and Kyle extended a hand to help her out of her seat.

His palm was rough against hers. His skin so very warm. She felt the strength in his arm when he boosted her upward, and she realized that he was much more muscular than his slenderness indicated. She had seen the exercise equipment in his home. He must put it to good use.

It was a new experience for her to be so primally aware of a man's strength. Of the way his hand felt at the small of her back. To be so focused on the sound of his breathing, and the scent of his soap and shaving cream.

She'd had a few crushes in her teens, a couple of boyfriends in college, but she had never spent as much time reliving every touch or obsessing over a single kiss as she had today. She couldn't remember ever aching quite this deeply for more.

Kyle parked the loaner car in the motel lot, then helped her to her room, even though she assured him she was okay on her own. Once again, their rooms had a connecting door, so he entered with her to ask if she needed anything else before they turned in.

She gave him a weary-feeling smile. "I'm okay. But thank you for taking such good care of me."

Pushing his hands into his jeans pockets, he shrugged. "It was my negligence that caused you to be hurt."

"Stop saying that," she ordered, tossing her crutches aside. "A board broke. I fell. You've more than made up for it by everything you've had to endure since."

"It hasn't been that bad. A couple of days in a car. Even the breakdown today was hardly a disaster. Waiting around most of the afternoon was sort of boring, but the steak I had for dinner was good. And that's the first movie I've seen in a theater in longer than I can remember. It was a nice evening."

He was trying to make her feel better, she realized, touched by his effort. He must have sensed her guilt that he had been so inconvenienced on her behalf. Maybe he'd picked up on her mounting tension all day, though she devoutly hoped he didn't suspect that it was her strong attraction to him that was causing her to be so nervous.

"I had a nice time, too," she told him quietly.

He stood there looking at her for a moment, and then he cleared his throat and nodded curtly. "Okay. Let me know if you need anything during the night."

He had said that the evening before, too. And, as had happened the last time, her mind immediately filled with fantasies about summoning him during the night. She was quite sure he hadn't meant anything along those lines when he'd made the perfunctory offer, but the images alone were enough to leave her flushed and restless.

"Well..." he said, taking a step toward his room.

Impulsiveness had always been a part of her personality. Sometimes the trait had been a help to her, other times a hindrance, but she had long since accepted that there were times she simply didn't choose to fight her instincts.

It had been her impulsiveness that had started her out on this quest to bring Kyle back to the ranch. It was a similar urge that made her blurt out, "You still haven't told me why you kissed me last night."

He shot her a warning look. "I thought you agreed to forget about that."

"I can't. I've been thinking about it all day."

"Well, don't."

He looked away, but not before she had seen the truth in his eyes. She wasn't the only one who had been thinking about that kiss.

It took only one step to put her between him and the door. She made it somewhat awkwardly because of the brace, but she managed to block his way just as he was preparing to bolt. "Kyle."

He looked as wary as a cornered animal. "What?"

"Kiss me again."

Maybe Kyle was getting to know her a bit too well. He didn't seem as surprised by her request as he probably should have been. Instead, he looked searchingly at her and asked, "Why?"

"Because then maybe I can stop thinking about it."

"How's that?" he asked suspiciously.

"Well, it probably won't be as big a deal this time. You know, without the element of surprise and the whole first-time aspect. It'll probably just be a regular, ordinary kiss—and then we can go back to being friends again."

He lifted a hand to the back of his neck and squeezed. His voice sounded rather strained when he repeated, "Just friends, huh?"

She nodded forcefully. "Just friends."

The way she was just friends with all her other former foster brothers, she told herself. The ones who had been drifting in and out of her life for almost twenty-four years. The way she was still friends with those few would-be lovers who'd quickly ended up seeing her as another great pal.

"So, let me get this straight. We're going to have a 'regular, ordinary kiss,' after which we'll be just friends with no sticky issues left between us."

Hearing him say it like that made her rethink the whole idea. Maybe just this one time she should have curbed her impulse rather than giving into it. "Um…"

A sudden look of resolve on his face, he moved toward her, his silent grace making his limp hardly noticeable at all. Second thoughts turning to third, Molly took a clumsy step backward. "Okay. I think…"

"Just a regular, ordinary kiss." He reached for her, his amber eyes glinting dangerously. "I suppose we should get it over with."

His mouth covered hers before she could tell him that she had changed her mind.

If this kiss was "ordinary," Molly thought a few moments later, then her previous experiences had been sadly lacking. Kyle's lips moved against hers with a clever skill that spoke of experience, despite his earlier claim that his friend had been the one to whom women had been attracted. She hadn't bought it then, and she didn't now.

She couldn't imagine many women who wouldn't be drawn to Kyle's air of deep, quiet, competent strength. Or his beautiful golden-brown eyes that spoke of the years of pain and disappointment that had left him brooding and reclusive—yet still so innately goodhearted that he had given a grieving couple someone new to love and fuss over. And then he had taken the responsibility to see Molly safely home after she had fallen on his porch, which she had pretty much invaded without an invitation.

What woman wouldn't be attracted to him? she asked

herself as her arms seemed to wind themselves around his neck. Or maybe she was just particularly susceptible to Kyle's unique charms.

Taking his signals from her, he wrapped his arms around her and pulled her more tightly against him. She reveled in his warmth. In the very masculine muscles roping his arms and legs. The solid width of his chest and the taut flatness of his abdomen.

Letting her attention wander even lower, she couldn't help but be aware that Kyle was also strongly affected by the kiss. And even as she shivered in purely instinctive reaction, she realized in despair that her naive plan had failed. Not only was this kiss more spectacular than she'd imagined, she didn't even try to convince herself that she and Kyle could be "just friends" now.

He ended the embrace very slowly, with a reluctance that might have indicated his belief that it would be their last kiss. Or maybe she was reading her own fears into his hesitancy.

She didn't want it to be the last kiss, she realized abruptly. Even though he was probably going to break her heart, she wanted to find out what it was like to be with a man who saw her as a desirable woman. A man who made her willing to place her own long-guarded heart at risk.

Kyle would be leaving again—she didn't pretend otherwise—but perhaps the memories she stored away would make the inevitable pain somewhat easier to bear.

"That," he said, his voice gravelly, "was a mistake."

Which she interpreted to mean that she wasn't the only one who had been shaken by their kisses. "Maybe. But now that it's already happened once…"

Leaning into him, she pressed her mouth to his again.

Kyle made a low, rough sound that was half laugh, half groan—and then he cupped her face in his hands and thrust his tongue between her lips. If he was trying to startle her, even to shock her into backing away, he did not succeed. She simply closed her eyes and opened to him, inviting him to take as many liberties as he liked.

Time became meaningless as they delved more deeply into the kiss. She couldn't have said how long they stood there, tasting, touching, exploring. They drew an occasional ragged breath, but her head still swam. She wasn't sure if it was caused by too little oxygen or too much sensation, but she was one kiss away from a complete meltdown. Judging from the way Kyle's hands trembled as they swept over her, he was on the verge, himself.

She wasn't sure what brought him to his senses. Maybe it was the way she moved against him when she shifted to take some of the weight off her injured leg. Whatever the reason, he tore his mouth from hers with a gasp and set her forcefully aside, leaving his hands on her shoulders only long enough to make sure she was steady on her feet.

"Enough," he said.

"Not nearly," she murmured, reaching for him again.

He avoided her with a quick side step. "Molly. No."

"No?"

"No."

She sighed and sank to sit on the edge of a bed, not certain her legs—even her good one—would support her any longer. "I guess I was wrong about it being ordinary."

"I guess you were."

He was gone before she had another chance to speak. He closed the connecting door firmly between them, and she heard the dead bolt lock on the other side.

Play the
Lucky
Hearts
Game

and get...
2 FREE BOOKS
and a FREE MYSTERY GIFT...
YOURS to KEEP!

yes! I have scratched off the silver card. Please send me my *2 FREE BOOKS* and *FREE mystery GIFT*. I understand that I am under no obligation to purchase any books as explained on the back of this card.

Scratch Here!
then look below to see what your cards get you... 2 Free Books & a Free Mystery Gift!

335 SDL EEX9 235 SDL EEWX

FIRST NAME LAST NAME

ADDRESS

APT.# CITY

STATE/PROV. ZIP/POSTAL CODE

(S-SE-02/06)

Twenty-one gets you **2 FREE BOOKS** and a **FREE MYSTERY GIFT!**

Twenty gets you **2 FREE BOOKS!**

Nineteen gets you **1 FREE BOOK!**

TRY AGAIN!

Offer limited to one per household and not valid to current Silhouette Special Edition® subscribers. All orders subject to approval. Please allow 4-6 weeks for delivery.

▶ DETACH AND MAIL CARD TODAY! ▶

© 2002 HARLEQUIN ENTERPRISES LTD.
® and TM are trademarks owned and used by the trademark owner and/or its licensee.

The Silhouette Reader Service™ — Here's how it works:

Accepting your 2 free books and gift places you under no obligation to buy anything. You may keep the books and gift and return the shipping statement marked "cancel." If you do not cancel, about a month later we'll send you 6 additional books and bill you just $4.24 each in the U.S., or $4.99 each in Canada, plus 25¢ shipping & handling per book and applicable taxes if any.* That's the complete price and — compared to cover prices of $4.99 each in the U.S. and $5.99 each in Canada — it's quite a bargain! You may cancel at any time, but if you choose to continue, every month we'll send you 6 more books, which you may either purchase at the discount price or return to us and cancel your subscription.

*Terms and prices subject to change without notice. Sales tax applicable in N.Y. Canadian residents will be charged applicable provincial taxes and GST. Credit or debit balances in a customer's account(s) may be offset by any other outstanding balance owed by or to the customer.

If offer card is missing write to: The Silhouette Reader Service, 3010 Walden Ave., P.O. Box 1867, Buffalo, NY 14240-1867

NO POSTAGE
NECESSARY
IF MAILED
IN THE
UNITED STATES

BUSINESS REPLY MAIL

FIRST-CLASS MAIL PERMIT NO. 717-003 BUFFALO, NY

POSTAGE WILL BE PAID BY ADDRESSEE

SILHOUETTE READER SERVICE
3010 WALDEN AVE
PO BOX 1867
BUFFALO NY 14240-9952

Was he locking her out, or himself in? Either way, he'd made it clear that there was more than a door keeping them apart.

Kyle opened his eyes the next morning to the sound of rain drumming against the windows. *Perfect,* he thought. Lousy weather to go with his lousy mood.

He'd spent the night alternating between urges to walk out of the room and head straight back to Tennessee, leaving Molly to find her own way home, or bursting through that damn connecting door and taking up right where they had left off earlier. Because his conscience wouldn't allow him either option, he'd spent another near-sleepless night wondering when The Longest Road Trip in Recorded History would end—and whether his sanity would hold out until it was over.

He'd slept finally, only to have weird dreams he couldn't really remember when he awoke. He was left with the haunting echo of Tommy McDooley's distinctive laughter in his ears—which was all he needed to get this day started badly.

He took his time showering, shaving and dressing in the last clean clothes he'd brought with him. He was in no hurry to face Molly again.

In the light of day—even a gray, watery day—he had to ask himself what had gotten into him last night. Had someone spiked the popcorn at the movie theater?

It had been the second time he'd let her goad him into acting without thinking, and this time it had taken him much too long to regain control. Had he not come to his senses at the last possible moment, he might have woken up in her bed this morning.

He was grimly aware of the regret that underscored

his relief. It would have been a huge mistake—she was Molly Walker, for Pete's sake—but judging from their kisses, it would have been amazing.

He called the garage before he made any effort to talk to Molly. He was assured that the part had already been ordered from Little Rock and was expected to arrive before noon—but even then, it wasn't a quick and easy repair. Even if everything went smoothly, it would be mid to late afternoon before the car would be ready.

Which left almost an entire day for them to kill. There were so many dangers inherent in that situation that he didn't even want to try to list them all.

The obvious solution was to stay away from her. She had a TV in her room, some books. She could entertain herself for a few hours. He could go hang out at the garage, harass the mechanics into rushing the job. The more he thought about it, the better that plan sounded.

He supposed he should feed her breakfast first.

Drawing a deep breath, he tapped on the connecting door, steeling himself for the sight of her. How would she behave with him this morning? Would she be withdrawn, as she had been yesterday morning? Confrontational? Or would she try again to treat him like a favorite brother?

He ruled out the latter the moment she opened the door and smiled at him. This was not a friendly, familial smile. This one had a shy quality to it, overlaid by a new awareness that could only be described as sexual.

"Good morning," she said, and even her voice had a huskiness that hadn't been there before.

He should *definitely* keep his distance from her today. He had already learned all too well that he couldn't depend on willpower alone to give him the strength to keep his hands off her.

"'Morning. Ready for breakfast?"

"Yes." She wore the navy-and-lime athletic outfit again. The top looked a bit damp around the seams, and he wondered if she had rinsed it out in her sink the night before. He imagined that she would be as glad to see the ranch as he would. She had to be tired of car rides and motel rooms, fast food and lousy company. "Just let me grab my purse."

"And your crutches," he reminded her as he watched her stump across the room. "You're supposed to keep your weight off that leg as much as possible."

She sighed heavily. "I hate the crutches."

"I know. But you need them."

Slinging the strap to her purse over her shoulder, she balanced on the crutches and moved toward the door. "I hope we can find someplace that serves a big breakfast. I'm really hungry."

At least some things hadn't changed, Kyle thought, following her out of the motel room with a shake of his head.

Despite all the useful things her parents had taught her, and all the fine schooling she'd received, Molly's education was sadly lacking when it came to the art of flirtation. She sat across the table from Kyle at a pancake restaurant located near the motel and tried her best to think of something clever and witty to say.

She had been babbling about herself and the ranch for days. She'd tried asking him questions about himself, which was supposed to be what men liked in a conversation, but whoever said that had never met Kyle Reeves. There was always the weather, but there was little to say about it except that it was gray and wet—hardly a romantic subject.

So she talked about the food, and about the people they had met during their journey. She smiled, she made sure their fingers brushed occasionally, she did everything but bat her eyelashes at him. He didn't seem notably overwhelmed. Just the opposite, in fact. He made eye contact with the syrup bottle more than he did with her.

How could he transform so easily from passionate lover to cool, near stranger? Was it really so easy for him to deny the emotions that had flared between them last night?

It was impossible for her.

"So what are we going to do now?" she asked as they finished their breakfasts. Rain still poured in sheets down the window next to their table, which didn't encourage any outdoor activities. As for indoor activities...she swallowed.

"I think I'll go over to the garage and check on the progress of your car. I'll drop you at the motel first and you can read or watch TV while you put your foot up and give that leg a rest."

He spoke casually, almost airily, but the words hit her hard. She didn't believe for a minute that Kyle wanted to spend several more hours in that depressing garage waiting room. Yet still he found that prospect more appealing than spending time with her.

Fine, she told herself, squaring her chin. If he wanted to get away from her, she certainly wasn't going to stop him. If he thought looking at old gossip magazines and drinking decaf sludge from a vending machine was preferable to her company, then he deserved what he would get. "Okay. I have a book I'd like to finish, anyway."

He looked momentarily surprised, as if he had expected an argument. Keeping her own expression as unrevealing as possible, Molly reached for her crutches without saying anything more.

Though she suggested that Kyle could just let her out at the motel and go on his way, he parked and ordered her to wait until he came around to her door with an umbrella. He kept her shielded from the rain as much as possible until she made it beneath shelter, and then he opened her room door for her. He was being just a bit too solicitous—only further indication, in her opinion, that he was feeling a little guilty about his plans for the day.

She was a bit surprised when he followed her inside. She had pretty much expected him to shove her inside the door and take off.

"Is there anything you need before I go?" he asked, hovering just inside the open door.

"No." She dropped into a chair and reached for the paperback she'd left lying on the table. "I'll be fine."

"Maybe I should get you a soda out of the vending machine, in case you get thirsty later."

"If I want a soda later, I'll get one for myself."

"No." He scowled and planted his hands on his hips. "You don't need to be going out of this room by yourself. It isn't safe. Besides, there's water on the pavement in places. Your crutches could slip and you'd fall flat on your face."

"I can take care of myself, Kyle."

"I want you to promise me you'll stay in this room with the door locked until I get back."

"No. I won't make that promise." She opened the book and looked pointedly at the pages. "Go do what you have to do. I'll probably be right here when you get back."

"Damn it, Molly."

She glanced up at him, letting just a hint of her irritation with him show. "You're the one who has told me repeatedly for the past few days that I shouldn't let anyone boss me around. I've decided I agree with you—and I'm starting now."

"You're mad because I'm leaving you here, aren't you?"

She shrugged.

"You could always go with me."

Apparently he thought they would be safe from their libidos in a public place, so it would be okay for her to accompany him. "No. I don't want to spend anymore time in that boring waiting room. But you feel free to spend the whole day there if you want."

"I just thought—"

She waved a dismissive hand. "I can certainly understand if you're getting tired of my company. I wouldn't blame you a bit, for that matter."

"Look, it's not like that."

"You don't owe me any explanations." She raised the book to hide her face.

Kyle reached out to push it down again. "I'm trying to be sensible here."

"I'm not stopping you, am I?"

"I think it's better if we don't spend a lot of time alone today."

"Right. I got the message. So, go."

"Fine. I'll give you a call when your car is ready."

She refused to look up from the book. "Do that."

Still he didn't leave. He just stood there. Looking at her.

She glared up at him. "Do you want to go or not?"

"I don't *want* to go."

She closed the book, her heart starting to beat a little faster. "Then stay."

"You know what will happen if I do."

She wondered almost absently how her heart could be pounding in her chest and her throat at the same time. She hadn't really expected Kyle to admit where they had been headed these past couple of days. His strategy so far had been to pretty much pretend it wasn't happening. When he wasn't kissing her senseless, anyway.

"Nothing has to happen if we don't want it to," she said reasonably. "We could just talk or play cards."

He looked doubtful. "I guess we could give it a try."

If she hadn't known better, she'd have thought he wanted to stay with her. Maybe…maybe he was afraid to stay. And wasn't that an intriguing thought? Kyle afraid of *her?*

She tried to make her smile reassuring. "I promise I won't jump you if you stay."

A mere hint of a rueful smile tugged at the corners of his mouth. "And if I jump you?"

She didn't think he would find it at all comforting if she told him she wouldn't even try to fight him off. It was probably better to say nothing at all.

Kyle looked at her smiling at him, then glanced out the door toward the gray, wet parking lot and the rain that was still falling in sweeping curtains. She would like to think she was the more inviting prospect.

Several long seconds passed before he made his decision. She let out a breath she hadn't known she was holding when he closed the door.

"Get out the cards," he said.

She reached for her bag.

With the steadily falling rain as a backdrop, they played gin rummy all morning. Perhaps they were rather stilted at first, but Kyle seemed to find Molly's cut-throat competitiveness amusing. He even laughed a couple of times.

And Molly learned all over again that Kyle's laughs were definitely lethal where she was concerned. It was all she could to do to speak coherently after he laughed, much less think clearly enough to play cards.

The rain was still falling, though more lightly now, when they grew tired of the game at just after noon. After calling the garage to learn that it would still be another couple of hours before the car would be ready, Kyle left to pick up some lunch. Molly could tell that he was much more relaxed about returning this time; their platonic morning of casual games had put him at ease that they could be together without losing control.

She put the cards away and stretched out on the bed to put her foot up for a few minutes while he was gone. It didn't really hurt since she'd been sitting all morning, but she had been instructed to keep it elevated as much as possible for the first forty-eight hours. Nestling her head on the pillow, she thought about how much she had enjoyed spending time with Kyle.

He wasn't the most loquacious of companions. He certainly wasn't one for flattery or flirtation. He didn't keep her in stitches, as some of her funnier friends did, nor did he engage her in clever repartee that kept her on her toes verbally. He wasn't the best-looking man she'd ever met, though his eyes could make her melt. He certainly wasn't the sunniest natured.

So what was it about him that fascinated her so much? What made her think he was the one who could make her fall head over heels in love for the first—and maybe the last—time in her life?

Listening for his footsteps outside the door, she allowed herself to drift into daydreams.

Her recent restless nights caught up with her as she lay there, and she fell into a light nap. She didn't hear Kyle's arrival until after he had entered and closed the door behind him. Her eyelids flew open when she realized she was no longer alone.

Kyle stood beside the table, studying her with a brooding expression. He had already set the bags of food on the table. She could smell the aromas wafting toward her.

She blinked and rubbed her eyes, trying to quickly clear her sleep-muddled mind. "I guess I dozed off."

"Yeah. Sorry I woke you."

She pushed herself up to one elbow. "That's okay. I didn't mean to go to sleep. The food smells really good."

He moved toward her and held out a hand, obviously intending to help her to her feet. She reached out to lay her hand in his.

She had been moving to stand, but the moment his fingers closed around hers, she froze. His legs were already braced to boost her upward, but he went very still as their gazes locked over their joined hands.

Maybe she tugged. Maybe he leaned forward. And maybe neither of them would ever know who initiated the kiss this time. Almost before Molly knew what had happened, Kyle was on the bed with her, and she was in his arms.

Chapter Nine

Molly speared her hands into Kyle's hair, loving the texture of it. It was still slightly damp, and the faintest scent of rain clung to him—more appealing, in her opinion, than the most expensive cologne. Their bodies were pressed closely together, and she reveled in the differences between them.

"Damn it," Kyle muttered against her lips.

She was startled into a giggle. She hadn't really expected Kyle to murmur sweet nothings, but this was ridiculous.

"I wasn't going to let this happen again," he said glumly, though he didn't release her.

She cupped his face in her hands and kissed his chin. "I know."

He gave her an accusatory look. "You aren't helping me prevent this."

Snuggling closer, she smiled unrepentantly. "What makes you think I want to prevent it?"

He started to disentangle himself from her. "Our food's getting cold."

"I don't care."

"Molly..." Propping himself on his right elbow, he gazed somberly down at her. "I'm not going to try to convince you that I'm not attracted to you."

Pleased that he had admitted even that much, she smiled. "You know I—"

"But—" he broke in before she could reveal too much "—this isn't going to happen."

She was tempted to point out that they were already lying on her bed with his arms around her and his left hand entwined in her hair, so something had already happened. It seemed like a good idea to keep quiet until she heard what else he had to say.

"I'm taking you to the ranch and then I'm going back to Tennessee."

She nodded, feeling the slight tug of her hair in his grasp. "I know. I wish you would consider staying until after the party Saturday, but of course I know you're going back home soon."

"Right. So, uh..." He seemed to have lost the point he was trying to make.

Still smiling slightly, she reached up to touch his face, her fingertips lingering on the scar that outlined his jaw. "Did you expect me to try to talk you out of going back at all?"

He made a face. "To be honest, I never know what to expect from you. Or what you expect from me."

"I don't expect anything from you, Kyle. I like you very much. I enjoy being with you. I also happen to be extremely attracted to you, which shouldn't be surprising since you're such a good-looking, sexy man. But that doesn't mean I'm expecting anything more than you're interested in offering."

It amused her that her almost offhanded compliments had made him flush in embarrassment. He pulled his hand from her hair and touched his own scarred jaw in a gesture that seemed almost subconscious. "Still, er—"

"Still, you're worried that I'm going to end up with a broken heart over you," she said with a sigh.

His color deepened, as did his sudden scowl. "I didn't say that."

"You didn't have to say it. I could tell what you were thinking."

"You're making me sound like a conceited jerk."

"No. Just another man with an overdeveloped sense of responsibility that makes you think you have to decide what's best on my behalf."

"You're comparing me to your brother again?" he asked in disbelief. "Now?"

"My brother. My father. My uncles, cousins and friends. Everyone seems to think I need to be protected from myself."

It always annoyed him when she compared him to anyone else, especially her brother. He leaned closer, his face very near to hers when he growled, "I am *not* trying to be your brother."

She ran her hands up his chest to encircle his neck. "I'm delighted to hear that."

"Behave yourself."

"Why?"

"Well…because."

She toyed with the hair at his nape. "We've already

established that I'm not expecting anything long-term, and that I'm fully capable of protecting myself from the emotional consequences of being with you. We've admitted that we're attracted to each other. So why should we have to pretend otherwise?"

He looked at her with a skepticism that might have annoyed her had she not known he was fighting his own desires in a misguided attempt to look after her. "But—"

Taking matters into her own hands, she tugged at his head, pulling his mouth closer to hers. She spoke against his lips when she said, "Sometimes you talk too much."

It was such an incongruous accusation for him, a man notorious for his terseness, that he was startled into a laugh. Enchanted as always by the rare sound, she muffled it with a kiss. And then he took over, in his usual manner.

Just this once, she thought as she closed her eyes and crowded more closely against him, she would let him get away with it.

Maybe if it hadn't been so long since he had been with a woman. Or maybe if he hadn't been alone with Molly so much in the past few days, allowing him to fall so completely under her spell. Or maybe if she weren't so sweetly, enthusiastically responsive to his every touch...

No. Kyle couldn't find any excuse for his lack of willpower when it came to Molly Walker. There was just something about her that was special. Something he couldn't resist, no matter how hard he had tried.

It might have been a bit easier if Molly had tried, too. Instead, she had smiled at him and laughed with him and kissed him as if he were the most exciting man she had ever met—a heady experience for him.

And then, when he had tried one final time to be noble and self-disciplined, she had convinced him that there was no need for him to deny himself on her behalf.

She had made him feel almost embarrassed about thinking he had needed to protect her from doing something foolish—like falling in love with him. She had assured him that she neither expected—nor even seemed to want—more from him than a pleasant, fleeting encounter.

He didn't know why that bugged him, he thought as he kissed her yet again. He should be relieved that she was open to some no-strings fun. She was, as he had repeatedly pointed out to her, a competent adult, old enough to know what she wanted. And she was giving him every indication that she wanted *him*—at least for now.

So what was holding him back? With a muffled groan, he lifted his mouth from hers. Without the kiss to distract him, he was able to focus on other things—like the way her body was plastered against his. How soft her smallish, but perfectly formed, breasts felt against his chest. The way her thighs cradled him so intimately.

The bulky brace on her right ankle didn't stop her from twining her long legs around him in a way that incited all sorts of heated fantasies. Her hand was inside his sweatshirt, her palm pressed against his back. He was aware that he still needed to gain some weight, and he imagined she could feel the scars that marred his skin, but she didn't seem to notice any imperfections. She looked at him as though she'd like to dip him in chocolate and swallow him in one gulp….

He groaned again. "Let's eat lunch."

She looked down at their bodies, her attention lingering pointedly on his hand, which was cupped rather intimately around her hip. "Now?"

He hastily moved his hand to a more innocuous position. "Yeah. The food's getting cold. If we don't eat soon, it'll be ruined."

She sighed. "Are you getting all noble again?"

"I'm not trying to protect you from yourself, if that's what you're asking. I've learned my lesson about that."

"So why are we stopping just when things were getting…particularly interesting?"

He wasn't prepared to examine the reasons too closely, himself. He said simply, "I'm hungry."

It was obvious that she sensed there was more to his sudden withdrawal than hunger pangs, but maybe she was having a belated attack of common sense, herself. She didn't try to stop him this time when he slid off the bed and walked rather gingerly toward the table.

With a sense of regret, Molly watched Kyle put distance between them. It wasn't a sudden return to sanity that gave her the strength to let him go, but the memory of what she had seen in his pretty brown eyes just before he'd drawn away. It had looked suspiciously like fear.

Who was he *really* protecting from the emotions that flared between them whenever they kissed—her or himself?

He had picked up a container of fried chicken, so the food tasted fine even though it had cooled during the twenty minutes that had passed since he'd returned. Coleslaw and biscuits were the side dishes, both of which Molly consumed with a surprisingly healthy appetite, considering the emotional roller coaster she had been on that day.

Kyle, she noticed, ate sparingly, his expression distant and distracted. "Have another piece of chicken," she urged, nudging the container toward him. "If we're able to get on the road this afternoon, you'll need your strength for the long drive."

He reached almost automatically for another piece. Watching him bite into it, Molly decided he had no idea what it tasted like. For all he knew, he could be eating a carrot. "You seem very far away."

He shrugged. "Just wondering if the car's ready."

"Bill said he'd call, didn't he?"

"Yeah." He glanced at his watch, causing Molly to check the time, herself. It was almost 2:00 p.m. If they left the garage any time before five, they'd still make it to the ranch before too very late.

She had mixed emotions about reaching their destination. While it would be nice to be home, comfortable again in her own surroundings and with her own things around her, it would mean the end of this time with Kyle. They wouldn't have the chance to be completely alone like this again once they were among her family and the other ranch residents.

And then he would leave. She would be surprised if she could even convince him to stay for the party.

But she wouldn't worry about that now. There would be time enough for what-might-have-beens after it was over.

After wiping his hands on a paper napkin, Kyle made a call to the garage. She could tell by his expression that he wasn't completely satisfied with the results. "It's going to be another hour—maybe an hour and a half before the car's ready to go."

She glanced toward the window. They'd drawn the

curtains, but she could still hear the rain falling lightly outside. "Whatever will we do to pass the time?"

Her tone made him look at her warily. "I suppose we could play cards again."

She stood and moved toward him, keeping as much weight as possible off her injured ankle, and ignoring the twinges of discomfort as she walked. "We could do that," she agreed equably.

"There could be something good on TV. An old movie, maybe..."

"That's a definite possibility." She walked her fingers up the front of his shirt. "Or...?"

He cleared his throat. "Charades?"

She giggled and leaned against him. "Okay. See if you can guess what I'm trying to say."

She tugged his head down to hers and pressed her lips to his.

His hands gripped her hips, as if he'd intended to set her aside. Instead, he returned the kiss almost angrily.

They took their time, one kiss leading into another, each one longer, slower, deeper. Kyle frowned down at her when he finally lifted his head. "You are..."

"Spoiled rotten," she supplied when he fumbled for a word. "Remember? I tend to get what I want."

"And what you want right now is...?"

She smiled. "Do I really need to spell it out for you? I want you, Kyle Reeves."

Something flared in his eyes, but he still looked nervous. "For, uh—for how long?"

"For as long as I can have you," she replied simply. "If that's only an hour and a half—well, I can live with that."

"You scare me, Molly Walker," he muttered, but he didn't release her.

She probably shouldn't have been so pleased by the admission. Rather than commenting, she lifted her face to his.

They sank to the bed together. Molly had her hands beneath Kyle's shirt again, stroking his warm back. Her fingertips lingered on the ridges of scars along his left side. They broke her heart, but they didn't make her want him any less.

His hands slid beneath the hem of her pullover, tracing her rib cage, resting his palm against her stomach. Moving slowly higher. Looming over her, he hesitated with his lips only a breath away from hers, his hand hovering just below her aching right breast. "Be sure, Molly."

She nestled closer. "I've never been more sure of anything."

He bit off a groan and crushed her mouth beneath his again, his hand closing over her.

She needed this, she thought with a last moment of coherence. And even more importantly, she believed with all her heart that Kyle needed her—at least for now.

There seemed to be no anger left in him now. No resistance. Only a tenderness she hadn't seen from him before. A hunger he had been trying to hide from her.

With a patience she wouldn't have expected, he removed her clothing and his own. He wouldn't let her take off the brace, which made her feel uncomfortable and clumsy at first, but it wasn't long before she forgot she was even wearing it. Any soreness she might have felt before swiftly evaporated in the heat of his caresses.

Amazingly enough, considering her lack of experience at this sort of thing, there was no awkwardness, no embarrassment. Nothing had ever felt more natural to her, no one more right for her than Kyle.

Somehow, at some time during the past few days, she had fallen in love with him, as surely as she had fallen through his porch. It had nothing to do with their shared past, which had been such a long time ago and at such different stages of their lives. She had fallen for the man she'd found brooding in a mountain cabin.

Whether it had been fate or coincidence or just a series of circumstances that had kept them together for several days after she'd tried to leave him, the result had been that she'd had enough time to get to know him. To tumble head over heels for him.

Yes, it had happened quickly, but she had always known it would be that way for her. Judging by family history, it was in her genetic makeup to fall hard and fast. It had been that way for her parents, who'd been happily married for twenty-five years.

Molly wasn't expecting a happy ending for her and Kyle. Not really. But if pain was inevitable, then pleasure should be savored while it lasted, she decided, arching into his searching hands.

Kyle lay on his back, staring at the ceiling, but he wasn't seeing the white acoustic tiles. Molly snuggled into his shoulder, soft and warm and nude against him, her long, thick hair tumbled around them. Her breathing was still a bit ragged, as was his own, but her heart was slowing to a steady thumping against his, rather than the frantic hammering of only a few minutes earlier.

That, he thought dazedly, had been an amazing experience. And it wasn't because it was the first time he'd been with any woman in more than a year. It was entirely because of Molly.

It should have come as no surprise that she made love

with the same spirit and enthusiasm with which she did everything else. She was obviously inexperienced in many ways, but touchingly eager to learn. No games, no artifice—just honest, undisguised desire and appreciation.

That sort of thing could all too easily become addictive.

"Kyle?"

He hoped she wasn't going to get all introspective now, wanting to talk about their feelings and the ramifications of what they had done—or expressing doubts and regrets now that it was too late to do anything about them. "Yeah?"

"Did you get anything for dessert?"

It took him a couple of beats to change mental gears. Glancing at the remains of their chicken lunch, he shook his head against the pillow. "I didn't think of it. Are you still hungry?"

"I could go for something sweet."

Okay, he was lying there reflecting about how his whole life had been turned upside down, and she was thinking about *food?* Maybe the experience hadn't been as spectacular for her as it had been for him.

Because he refused to get into one of those painful, was-it-good-for-you conversations, he reached for his pants. "I'll see what I can find in the vending machine."

"Anything chocolate would be good."

"Chocolate. Right." Grabbing the rest of his clothes, he limped self-consciously into the bathroom and closed the door.

He felt like a fool now for worrying about Molly's tender sensibilities. Obviously, she wasn't nearly as enamored with him as he had feared.

He had apparently fallen victim to an uncharacteristic attack of swollen male ego.

* * *

Waiting only until the motel room door had closed behind Kyle, Molly shed her brace and hurried for the shower, clinging to furniture on her way to support her ankle. She closed the bathroom door and climbed beneath the spray before the water had even warmed, only then allowing the trembling to overtake her. She had a sneaking suspicion that there were tears mixed with the shower water streaming down her face.

She had desperately needed this brief time away from Kyle. After assuring him that she could handle their lovemaking, it wouldn't have been at all good for her to burst into tears in his arms. Or to tell him that she had fallen hopelessly in love with him. Or to beg him to give them a chance at a long-term commitment.

Kyle hadn't wanted to hear any of those things. He would have made a hasty and complete emotional retreat if she had said them—so she had given herself time to regain control in private.

She wasn't sure how more experienced, more sophisticated people behaved after dazzling lovemaking. Probably they didn't immediately request chocolate and leap into the shower—but maybe she had reinforced her false assertion that her heart was not at risk with him.

At least the question of birth control had not been an issue. Earlier that year she had been prescribed birth control pills to alleviate cramps and monthly migraines. Though she hadn't explained the reasons, she had assured Kyle that she was protected—which might have gone even further toward convincing him that making love with him wasn't a huge, momentous, life-changing event.

Maybe he had simply wanted to believe it was no big

deal to her—wanted it enough to ignore the signs that it had been a very big deal, indeed.

He hadn't told her he loved her. He hadn't said much at all, actually. He had made love to her with a quiet, intense concentration that had sent a pang through her heart even as it had made her soar to heights she had never imagined possible. He was so lonely, so hungry for love and acceptance—yet so deeply guarded that he would never admit he needed anyone.

So she had been breezy and blasé, careful not to reveal anything that would have scared him off. She'd bought herself a few minutes of privacy to have her little mini-breakdown. Now maybe she would be able to face him without falling to her knees and begging him to love her.

Braiding her wet hair into a long plait, she wrapped herself in her green terry robe, drew a deep breath and opened the bathroom door.

Kyle stood when she entered the room. He studied her face searchingly, but she kept a bright smile firmly in place. "Did you find chocolate?"

"Yeah." He waved a hand toward the table, where a package of chocolate cupcakes sat next to an assortment of candy bars and a couple of canned drinks. Apparently, he'd bought every type of chocolate treat in the machine, she thought with a lump in her throat. "Take your pick."

Hoping she would be able to swallow now that he'd gone to this much trouble, she nodded toward the pile. "Looks like we can go on a serious sugar binge here."

"Actually, we'll need to have dessert-to-go," he replied. "The guy from the garage called while you were in the shower. Your car is fixed."

"So we can get on our way again?"

He nodded. "As soon as you're ready."

She found that she wasn't ready at all for the last leg of her time with Kyle. But she hoped her heartbreak wasn't visible in her eyes when she looked at him with a bright smile and all but chirped, "I'll hurry."

He turned away. "Good."

Molly kept the CD player going as they got back on the road toward Texas. She selected lively country music turned to a volume that would have made conversation difficult, even had Kyle been inclined to talk. Which he apparently wasn't, since he drove in silence without taking his eyes off the road.

She made a few random comments about passing scenery—just so he wouldn't think she was being all broody and moony about the events of the day—but he answered in monosyllables. Eventually she stopped trying and settled back into her seat, letting weariness overtake her.

She was a bit sore in a lot of places, but her ankle was really throbbing now. Maybe she hadn't been taking care of it quite as diligently as she should have.

Though she didn't want to call attention to her discomfort, she finally decided she needed to take something for the pain. She dug into her purse for the mild pills she had been given when she'd left the hospital, washing one down with the bottled water she kept in one of the two console drink holders.

"Hurting?" Kyle asked, glancing her way.

"Just a little sore."

He probably knew it was more than that or she wouldn't have resorted to medication, but all he said was, "Why don't you lean your seat back and get some rest? You don't need to keep me company."

His tone seemed to imply that he would be happier if she didn't try to make conversation. She reclined her seat a bit and bunched up the light jacket she usually kept in the back seat, using it for a pillow. The combination of pain, medication and emotional overload made it easy for her to shut down for a while.

She would save her worrying for later, she decided, when she was better rested. She didn't even try to convince herself it would be any easier then to face separation from Kyle—but she would need all her strength to get through it.

Molly slept for quite a while. Remembering how medications affected her, Kyle wasn't surprised that the pill had knocked her out. Even in her sleep, she frowned occasionally and shifted her injured leg.

He hoped he hadn't twisted it or anything when they'd made love. He'd tried to be extra careful, but… well, there had been an interlude when he hadn't exactly been thinking clearly.

As for himself—he felt great. Better than he'd felt in months. Yeah, he still had his usual aches and pains, but right now they just didn't seem to matter.

It had been just what he needed. Mind-blowing sex with a lovely, eager woman who wanted nothing more from him than an afternoon of pleasure. There'd been no awkward attempts at heart-to-hearts afterward, no hint that she would get clingy when they went their separate ways. He should be fully satisfied right now, no complaints at all.

And yet…

He looked at her again. She was sleeping deeply now, the frown lines smoothed into an utterly peaceful expression. He had a hard time reconciling the beautiful woman he saw now with his hazy memories of the carrottopped, gap-toothed, gawky little girl he'd known so long ago.

When he had paid any attention to her then, he'd thought of her as a sheltered, pampered, indulged daddy's girl. She had been well behaved—friendly and happy and kindhearted. No tantrums or bratty behavior that he remembered, but her life experience had been so removed from his own that he'd had a difficult time identifying with her. Two loving, protective parents; an adoring older brother; a huge, supportive extended family; a nice, safe, relatively peaceful home filled with love and laughter and the smell of home-baked cookies—all so different from his own tumultuous, unsettled childhood.

That upbringing had produced a young woman who was headstrong, impulsive, uninhibited and blithely certain that everything would turn out just the way she wanted. She was young, pretty, happy with her circumstances. It was no wonder, he supposed, that she was in no hurry to entangle her life with anyone else.

She certainly wouldn't want to get mixed up with a burned-out, battle-scarred, embittered ex-soldier with a painful past and a precarious future. And he couldn't blame her for that.

He'd been driving for almost two hours when physical demands and an emptying gas tank made a stop necessary. He pulled into a clean-looking convenience store with gas pumps and a fast-food restaurant attached. "Molly," he said, placing a hand on her shoulder. "Wake up."

She opened her eyes and gave him a sweet, sleepy smile that went straight to his gut. "Where are we?"

"We're in Texas. I need a break. I thought you might need one, too."

She gave it a moment's thought, then nodded. "I could use a stretch. Hand me the stupid crutches."

He smiled slightly in response to her resigned request for the hated crutches. And then he opened his door. Barring any further unpleasant surprises, this would be their last extended stop before reaching the ranch.

He supposed he should be impatient to reach their destination—and he was tired of being in the car. But he couldn't say he was looking forward to revisiting his past. Or to seeing Shane Walker again—which was definitely going to be awkward now, with the memory of making love with Molly so fresh in his mind.

The awareness that the journey's end put him that much closer to parting with Molly nagged at the back of his mind, as well. He told himself he was ready to say goodbye—but deep inside, he knew that wasn't true.

Chapter Ten

The lights were on inside Shane's house as they passed it on the way to the main house. Molly had called a few minutes earlier to let her brother know they were close to arrival, so she knew Shane was watching to make sure they made it safely home. The windows of the building that served as the boys' dormitory were also alight behind the blinds; the boys were all supposed to be inside at this hour, and it wouldn't be long before lights out.

Lights were on at the main house, too, even though her parents were still away. Shane must have turned on the porch lights and a few lights inside for their benefit, so they wouldn't have to return to a dark house.

She glanced at Kyle, trying to see his face in the pale green lights from the dashboard. She couldn't quite read his expression. What was he thinking as he drove onto the ranch where he'd spent more than a year of his youth? Was he noting the changes or seeing it as it had been a decade earlier? Was he remembering the fun times he'd had here, or the unhappy circumstances that had brought him here in the first place?

"We've changed a few things since you lived here," she said.

"So I see." He nodded toward the dormitory, which had once been a barn. The new barn was now located behind the old one. "Shane's house has a whole new wing on it, too."

"Yes. He added that about five years ago."

"You said there are four boys in residence now?"

"Right. Jacob, Colin, Elias and Emilio, who are brothers. They range in ages from eleven to seventeen."

"And they all stay in that building?"

"The dormitory. Yes. There's a very nice couple who live in one end of the building. Memo and Graciela Perez. They serve as dorm parents. Memo supervises the boys' ranch chores and Graciela's in charge of the kitchen and laundry. The boys take turns helping with those chores, too. They leave here completely prepared to take care of themselves."

"Your mom made sure I could cook and clean for myself before I left here. Since I've been living on my own, I've put her lessons to good use."

"She'll be happy to know that."

Following her instructions, he drove into the three-car garage and parked in her usual bay. He carried her crutches around to her side of the car and helped her out. The door that led into the kitchen opened just as Kyle closed the passenger door of her car.

Molly wasn't particularly surprised that Shane had been waiting for them to arrive. As much as he'd tried to sound resigned to her encountering so many problems on her solo mission to Tennessee, she knew he must have been worried.

Though she was admittedly biased, Molly had always thought of her brother as one of the most handsome men she knew. A tall, lean cowboy, he had still-thick brown hair dusted at the temples with the merest hint of silver. His piercing blue eyes had been making feminine hearts flutter since he was fourteen, though the only females he had cared to charm lately had been his lovely wife, Kelly, and their adored young daughters.

Before he greeted their guest, Shane stepped forward and gave Molly a quick, but thorough, visual onceover, his attention lingering on her braced leg. "How bad is it?"

"Just a bad sprain," she assured him gently, knowing he was genuinely concerned. "It hardly hurts at all."

Her leg was actually throbbing from her toes to her hip, but he didn't have to know that. She tilted her face up to kiss his cheek when he gave her a hug, even though she knew he was as tempted to yell at her as he was to embrace her.

Satisfied that she was in one piece, he turned to the man hovering self-consciously in the background. Molly stood aside as her brother looked Kyle over, much as he had her. "Hey, Kyle," he said finally, as casually as if they had last seen each other only a few days before.

"Hey, Shane." Kyle stuck out his right hand with a touch of shyness that Molly found endearing. She noticed with underlying amusement that Kyle's own Texas accent had suddenly intensified now that he was back at the ranch.

"You're looking good. I was really sorry to hear about your injuries."

"Thanks. I'm almost back to full speed."

"Glad to hear it. Here, let me help with the bags."

Clutching his own bag, Kyle gave Molly's over to her brother, then followed as they turned to head inside.

Molly wondered if Kyle noted the changes that had taken place inside the house since he'd left. They had redecorated at least once since then, of course, though the furnishings were still simple, sturdy and homey. Cassie and Jared both liked satin-finished wood furniture and painted walls. Lots of green, their favorite color. Plenty of comfortable and inviting chairs. And framed photographs covering nearly every vertical and horizontal surface, documenting twenty-five years of marriage and family.

Covered dishes sat on the table when Molly entered the big, country kitchen. "Kelly thought you might be hungry when you got home," Shane explained. "If you don't want anything now, we'll put this stuff in the fridge and reheat it tomorrow."

"That was thoughtful of her. Tell her thanks for me."

"She would have been here to greet you personally, but the girls are already in bed, so she'll see you tomorrow."

Though Shane suggested that Molly stay in her parents' bedroom downstairs, she insisted she could handle the stairs to her own room. Now that she was home, she wanted her own things around her.

Leaving the crutches at the bottom of the stairs, she clung to the banister and made her way carefully up to the second floor. The walls of the stairwell served as a photo gallery, lined with dozens of framed portraits and snapshots. Molly was aware that Kyle studied those pictures as he followed her and Shane upstairs.

She wondered if he was searching for familiar faces. He had met most of her extended family during his stay here, since the Walker clan tended to congregate at the ranch at every opportunity. Of course, everyone had changed during the past dozen years.

Shane dropped Molly's bag in her room, then turned to Kyle. "The room at the end of the hallway is still used as a guest room."

It was the room that had been Kyle's when he'd lived with them in the predormitory period, back when the ranch had housed only one foster boy at a time. Kyle nodded and followed Shane down the hallway, leaving Molly alone to freshen up.

She sat for a moment on the edge of her bed, reacclimating herself to being home. She had the oddest feeling that she had been gone longer than six days—and that she had returned a different person than she'd been when she left.

The room, itself, hadn't changed, of course. An iron sleigh bed dominated her bedroom. She had used a hand-pieced Lone Star quilt in dark greens and burgundies on cream for a spread, pairing it with a cream dust ruffle and multiple pillows in coordinating colors. The hardwood floor was warmed by a couple of thick rugs. An antique chest and matching double dresser with a beveled glass mirror held her clothes and personal items, and an old wooden icebox served as her nightstand, holding a wrought-iron lamp, a telephone and a clock radio.

Other than a few scented candles and a couple of family photos in antique frames, she had kept ornamentation to a minimum. There were none of the stuffed animals or riding trophies or childishly handcrafted decorations that had overfilled her girlhood room. The only relic of her youth that hadn't been packed away was a favorite antique doll that sat in an old wooden rocker in one corner of the moss-green painted room. A writing desk was tucked into another corner, holding her notebook computer, a small printer and a stack of books and supplies for tutoring the boys.

This was her refuge when she needed time alone, her place to plan and dream and unwind. It wasn't the room she'd slept in as a child; that one was downstairs, close to the master bedroom. She had moved into this room—the one that had been Shane's before he'd built his own house next door—after she'd received her degree in Houston and had moved back home full-time while she looked for a permanent teaching position.

She had needed that transition from her childhood. While her family still occasionally treated her like "little Molly," at least she thought of herself as an adult.

She glanced down at her braced foot, wiggling her toes inside her soft white sock. Starting tomorrow, she was supposed to start exercising her ankle, rebuilding strength and mobility, and she had been advised to see her own doctor in a few days to check the progress of her healing. Within a few weeks, she would be completely back to normal, with no physical evidence of her time with Kyle.

Only she would know how much she had changed on the inside.

Pushing herself to her feet, she moved gingerly toward the door. She heard Shane and Kyle talking as she reached the stairs. She looked down to see them standing at the bottom, Shane completely at ease, Kyle a bit stiff. Though she didn't realize she'd made any noise,

Kyle seemed to sense her presence, his gaze meeting hers as he glanced up.

His expression didn't change, and she made sure hers didn't, either—but something passed between them, anyway. Whatever it was, she hoped it had bypassed Shane's usually acute radar.

Kyle started up the stairs, pausing in front of her. "We thought you might need help getting down the stairs," he said, holding out an arm.

Touched by the courtesy, she braced a hand on his arm, using him to support the weight on her right foot as she descended the stairs. Shane handed her the crutches when she reached the bottom. "You're sure you're okay?" he asked, looking down at her foot. "We can give Joe a call—I'm sure he'd be happy to take a look at your ankle."

"Tonight? Don't be silly. That isn't necessary."

Their cousin Brynn had married an orthopedic surgeon, Dr. Joe D'Alessandro. Molly had no doubt that Joe would see her—or even make the hour-long drive to the ranch if Shane called him—but there was absolutely no need.

"We'll call him tomorrow, then," Shane conceded.

"Stop fussing. It's just a sprain."

Correctly reading her tone, he backed off. "Are you hungry?"

"I could have a snack." She thumped toward the kitchen, downplaying the awkwardness of her injury as much as possible.

Fortunately, she thought a few minutes later, awkward silences were rarely a problem when Shane was around. While she tended to babble to fill such moments, she didn't have to resort to that as they sat around the kitchen table, eating the ham and cheese sandwiches and potato salad Kelly had sent for them. Having already dined, Shane had a cup of coffee while they ate, chatting with the comfortable ease that came so naturally to him.

"So, Kyle, you've got a place in the Smokies now. My dad and I went through there years ago, back when I was a kid. Before he even met Cassie. I remember it being really beautiful there."

"Prettiest area I've ever seen," Kyle answered simply. "First time I visited there, I knew I would live there someday. Just never thought it would be so soon."

Molly remembered him saying there was nothing left for him in Texas, but maybe she hadn't realized quite how permanently he had settled in Tennessee. Had she harbored some faint, secret hope that he would decide to stay here on the ranch with her? If so, how foolish of her.

She had known from the start that her time with Kyle was temporary. He had certainly made it clear enough that he wanted nothing more.

Though her appetite had dissipated, she finished her meal while Shane skillfully drew a few more remarks out of Kyle. Only when she noticed that Shane was starting to give her a few searching looks—probably in response to her uncharacteristic silence—did she make an effort to join the conversation. "How are the boys?"

A quick frown crossed her brother's face. "They're doing okay, I guess."

"What's wrong?"

Looking a bit rueful that he hadn't done a better job of hiding his concerns, Shane replied, "It's Jacob again."

Now it was Molly's turn to frown. "What's he done?"

"No, it isn't him. It's his father. Gene Hayes."

"Oh, no. Don't tell me he's shown up again."

"Yeah. He crawled out from under a rock during the weekend. Showed up drunk on my doorstep demanding that we turn his son over to him. Kelly had the phone in her hand to call the police when he finally decided to leave on his own—but I'm afraid he'll be back."

"He was driving drunk? Shouldn't you have turned him in for that?"

"Someone was driving him. A woman—she stayed in the truck, so I never got a good look at her."

"There's a restraining order against him. He has to leave Jacob alone."

She watched Shane and Kyle share a look before Shane murmured, "Yeah, well, sometimes restraining orders aren't enough. Especially when you've got an aggressive drunk with no respect for or fear of the law."

"Does Jacob know his father was here?"

"No. Kelly and I decided not to tell him."

Molly glanced at Kyle, who was chewing the last bite of a brownie while listening to every word they said.

"Jacob was taken away from his father almost a year ago," she explained for his benefit. "The man is a mean, abusive, irresponsible alcoholic. When he was brought here a few months later, Jacob still had old bruises, poorly healed broken bones and slight hearing loss from being repeatedly hit in the head. He flinched every time anyone came close to him, and he suffered from nightmares. He was several years behind other kids his age educationally because his father hadn't bothered to send him to school on a regular basis. He's much better now, though he still has plenty of emotional healing to do."

"How old is he?"

"He's fifteen. He's crazy about Mom and Kelly and seems fond of me, but he's still a little skittish around Dad and Shane and Memo, even after almost two years."

Kyle nodded. "Makes sense. He's used to male authority figures using him as a punching bag."

"Exactly."

"What about his mother?"

"Gone," Shane replied. "From what we've been told, she wasn't much better than his father."

"Yeah, well, not all women come equipped with maternal instincts," Kyle muttered.

Shane's expression darkened. "Tell me about it."

Molly's throat went tight. She knew Shane was remembering his own early childhood with a neglectful, alcoholic mother and a cold, uncaring stepfather. Jared had been an absent father then, a sailor who spent months at sea—something he regretted to this day.

It had taken a drastic move on Shane's part to change the situation—running away from home at the young age of twelve and living on the dangerous streets of Memphis until his father found him several weeks later. Jared had been so shaken by almost losing his son that he had left the navy and assumed full custody of Shane, vowing to be a better father from that point on. He had kept that promise faithfully, becoming the best father either Shane or Molly could imagine having.

She had wondered at times if Shane ever resented that her own childhood had been so sheltered and privileged compared to his. Yet, because of the loving and generous man he had become despite his own disadvantages, she knew he was happy for her. He had, in fact, done everything he could to contribute to her happiness.

"Maybe Hayes won't come back again," she said

hopefully. "Maybe once he sobered up, he thought about how much trouble he could get in if he didn't move on."

"Maybe," Shane agreed, but he sounded doubtful.

"Don't you think the boy should be warned that his father's been here?" Kyle asked—and then quickly backed off by saying, "Not that I'm an expert on this sort of thing. You guys probably know what you're doing—I just know how I'd feel in his position. I'd want to know."

"Jacob has only recently started to respond to Dad and me," Shane explained. "I really hate to remind him of the reasons he was wary of us in the first place."

"Like I said, you probably know what you're doing. I don't know anything about kids." And his tone suggested he didn't want to know more.

"If Hayes comes around again, I'll figure out a way to warn Jacob without sending him back into his shell—I hope," Shane added. "You're right that he should know to stay on guard."

Seeing that both Molly and Kyle had finished their meals, Shane reached for their dishes. "I'll clear this stuff away. I'm sure you're both tired. You had a long, eventful trip."

"Tell us about it," Molly said with a groan. "I'm wiped out, and I'm sure Kyle is, too."

"I could use some rest," Kyle admitted.

"There's no reason for either of you to get up early in the morning," Shane said as he stacked plates in the dishwasher. "The boys will be in school, and everything else is under control. Just give us a call when you're up and about and Kelly and I will come over."

He didn't linger much longer. Saying they would visit the next day, after Kyle and Molly rested, he let himself out with a warning to Molly to be careful on the stairs.

Kyle pushed a hand through his hair and glanced at Molly. "I guess we should try to get some sleep."

She nodded and shoved her chair back, reaching for the crutches. Kyle followed her out of the kitchen, turning out lights behind them as they made their way toward the stairs. Once again, Molly left the crutches at the bottom of the staircase, clinging to the banister to support her weight on the way up. Kyle hovered close by, one hand partially extended in her direction as if to catch her if she stumbled.

They both paused in front of her bedroom door. Turning toward him, Molly locked her fingers in front of her. "So, um—do you need anything?"

The question seemed to hang in the air between them, inviting several possible responses. She could almost see Kyle considering and rejecting several replies before he finally shook his head. "I'll find whatever I need."

"Okay. Well...good night."

"G'night." He turned toward his room.

"Kyle," Molly blurted before he had taken a second step.

He looked over his shoulder. "Yeah?"

"You don't have to go to your own room just yet."

Turning his head to focus on the room at the end of the hall, he murmured, "I think it's best if I do."

"Not for my sake."

He glanced back at her quickly, and then quickly away. "Maybe I'm going for my own sake."

She would have given a great deal to know exactly what he meant by that. "Are you still planning to leave tomorrow?"

"If I can make arrangements, yes."

She swallowed. "Then would it really be so bad for us to spend these last few hours together?"

"I just don't want anyone to get hurt."

"There's no reason for anyone to be hurt, is there? After all, we both know the score here. Neither of us expects anything after this one night, right? No strings. No clinging. No tearful goodbyes. Right?"

He didn't look like a man who had just been offered exactly what he wanted. Just the opposite. He looked almost annoyed, in fact.

So maybe, she thought with a sinking feeling deep inside her, their lovemaking hadn't been as spectacular for him as it had been for her. Maybe he had simply acted on impulse, and was now sorry it had ever happened at all.

Lifting her chin in an effort to salvage what little pride she had left, she gave a crooked smile. "Then again, you're probably tired. I wouldn't blame you if you want to just crash and..."

He put his hands on her shoulders and jerked her toward him. His lips settled firmly, almost possessively against hers.

As she wrapped her arms around his neck, Molly wondered if she would ever learn to predict what Kyle would do next, even if she'd had a lifetime to spend with him. Every time she thought she'd figured him out, he did something completely opposite from what she'd expected.

Funny how that very unpredictability was so mesmerizing to her, even as she wondered if anyone would ever really know him.

"Maybe you're right," he muttered, backing her through her bedroom doorway. "Maybe this is just what we both need."

He didn't give her a chance to reply before he swept her off her feet and onto the bed.

* * *

Molly woke alone the next morning. She didn't remember Kyle leaving during the night, but she wasn't surprised he had. He wouldn't risk being caught in her bed by her brother or any of the other ranch residents. It had been enough of a risk, in his opinion, to spend any time there at all.

Sore muscles protested when she rolled to sit up on the side of the bed, proving that Kyle had made the most of the time he had spent with her. She wasn't wearing the brace yet; tentatively, she flexed her still-swollen foot, wincing with the movement. She worked her way carefully through the gentle exercises she had been instructed to start out with, then made her way to the bathroom to shower and dress.

She emerged from her bedroom a short while later, wearing a long-sleeved yellow T-shirt with a denim skirt that wouldn't interfere with her brace, and a white sneaker on her uninjured foot. It felt good to be wearing something other than the two athletic suits Jewel had provided for her, even though she'd have rather worn her jeans and boots.

She thought wistfully of her mare, Taffy. She supposed she wouldn't be able to ride again at least until she'd shed the brace, which wouldn't fit into a stirrup.

The door to the guest bedroom stood open, and the room was obviously empty. She thumped toward the stairs, half expecting Kyle to be lurking there to help her down. Instead, her sister-in-law appeared out of nowhere when Molly had descended only two steps.

"Here, let me help you." Her dark blond hair pinned into a casual twist at the back of her neck, Kelly wore a red denim shirt and a pair of jeans, yet still managed to look stylish and attractive.

A licensed audiologist for the local school district, she had cut back to a three-day workweek after her girls were born. Cassie and Graciela had helped Shane with the girls on the days that Kelly worked, and continued to do so with four-year-old Lucy now that seven-year-old Annie was in school.

"I can make it down the stairs pretty well on my own—but stay close, just in case." Molly clutched the banister and hopped down another step. "Where's Lucy?"

"She and Shane are taking Kyle on a tour, showing him the changes that have taken place since he left."

Molly tried to wrap her mind around the image of Kyle spending time with her talkative niece. When that proved impossible, she gave up the attempt and concentrated on getting down the stairs in one piece.

"Shane told Joe about your ankle this morning," Kelly confided. "Joe wants to take a look at it tomorrow."

Molly sighed. "Why did Shane do that? I'm perfectly capable of calling Joe, myself."

"Actually, Brynn called me and I mentioned your ankle and Joe happened to overhear her part of the conversation and then Shane—oh, never mind. The point is, Joe wants to make sure you're healing properly."

Kelly had grown up with Molly's cousin, Brynn, Joe's wife, and Kelly and Brynn were still best friends. They considered themselves as close as most sisters.

"All right, I'll call Joe's office later today and ask when he wants to see me."

"I'm sure Shane will be happy to drive you."

"I'm sure he will." And would probably insist on seeing the X-rays for himself, Molly thought with a sigh.

"So, do you think Kyle will stay for the party?"

"I doubt it." Resting her weight on the crutches, Molly made it into the kitchen, where tantalizing scents told her Kelly had been busy. "Do I smell cinnamon rolls?"

"Mmm-hmm. They're just coming out of the oven. Sit down, and I'll get you a couple."

Molly lowered herself into a chair. She took a sip of the coffee Kelly poured for her. "Tastes good."

Kelly set a plate of still-steaming cinnamon rolls in front of her, then took a seat across the table with a cup of coffee for herself. "Kyle's changed a great deal since he left here, hasn't he? Of course, I only met him a few times before he went away."

"And I was very young when he was here—but I can assure you he has changed a great deal. He's had a tough time the past year."

"So I understand."

Kelly probably referred to Kyle's injuries. She couldn't know that the physical pain was the least of what Kyle had suffered.

Glancing toward the kitchen window, Molly wondered if anyone in her family would notice the changes that had taken place in *her* during the time she had spent with Kyle.

Chapter Eleven

"And my daddy said when I get bigger I can ride in a barrel race. Have you ever seen a barrel race, Mr. Kyle? Daddy used to do rodeo, but he wasn't very good."

"Hey, I wasn't *that* bad," Shane protested, placing a hand on his daughter's bobbing blond head. "I just had other things I wanted to concentrate on. Like keeping all my bones intact," he added in an aside to Kyle.

Kyle smiled obligingly as they made their way across the sweeping back lawn toward the main house, but his head was still spinning from spending the better part of an hour with Shane and Lucy. Kyle had noted on more than one occasion that Molly liked to talk, but she couldn't hold a candle to her four-year-old niece. At least Molly had to pause for air occasionally.

"Run on into the house, honey, and ask your mommy

for a glass of milk or something," Shane instructed, giving Lucy a little push. "We'll be right in."

Lucy disappeared into the house. Shane turned to Kyle, motioning toward one of the wrought-iron rockers grouped invitingly around the brick patio that stretched across the entire back of his parents' home. "Have a seat, Kyle."

He chose a rocker warily, wondering what was coming next. An interrogation? Had Shane somehow sensed that he and Molly were involved in...well, in something?

Shane dropped into one of the nearby chairs, stretching his lanky, denim-clad legs in front of him, battered boots crossed at the ankle. "Does the ranch look pretty much the way you remembered?"

"With a few exceptions, yeah, it's the same."

"You ever think much about your time here?"

"Occasionally. It was the one good time during a generally lousy period in my life."

"You've always been welcome to come back for a visit, you know."

Kyle nodded. "I figured. Time just got away. Things changed. You know how it goes."

"Yeah, I know. You start feeling like a different person. Not sure how you'll connect again with the people who knew you the way you were before."

"That sums it up pretty well." Kyle was surprised Shane understood.

"I've been talking to Daniel Andreas since he married my cousin B.J. He said that's sort of the way he felt when the thought of visiting crossed his mind during the past few years."

Recalling a hazy memory of a slender, dark-haired youth about his own age, Kyle nodded again.

Shane wasn't discouraged by Kyle's lack of verbal response. "You know, the big party for Dad and Cassie is only four days away. If you don't have anything pressing to get back to this week, we'd sure like it if you could stay long enough to visit with them for a while."

Anything pressing. Kyle rolled the phrase around in his mind for a moment, wondering if working out, watching TV and stewing about his future counted as "pressing." It wasn't as if he had to hurry back, but he still wasn't sure he wanted to stay for the party. Even at his best, he wasn't much of a party guy.

Maybe it wasn't as uncomfortable as he had feared, being back at the ranch, faced with so many old memories. And maybe he wouldn't mind seeing Cassie and Jared again. It was the thought of all those other people—strangers, extended Walker family members who would look vaguely familiar but whose names he would probably never recall—that made his palms go damp.

Not to mention the awkwardness inherent in seeing Jared again after sleeping with Jared's daughter.

It was that last thought that made him stammer a little when he said, "I, uh, don't know that I can stay that long."

"I'm not going to pressure you. I just wanted to assure you that you're more than welcome to stay. Molly's been working on this party for months, with some help from Dad's sisters, Layla and Michelle. She's determined to make everything work out perfectly—hence, her trip to Tennessee to drag you back here."

"I don't really think she sprained her ankle just to get me here."

Shane chuckled. "I wouldn't put it past her."

"She's got a big heart."

"The biggest." Shane laced his hands on his stomach

and gazed at his boot tips. "Of course, she can nag you half insane when she sets her mind on something—this party, for example. She came to me last April and told me about her idea, and she's been working and planning on it ever since."

"That long, huh?" It had been late July when Kyle had first been contacted; he supposed it had taken them that long to track him down.

"Oh, yeah. It's been all she's thought about for most of the year. It's a wonder Dad and Cassie haven't figured out that something was going on, but I think it's still going to be a surprise for them."

Kyle was starting to feel guilty. He wondered if that was Shane's intention, telling him how long and hard Molly had worked to make this party so special for her parents.

He told himself that he didn't owe this family anything—but even before he had completed the thought, he knew that wasn't true. He owed the Walkers a great deal. More than he could repay. Put in that perspective, staying a couple extra days for a party didn't really seem like too much to ask.

"I guess I could stay for the party—since it means so much to Molly," he heard himself offering almost before he knew he'd come to the decision. "I'll make arrangements for a flight out late Saturday night."

"Airfare will be cheaper if you wait until Sunday morning," Shane pointed out.

"Yeah. Okay. Sunday morning, then."

"I'll drive you into Dallas, myself. Just let me know when you need to be at the airport."

It seemed to be all settled. Looked as though Kyle would be staying for that party he'd been trying to avoid for several months.

He gave Shane a quick, suspicious look, but Shane's expression was still serene. He didn't look particularly smug at having just skillfully manipulated Kyle into the answer he had wanted to hear. Yet, somehow, Kyle still had the sneaking suspicion he'd just been conned by a master.

Having sent Lucy into the den with a spill-proof cup of milk, a cinnamon roll on a plate and permission to watch television for a short while, Kelly glanced out the kitchen window toward the patio. "They're still sitting out there talking."

Molly tried not to reveal how nervous that made her. "I wonder what they're talking about."

"Probably just catching up. Maybe I should make a fresh pot of coffee for when they decide to come in."

"Not for Kyle's sake. He doesn't drink caffeine."

"Oh. Should I make a pot of decaf?"

"I don't think he cares for coffee at all. He likes herbal teas, though. I know Mom keeps several varieties on hand."

"Then I'll put on a kettle of water."

Molly nodded and glanced toward the back door again, hoping the guys wouldn't stay out there much longer. Her curiosity was driving her crazy.

"You've spent a lot of time with Kyle during the past few days."

"Yes. More than I had intended, of course."

Kelly shot her a quick smile from the sink where she was running water into a copper-bottomed aluminum teakettle. "It doesn't seem as though you've found it too much of a trial."

"No. We've gotten along fine."

"Funny. I'd gotten the impression that he was sort of surly and antisocial."

Since he had sent two representatives back with metaphorical tails tucked between their legs, Molly knew where Kelly had come by that impression. "He can be a little grumpy," she admitted. "But I learned pretty quickly how to handle him when he gets that way."

"If I didn't know better, I'd think you have a little crush on him. Just something about the way you look when you talk about him."

Molly felt her cheeks warm. "Don't be silly," she said, but she didn't meet her sister-in-law's eyes.

"Deny it all you want, but there's something there."

"Even if there were, it wouldn't really make any difference. Kyle's a confirmed loner. He's going back to his little mountain hideaway as soon as he can book a flight. What ties he has to anyone are back in Tennessee, not here in Texas."

"That is quite a way from here," Kelly conceded.

It hadn't seemed so far when Molly had set out on her trip to find Kyle, but she knew it would seem a half a world away after he left. Even had he wanted her to go back with him, which was highly unlikely, she couldn't imagine living that far away from her family. Her aunt Lindsey lived in Little Rock, not even halfway to Kyle's place, and Lindsey had never been able to participate fully in all the family get-togethers and impromptu parties.

Not that Kyle would ask, of course. More likely he'd be glad to see the last of her when he left. She couldn't even talk him into staying a few more days for the party.

The back door opened and Shane ambled in, followed by Kyle. Shane draped an arm around his wife's shoulders and kissed her cheek. "Where's Lucy?"

"Watching cartoons in the den." Kelly smiled at Kyle. "I've heated some water for tea. Would you like a cup? We have several herbals without caffeine. And fresh cinnamon rolls, if you're interested."

"I'm interested in both. Thanks." He pulled out a chair and sat next to Molly, his gaze meeting hers for a moment and then sliding away.

"Kyle's decided to stay and join us for the party Saturday," Shane announced cheerfully. "You don't mind having a houseguest for another few nights, do you, Molly?"

She blinked, but managed to contain her surprise, though her curiosity was running rampant. How on earth had Shane talked Kyle into staying? "I'd be delighted," she said brightly, without looking at Kyle. "Mom and Dad will be so pleased."

"They're going to be so surprised," Kelly predicted. "I can't believe how much Molly has gotten done without even letting a hint of her plans slip to her parents."

Molly smiled modestly. "I really wanted to do this for them. But I've had a lot of help, you know. You and Shane, and aunt Layla and aunt Michelle. Everyone at Walker Investigations who helped me track down the foster boys we'd lost contact with."

"So everything is pretty much on track on your end?" Shane asked.

"It's going to be a busy week, but nothing I can't handle."

Shane nodded and glanced at Kyle. "Since you're going to be here anyway Kyle, maybe you could give me a hand for the next couple of days with some of the outside preparations."

Molly watched as Kyle gave Shane a look of guarded intrigue. "I'd be glad to help out."

She thought he sounded almost relieved to have the prospect of something to do for the next few days.

As for herself, she couldn't help wondering about the next few nights.

Molly didn't see much of Kyle that day, since he spent a lot of time outside with Shane. In the meantime, she and Kelly—with a little "help" from Lucy—made a half-dozen lists of details to be seen to before the party.

Working on the party plans gave her something to do besides brood about Kyle, but didn't stop her from wondering about him periodically. Specifically, she wondered what he and Shane were talking about out there.

"...as for the logistics of housing everyone, it looks as though all the arrangements have been made," Kelly said, breaking into Molly's reverie. "Most everyone from out of town prefers to stay in a motel, and they've already made reservations. Everyone else lives close enough to drive back and forth."

"I assume Lindsey and Nick and their kids are staying with Michelle and Tony?"

"Yes. They'll drive to Dallas on Friday. By the way, I don't envy you having to admit to Lindsey that you drove right through Little Rock—twice—and didn't even call her."

Molly shifted guiltily in her chair at the kitchen table where they had spread all their paperwork. "If I'd called on the way to Kyle's house, she'd have tried to stop me, or would have insisted on someone accompanying me the rest of the way. I didn't call on the way back because Kyle was with me and it would have been too awkward."

"Mmm. Maybe you'll get away with those excuses."

They both knew she wouldn't, of course. Lindsey

would have a few things to say—but since she'd have to get in line behind Jared and the other relatives, Molly figured it would be routine by then to say she was sorry and promise never to do such a reckless thing again.

The phone rang then, and Kelly jumped up to answer the kitchen extension. Molly dutifully admired the picture Lucy had drawn with colored markers, then looked up when Kelly held the receiver out toward her. "It's your mom."

For the first time in her life, Molly hesitated before reaching for the phone to speak to her mother. She could only hope Kelly would attribute her sudden surge of nerves to her determination to keep the anniversary plans secret.

"Hi, Mom. Are you having a good time?"

Cassie's rich voice came through the line with a vibrant clarity that made Molly ache to hug her. "We're having a wonderful time, even though your father is already getting restless to get back home."

"Tell him he'll be home soon enough. You should both enjoy every minute of this trip. You've had so few of them together."

"How is everything there? Going smoothly, I hope?"

Molly glanced at the papers scattered across the kitchen table. "So far."

"How are the boys?"

"All doing well." She saw no need to mention Hayes's unpleasant appearance at Shane's door.

"Good. And you? Are you okay?"

She looked down at the brace on her right leg. "I'm fine. Tell me about everything you've seen this week."

Cassie laughed. "I couldn't possibly do that in one phone call, but I'm taking lots of pictures."

They chatted for a few more minutes, and then Cassie announced that she had to end the call. "I'll see you Saturday, sweetheart. Your Daddy sends his love."

"Give mine right back to him. And to you, too. Bye, Mom."

She handed the receiver back to Kelly, who waited to replace it in the cradle so Molly wouldn't have to get up. She wasn't sure she had done a very good job of sounding entirely natural with her mother, but she was confident that she hadn't let anything slip—about the party or the fact that since she'd last seen her parents, Molly had fallen head over heels in love.

In addition to the party, the entire family's anniversary gift to Cassie and Jared was a new outdoor kitchen for the parties they were so fond of hosting. While most of the clan had donated financially to the cause, Shane and Memo had done the actual work, with help from the foster boys after school and on weekends.

The Walkers had always believed in the benefits of honest physical labor, Kyle reflected, wiping a film of sweat from his forehead. He and Shane had just wrestled a large, stainless steel, built-in grill into place, and now Kyle stood aside while Shane connected the gas lines.

It felt good to be useful. To be treated like an able-bodied man again. Shane cut him little slack, crediting him with enough sense to decide for himself how much he could comfortably handle.

Memo, a quiet, easygoing man who reminded Kyle a bit of his friend Mack, had left a while earlier to pick up the boys from school. While Shane finished connecting the grill, Kyle studied the kitchen, which was almost complete.

Protected from the elements by a slate-roofed, open-sided wooden structure, the kitchen consisted of a stainless steel sink, small refrigerator and the massive grill–rotisserie–gas burner unit they had just installed. Lights were strung overhead for evening entertaining, and a fire pit was surrounded by a Mexican tile floor that would hold a couple of café tables and several chairs. Certainly not enough seating for the crowd expected that weekend, but enough for smaller family dinners outdoors.

Shane had explained that Molly and Kelly would place big Mexican pots filled with hardy plants along the borders of the outdoor room. Future plans included a water garden with a small waterfall nearby, to add the soothing sounds of water to the backyard retreat.

"And more bird feeders," Shane added, taking a step back to catch his breath and admire their handiwork. "Mom's a nut for the birds."

There were already several feeders and baths scattered around the yard. Kyle looked beyond the outdoor kitchen to the dormitory, the barn and the green pastures beyond. "I can see why you and Molly enjoy living here so much. It's a great place."

"A different view from what you see in the mountains, but this is pretty much paradise, as far as I'm concerned," Shane murmured, his gaze following Kyle's. "I know Dad feels the same way. This is exactly what he and I always wanted during the years we drifted around looking for a place to settle, before he met Cassie or reconnected with his brothers and sisters. I don't know if you remember the story about Dad finding his siblings twenty-five years ago?"

Kyle frowned. "I remember hearing something about

them all being separated as children, then coming back together years later. Your dad spent a lot of time in foster homes, himself, from what he told me."

"He did. He was the eldest of seven kids who were separated when their parents died when Dad was eleven. My aunt Michelle was the one who brought them back together. She'd been adopted as a toddler and didn't even remember her biological family, but she found out about them after her adoptive mother died. She hired Tony—whom she married shortly afterward—to find her siblings. He put his investigators to work, and within a couple of years, they'd located everyone except a brother who died years earlier, leaving one daughter, my cousin Brynn. The one who's married to the orthopedic surgeon who's going to look at Molly's ankle."

Following the story easily enough, Kyle nodded. "They've all become close since they were reunited. I remember seeing them all together at family barbecues here when I was in high school." And envying the family bonds between them he'd never experienced for himself, he added mentally.

"They're very close. You'd never know they weren't raised together. But I guess that's why they like to get together so often now—to make up for lost time. Michelle and Lindsey were the only ones adopted into new families. The others were all older, and remembered being together for a time. All of them spent a lot of years missing their family and searching for a place to call home."

Kyle could empathize with the need to find a place to belong. That was exactly what he had faced as he'd lain in a hospital bed in Germany, his best friend dead, his military career at an abrupt end. He hadn't had a clue where to turn—and then Mack McDooley had shown up at his bedside to assure him that he did have someplace to go.

It had touched Kyle immeasurably that Mack had gone to that effort, even in the depths of his own grief over the loss of his son. Knowing that Kyle had no family of his own, Mack and Jewel had taken him into their family, helping him find a place to live, patiently drawing him out of his depression, offering him hope for his future—much as Jared and Cassie had done a dozen years earlier.

For a guy who'd had his share of hard luck, he'd been extremely fortunate to have had the Walkers and the McDooleys in his life, he mused.

Speaking of boys who had been lucky enough to come into this family…

Kyle looked around as Memo Perez ushered the four foster boys out of the dormitory. "You got things for this crew to do, Shane?" Memo called out.

Shane grinned. "Always."

As the boys groaned, Shane turned to Kyle. "Kyle, meet the gang. Jacob, Colin, Elias and Emilio." He pointed to a gangly fifteen-ish redhead, a chubby towhead about the same age and a pair of dark-haired, dark-eyed boys who were obviously brothers, the older perhaps seventeen, the other five or six years younger. "Guys, meet Kyle Reeves. He lived here for a while when he was a teenager."

"You was a foster kid?" the towhead, Colin, asked.

Kyle nodded. "I was here for just over a year when I was seventeen. I left after I finished high school."

"They make you muck out stalls?" Elias asked, his lip curling.

"Every afternoon. Can't say it was my favorite chore, but I lived through it."

"How'd you get that scar on your face?" Emilio, the youngest boy, inquired.

"Emilio, that's not polite," Memo chided with an apologetic frown toward Kyle.

Kyle shrugged. "It's okay. I was wounded overseas by a roadside bomb. I was in the Marines."

All four boys looked at him with widened eyes, obviously intrigued by meeting someone with such an adventurous past. The scar, rather than an oddity, had now become a mark of heroism to them. Because he wasn't comfortable with the image of himself as a war hero, Kyle turned abruptly to Shane. "I'm getting pretty thirsty. If you don't need me for anything else right now, I'll go inside for a while."

"Yeah, go sit and relax for a bit," Shane encouraged him. "We've put in a hard afternoon."

Kyle hoped he had worked hard enough that he would be able to sleep that night. Alone. Without spending hours lying in his bed aching to go to Molly.

But then again, he didn't think it was possible to work himself to that point.

Late that afternoon, Shane insisted that Kyle should get on a horse. "Can't have you turning into a city boy," he said with a laugh, leading a glossy, brown, saddled gelding around the end of the barn while Molly and Kelly watched. "Jump on. Bodie here needs some exercise."

Kyle made a face. "It's been three years since I was on a horse, and I was in much better shape then," he demurred. "I'll probably fall right into the dirt."

"Nah. It's like riding a bike. You never forget." Grinning, Shane motioned toward the stirrups. "C'mon, Kyle, it's not like I'm asking you to rope a calf or race to the back property line. Just ride around the yard here. Show me that you remember everything I taught you when you were a skinny, funny-looking kid. Rather than the skinny, funny-looking guy you are now," he added, mischievously.

Molly was pleased that Kyle chuckled in response to Shane's cheerful put-down. Though he cautiously approached the right side of the patiently waiting horse, he still seemed concerned about climbing on. "No laughing if I fall on my butt," he warned Molly.

She grinned. "Sorry, greenhorn. No promises from me on that count."

For all his protests, Kyle wasn't nearly as rusty as he'd feared. Placing his right foot into the stirrup, he swung himself into the saddle almost as easily as if it were something he did everyday. Once again, Molly was struck by how gracefully he moved, despite his physical limitations. She wished she could better remember what he'd been like as a teenager. Had he always been so well coordinated, or had that developed during his rehabilitation?

"Not bad," Shane approved. "Careful, though. Tennis shoes aren't made for stirrups, the way boots are."

Kyle nodded and wheeled Bodie around to trot briskly around the perimeter of the big yard. He looked as though he enjoyed being on horseback again.

Molly looked down regretfully at her brace and crutches, wishing she could join him for a nice, long ride. By the time she got rid of these things, he would be gone, and there would be no chance to ride with him, she thought wistfully, her chest aching with the thought.

"Wow," Kelly murmured, moving close to Molly's side. "He looks good up there, doesn't he? I guess I'm just now realizing how attractive he really is, once he relaxes and lets himself smile."

"Yes, he is nice looking." Molly tried to speak casually, but the look her sister-in-law gave her said she hadn't done a very good job of it.

"Yeah, right," Kelly said with a sudden, wicked smile. "Like you've hardly noticed in the past few days."

"Haven't noticed what?" Shane asked, joining them just in time to hear the last few words.

"Nothing that's any of your business," Kelly shot back, playfully punching his arm.

"Where are the girls?" he asked, looking around for his daughters. "I thought they wanted to ride before dinner."

"Last I saw, they were playing a video game with Emilio. I'll go get them."

Kelly turned and walked away. Shane and Molly both looked at Kyle again. Perhaps Shane was still remembering the boy he'd known in the past—but Molly was much more interested in the devastatingly sexy man she saw in the present. Now if only she could do a better job of hiding that reaction from her much-too-perceptive older brother than she had with his equally observant wife.

Chapter Twelve

Molly spent an hour in the dormitory before dinner that evening, catching up with the boys, reviewing their schoolwork, working with Colin on a math assignment and with Emilio on a reading assignment he was finding particularly difficult. Afterward, while the boys ate in the dormitory dining room—delicious, healthy food prepared fresh in the dorm kitchen by Graciela—Molly and Kyle dined with Shane, Kelly, Annie and Lucy.

Kyle was quietly courteous during dinner, responding politely to conversation, and watching the girls with a cautious fascination that Molly found amusing. It was obvious that he hadn't spent much time with children.

She had a vague memory of him looking at her much the same way all those years ago.

He walked her back to the main house after dinner. "Kelly's a good cook," he said, making small talk as they moved slowly down the pathway between the two houses. "I enjoyed the dinner."

"She likes to cook almost as much as Mom does. Which is why Shane's always fussing about having to watch his weight—not that he ever slows down enough to have to worry about calories," she added.

"It felt strange to be on horseback again. I guess you'll be glad when you can ditch those crutches and get back into the saddle. Shane showed me your mare. She's a pretty one."

"She's a sweetheart. And yes, I will be glad to get rid of these things—for lots of reasons."

Kyle reached for the back door, pushing it open to allow her to precede him inside. "Do you still ride in horse shows and things?" he asked, following her into the kitchen. "I seem to remember you having a bunch of trophies and ribbons even when you were just a little kid."

"I rode through high school, but I stopped competing when I left for college. I just didn't have the time for it anymore."

"Do you miss it?"

"Not really. It was fun when I was a kid, gave me something to do to keep me out of trouble, but now I just enjoy riding for pleasure."

"I see." Without quite looking at her, he put a hand to the back of his neck, squeezing as if the muscles there were tight. "I guess I'll turn in early tonight. I've used muscles today I'd almost forgotten I had. Think I'll take a hot bath, read for a while, then get some sleep."

A little startled, she blinked. "Oh. Okay—is there anything you need before you go upstairs?"

"Nope. But thanks, anyway. See you in the morning."

He could move surprisingly fast when he wanted to, she thought moments later, when she stood alone in the kitchen staring at the place where he had been.

He hadn't even kissed her good-night.

She tried not to take his desertion too personally. He probably *was* tired, she told herself. She had seen for herself how much he and Shane had accomplished that day. He seemed to have been limping a bit worse than usual as they'd made the short walk from Shane's house, though of course she had known better than to comment.

Yet, as much as she tried to rationalize, she knew weariness had little to do with him bailing out on her so early. Obviously, Kyle had simply had too much "togetherness" for one day. Too many reminders of the past. Too much evidence, perhaps, that Molly's life was still very different from his own.

All she could do, she thought with a wistful sigh, was to give him the space he needed. And if he didn't come close to her again before he ran back to Tennessee... well, she could deal with that, too.

Kyle sat sprawled in one of the spring rockers on the back patio, idly watching a cow and her calf eating grass in the distance. A glass of lemonade rested on a small iron table beside him; Kelly had actually squeezed fresh lemons to make it for him.

These people were unbelievable.

It was Thursday afternoon, and it was the first time since he'd arrived at the ranch that he'd been alone outside his bedroom. He'd spent Wednesday finishing the outdoor kitchen with Shane, both of them working until they were too tired to do more than grunt during the dinner they shared with Molly, Kelly and the girls. Afterward, Kyle had locked himself in his bedroom, relieved that the physical exertion had exhausted him enough to sleep through the night without waking.

Hard work, he had discovered, was better than a cold shower when it came to avoiding any further intimate contact with Molly. As much as he still wanted her, he had decided there would be no more late-night visits to her bedroom. It didn't seem right, somehow, to violate Shane's trust—not to mention that Jared would absolutely hate it. And besides, it wasn't as if anything would come of it, since he would be leaving in a few days and might never see Molly Walker—or any of her family—again, he reminded himself with a hard, rather painful swallow.

Shane had driven Molly to Dallas that afternoon to see her cousin's husband, the orthopedic doctor. They hadn't yet returned. Kelly had gone shopping with the girls after school, and Memo had the boys doing their chores.

Having declined Shane and Molly's invitation to accompany them to Dallas, Kyle had taken advantage of the peace and quiet to rest and regroup. He'd needed this time to brace himself for the rest of his visit, he thought, though he wasn't sure it was possible to fully prepare himself for the upcoming party.

A shuffling sound from behind him caught his attention, and he turned his head to investigate. The lanky redheaded kid, fifteen-year-old Jacob Hayes, had just stepped around the corner of the house. He hesitated when he saw Kyle, then moved tentatively forward. "Hi."

"Hi. Finished with your chores?"

Jacob nodded. "Memo said we could entertain ourselves for a while before dinner. The other guys are playing video games."

"You don't like video games?"

"I just wanted some quiet. They get kind of loud sometimes. And Elias and Emilio always end up fighting. I guess brothers do that a lot."

Kyle chuckled. "I need quiet time, myself, every once in a while. You want some lemonade?"

Jacob's eyes lit up. "Yeah, sure."

Pushing himself to his feet, Kyle motioned toward a chair. "Sit down. I'll be right back."

He returned carrying a glass of lemonade for Jacob and a handful of cookies for both of them. He wasn't sure what the rules were on predinner snacking, but as skinny as this kid was, he didn't figure a couple of Oreo cookies would do any permanent damage.

"Thanks." The boy accepted the snack with the eagerness of the average hungry teenager.

"If this is against the rules, you were never here."

Jacob grinned. "Gotcha." He twisted a cookie apart and licked the filling.

Kyle took a bite of his own cookie and washed it down with a swallow of tangy lemonade. He hadn't asked why any of the boys had been placed here at the ranch, but he was pretty sure Jacob was the one with the abusive, alcoholic father. Which probably explained the boy's noticeable nervous twitches, he thought sympathetically.

"How do you like it here on the ranch?" he asked the boy, feeling the need to initiate some sort of conversation.

Jacob shrugged. "It's not so bad. Graciela's a good cook. Cassie makes cookies for us sometimes. Shane talks tough, but he's pretty easygoing, really."

"What about the others?"

"Memo and Jared don't say much, but everyone

knows you better listen when they do. We're not scared of them or anything," he added quickly, "it's just…"

"You don't like disappointing them." Kyle remembered the hollow feeling he'd get after he'd broken some house rule and Jared had given him the look that said he'd expected better. Earning a smile or an approving pat on the shoulder from Jared Walker had been a heady reward for a kid who practically idolized the taciturn cowboy. He wouldn't be surprised if all the foster boys came to feel that way about Jared.

"And Molly?" he asked, thinking of the one family member Jacob hadn't yet mentioned.

Jacob rolled his eyes. "I know she's your girlfriend and all, but she's a real pain when it comes to schoolwork. I mean, we all like her, but sometimes we're just not in the mood for homework and stuff. Other guys at school blow off their homework all the time, but we've always got to turn ours in, even if there's a good TV show or a ball game or something on. Elias calls her the homework tyrant."

It took Kyle a few moments to catch up, since his brain had sort of frozen in response to Jacob's opening comment. "First, Molly's not my 'girlfriend,' she's just an old friend from when I lived here myself. As for the schoolwork, I know you think it isn't important, but it is. Those other guys blowing off their homework and thinking they're too cool to study? Check with them in ten years when you've made something of yourself and they're still asking, 'Do you want fries with that?' "

Jacob sighed. "That's the kind of thing Jared's always saying."

Kyle chuckled. "Where do you think I learned it?"

The boy munched another cookie, took a sip of lemonade, then asked, "So what was *your* story? How'd you end up here?"

Kyle didn't take offense at the question, since he had initiated the conversation, but he wasn't fond of talking about his past. He answered without embellishment, "My single mom got sick and couldn't take care of me. She died while I was in my second foster home, before I came here."

"My mom ran off a few years back," Jacob murmured, gazing down into his lemonade with another twitch of his facial muscles. "She got tired of my dad yelling at her and hitting her—and I guess she got tired of me, too, since she didn't take me with her."

Kyle knew how much it hurt to be abandoned by a mother—his own had pretty much turned her back on him even before she'd gotten sick. But because he knew that a kid needed something positive to hold on to, he said, "Maybe she wanted to take you with her, but she didn't think she could take care of you."

Obviously, it wasn't the first time Jacob had been offered something along those lines. "Yeah. Maybe."

"You've had a tough time, and it isn't fair that you had to go through it," Kyle said bluntly, remembering what he'd heard about the boy's father. "Still, you should consider yourself lucky that you ended up here. Take advantage of what you've found here, okay? Let the Walkers show you how to stay on the right path, so you don't end up making the same mistakes your parents made."

"Were you lucky to be here?"

"You bet. The other homes I was placed in—well, they didn't work out. I was starting to get really bitter, thinking maybe no one in the world cared about me—and then I came here."

Jacob nodded. "That's the way I was at the other home. I didn't like the people there, and I don't think they liked me much, either. It didn't help that my dad kept showing up and making trouble for them. They hated that. But Jared said he could handle it."

"He can handle it." All these years later, Kyle still tended to believe that Jared Walker could pretty much handle anything.

"Yeah. Even though Jared's older than my dad, he stays in real good shape. I'm pretty sure he could take him."

"I don't think it will come to that. But you can feel safe here."

Jacob seemed to sink a bit more deeply into his chair. "He was here a few days ago. My dad. They don't think I know, but I heard him yelling and I looked out the window. I heard him say he'd be back."

Which only proved that Kyle's gut instinct had been right this time. Someone should have talked to the boy after his father's appearance, rather than letting him struggle alone with his fears. "Shane didn't know you saw them," he tried to explain. "He thought it would upset you if you found out. He was trying to protect you."

"I know. But Shane doesn't know my dad like I do. Shane's too nice to everyone—too easygoing, you know? I'm—" He stopped short of admitting that he was afraid.

Kyle didn't allow that evasion. "You're afraid your father will hurt Shane. Or yourself. Or someone else here on the ranch."

Jacob nodded miserably, his knuckles white around his lemonade glass. "Maybe you could warn them to be careful? I mean, you were, like, a marine and you went to war. Even if you got blown up and now you limp and all, you know about things like not underestimating your enemy and being prepared and stuff, right?"

Suddenly feeling much older than twenty-nine, Kyle pushed a hand through his hair with a deep sigh. What he had learned was that no one could ever be fully prepared for everything life could throw at you. That the most carefully mapped-out plans could disintegrate in an instant. And that people you had come to rely on and care about could be taken away in a heartbeat.

Torn between offering reassurance and telling the kid the hard truth, he said merely, "I'll tell them you want them to be careful."

Jacob nodded, apparently settling for what he could get. "So, how long are you staying here?"

"Until Sunday. I'll be here for the party Saturday, but after that I have to get back home."

"Where's home?"

"East Tennessee." Funny how quickly it had come to be home to him, Kyle mused.

"You got family there?"

"I have friends."

"So you're not, like, married or anything?"

"No."

"Oh. So maybe you and Molly…?"

Kyle raised an eyebrow in the young, would-be matchmaker's direction. "That's not likely. I like my life there, and she's happy here."

Not to mention all the more significant differences between them, he thought. But the kid didn't need to hear about that.

Still young enough to be satisfied with relatively

simple answers when it came to male-female relationships, Jacob nodded. "I don't think Molly would like living anywhere else. She and her family are pretty tight."

"I know." And because he knew, he wondered why hearing it confirmed by someone else made his gut tighten. It wasn't as if he'd have asked Molly to go back with him even without that obstacle, he reminded himself, thinking of all the other differences he had just mentally listed.

"Besides," Jacob added around the last mouthful of cookie, "I guess I—I mean, the guys and me—wouldn't really want you to take her away, anyway."

"Even if she is a homework tyrant?" Kyle teased, forcing a smile.

Jacob shrugged and scuffed a sneaker toe against the patio bricks. "At least she cares about us," he muttered.

"Yeah," Kyle said, letting out a slow breath. "She cares very much."

Jacob set his empty glass on a table and jumped to his feet. "Speaking of Molly, I'd better go. I'm supposed to have an essay written before she comes in to tutor later, and I'm only half-finished."

"Better get with it, then."

"Okay. See you, Kyle."

"See you, Jacob."

Kyle found himself oddly drained after the boy left. Funny how a relatively brief conversation with a gawky kid was more wearying—at least mentally—than a couple of hours of hard manual labor.

Kyle was sitting in the den, reading one of Jared's ranching magazines, when Molly entered the room later that evening. They'd had dinner earlier, and then she had gone back to the dormitory to work with Emilio. That had been more than an hour ago.

Kyle glanced up when she came in. "Hi."

"Hi. Sorry I took so long. The boys had a lot of extra schoolwork tonight."

Kyle shrugged. "I can entertain myself. I figured you were busy."

He watched as she crossed the room to sit in a chair near his. "How's the cane working out for you?"

"Much better than the crutches. Joe said I shouldn't even need the cane in another couple of weeks if I'm faithful about the ankle exercises."

"You should make sure you do them, then."

"Trust me, I will. I can't wait to be back to full speed."

He nodded without looking at her. She bit her lip, wondering if he was thinking about how he would never fully recover from his own much more serious injuries.

As relatively minor as her own injury was, it had been both painful and frustrating to be incapacitated for even a short time. She couldn't imagine how much worse it had been for Kyle.

"I hear you talked to Jacob this afternoon," she said, deciding to change the subject.

"He told you?"

"He mentioned it."

"Did he, uh, say what we talked about?"

Something about the way he asked made her wonder just what she had missed. "No. He just said you gave him a glass of lemonade. He was very cool and casual about it—you know, as if it were no big deal. I'm sure he was trying to make the other boys jealous."

Kyle looked startled. "What would they be jealous about?"

She smiled a little in response to his cluelessness. "You're older, you were a marine, you left here to have adventures like the ones they read about in books. Or at least, that's the way they think of you."

"Yeah, well, they've got the wrong impression."

"They're troubled boys in search of male role models," she reminded him. "Dad and Shane and Memo all represent different qualities to them, but you're a little more exotic, in their eyes, than the settled, married men who live here on the ranch."

"They'd do better to look to your father and brother," he muttered. "I don't even know what *I'm* going to do from this point. I'm sure as hell in no position to serve as a role model for anyone."

"Apparently, you did just fine with Jacob. He seemed a bit more relaxed than usual this evening."

"He told me what's been bothering him this week. He knows his father was here," Kyle said bluntly. "He's been worrying himself sick about it. I told you someone should have talked to him."

Molly shook her head regretfully. "I had no idea. How did he find out?"

"He saw him through the dorm window. He asked me to warn the family to be careful. He seems to be worried that his father will hurt someone here."

"He wouldn't dare."

"It's still a good idea to be on guard. Especially for Lucy and Annie's sake."

Molly could almost feel the blood drain from her face. It had never even occurred to her that Hayes could be so angry about having his son taken away from him that he would be tempted to turn the tables on Jacob's foster family. "I'll talk to Shane."

"Do that."

Pushing her uneasiness to the back of her mind by assuring herself that Hayes had more sense than to risk anything that reckless, she glanced toward the kitchen. "Can I get you anything? A cup of herbal tea, maybe?"

"No, I'm fine, thanks. It isn't necessary for you to play the hostess. If I want tea, you've shown me where to find everything I need."

She relaxed into her chair again—at least, as much as possible with Kyle sitting so close by. "Um, Kyle…?"

"I talked to Mack today," he said suddenly, the change of topic startling her for a moment. "I called to check in and let him know what time my flight will arrive on Sunday. He agreed to pick me up at the airport."

"So you've made your reservations?"

"Yeah. I got a pretty good rate by accepting a fairly long layover. I'll take a couple of books to make the time pass more quickly."

She nodded, making a massive effort to keep her expression nothing more than politely interested. "How are Mack and Jewel?"

A little frown creased his forehead. "Mack said he thinks Jewel's coming down with a cold. But she said she's fine, and for me not to worry about her."

He would, though, Molly mused. Kyle felt responsible for the couple, as if he were trying to care for them the way their own son would have done. He was obviously anxious to get back home—and Tennessee was home to him now, she thought with a sigh. She wondered if he had realized yet, himself, just how deeply he'd already put down roots there.

"They both sent their best to you, by the way," he added. "Jewel said to remind you of the advice she gave you."

Molly smiled slightly, remembering their conversation about not letting other people run her life for her. "I'm working on it."

"I don't suppose you want to expand on that?"

"Not right now, no."

He nodded. "Fair enough."

The phone rang, and Molly reached for the cordless extension close to her chair. It was her aunt Michelle, calling to talk about last-minute party details and to ask about Molly's ankle.

Assuring her aunt that she was fine—and yes, she knew she should have asked someone to accompany her to Tennessee—Molly managed to get through the well-intentioned lecture meekly enough. She changed the subject by asking about her cousin Carly's new boyfriend. Richard Prentiss was divorced and several years older than twenty-year-old Carly, details that had given Michelle and Tony a few qualms about the relationship.

Before that conversation was over, she heard a beep that signified another incoming call. Michelle concluded her call with a promise to check in again the next day. Molly clicked over to the other caller—who turned out to be her aunt Layla, with much the same reasons for calling.

Molly listened dutifully to another lecture about how dangerous it was for a young woman to travel alone, assured her most worry-prone aunt that her ankle was healing nicely, then soothed Layla's worries about the million last-minute details concerning the upcoming party. She was finally able to disconnect with yet another promise to be careful and take better care of herself.

She glanced at Kyle, who was still reading the magazine, though she had noticed he hadn't turned a page in a while. "My aunts," she said.

"So I gathered."

"Everyone's getting a little nervous about the party. You know, the last-minute details."

"I thought you said it was going to be a casual affair. An informal outdoor cookout, at which everyone can just mingle and wish your parents a happy anniversary."

He was quoting things she had said to him, which proved he'd listened to at least some of her babbling. "Yes, that's exactly what we're planning, but you know how it is when you're hosting a party. You still want to make sure everything comes off okay."

"I wouldn't know, actually. I've never hosted a party. But I'll take your word for it."

"At least the weather is supposed to cooperate. Every forecaster I've listened to predicts sunny skies and temperatures in the high seventies."

"What would you have done if it rained?"

She groaned. "Don't even say that. However, we did have a contingency plan. The church Layla attends has a big fellowship hall that she reserved on a just-in-case basis until last week, when we were confident enough to let it go. I'm just so glad there's almost no chance of rain, so we can have the party here."

"So, how's it all going down Saturday? Last I heard, you and Kelly were still working out the details."

"I think we've got it all mapped out now. Shane's picking up Mom and Dad at the airport Saturday morning at eleven-fifteen. I hope their flight isn't delayed or anything. He'll drive them back here, trying to arrive somewhere between twelve-thirty and one o'clock. In the meantime, everyone is supposed to gather here Saturday morning to get lunch preparations underway. Someone will stand lookout while everyone else waits in the backyard, grouped around the new kitchen. We'll all yell 'surprise' when Shane leads Mom and Dad around."

Kyle looked amused. "I've participated in military operations that weren't this well planned."

"Yeah, well, there are about a zillion things that can go wrong, so we'll just have to hope for the best."

"So, how many people are you expecting?"

Hearing the slight nervousness in his voice, she gave him a sympathetic smile before breaking the total to him. "Counting children, we've invited just over sixty people."

She watched the color drain from his face. "I, uh, knew there would be a lot, but I didn't realize…"

"Well, think about it. Dad has five siblings, all of whom are married and have kids of their own. Some of those kids are married, others involved in relationships, and everyone's invited, of course. We contacted a dozen former foster boys—not counting the four here now. Counting you, nine are able to attend, and four of them are married with children. My mom's brother and his wife are flying in from Alaska for the event. A few longtime friends couldn't be left out, so the guest list grew pretty long, even though we tried to pare it down a little."

He still looked dazed. "You mean there are people you *didn't* invite?"

"Oh, yes." She sighed regretfully. "We couldn't invite many of the D'Alessandro family, except for the two brothers who married Walkers, of course, and their parents, Vinnie and Carla. We've been friends with the whole family for years, but there are just so many of them…."

"Unlike your own family," Kyle muttered ironically.

She couldn't help laughing a little. "You sound as

though this isn't a usual type of thing for us. I know you were here for some of the big barbecues in the past."

"I remember a couple of big parties, but I didn't recall them being this huge."

"The family has grown since you left."

"No kidding."

Her sympathy returned. She knew Kyle wasn't accustomed to big social gatherings. He hadn't met many of the guests who would be in attendance, and the ones he had met, he hadn't seen in years. Both he and they had changed a great deal since then. "It will be fun. You'll see."

"If you say so."

Suddenly tired, Molly pushed a hand through her hair. "As much as I'm looking forward to it, it will be nice when it's all behind us."

"I've heard you've been working on the party for a long time."

She smiled weakly. "Seems like years, though it's only been a few months."

"I guess you'll be relieved when your guests have gone home and your life is back to normal."

Reading between his words, she knew he included himself in the guests who would soon be leaving. "I'm not in any hurry for you to be gone," she answered candidly—the only way she knew how to reply.

He gave her a brooding look. "You'll get over that soon enough."

"I'm not so sure that I will," she murmured. "And what about you, Kyle? Will you get over it quickly? Or is there anything for you to get over?"

He released a long breath. "I'll carry a few new scars back with me," he admitted after a pause. "But I'm getting used to that."

A little annoyed by his response, she shook her head. Kyle was so accustomed to thinking of himself as a battered survivor that he couldn't seem to visualize himself actually coming out a winner. When someone became that accustomed to disappointment, didn't it become too easy to simply settle for whatever he could get?

Chapter Thirteen

Abruptly deciding that she didn't want to be the temporary diversion Kyle settled for, Molly squared her shoulders with a sudden surge of pride. She had pretty much done all the pursuing in this awkward affair of theirs, promising not to ask for more than he was willing to give, keeping her own desires to herself, treading carefully to avoid stepping on his ego. But enough was enough.

"It's too bad," she said, "that I never learned to protect myself as carefully as you do. Even though I knew what to expect when we became involved, I don't think it will be quite so easy for me to say goodbye as it will be for you."

He looked surprised by her sudden curtness. "I didn't say it would be easy."

"No," she agreed coolly. "You just implied that your familiarity with goodbyes makes it less difficult for you to accept."

His face hardened. "Just hope you never have to learn the way I did."

"I know you've been through some very hard times," she replied, choosing her words carefully. "But that doesn't mean you should just give up on ever having better times. Despite what you may think, I'm not talking about us, but about your attitude in general. You've become a defeatist."

He took immediate offense at the word. "I am not a defeatist."

"You always expect the worst. You sit up there alone in your mountain cabin, brooding about the past, afraid to say what you really want for your future in case that doesn't work out, either—"

"You're one to talk, aren't you?" he snarled. "Sitting here safe in Mommy and Daddy's house, letting everyone make your decisions for you so there's no chance you'll make any big mistakes on your own."

She gasped. "That is so unfair. I told you I'm going to find a place of my own as soon as…"

"As soon as you find a job close enough so you'll still be within minutes of daddy's protection."

She stood furiously, wincing when the movement jarred her injured ankle. But because she refused to show him how much her carelessness had hurt, she ignored the pain and kept her chin high. "I'm going to my room. If you need anything during the night—get it yourself. That's the way you prefer to do things, anyway."

She thumped rapidly out of the room without giving him a chance to respond. Only when she reached her own room and slammed the door behind her did she admit to herself how disappointed she was that he hadn't even tried to detain her.

Tommy looked as young and healthy as he had during their last leave together. They stood in the living room of Kyle's mountain cabin, both dressed in flannel shirts and jeans and hiking boots, ready for an outdoor adventure.

"Nice place," Tommy commented, looking around the sparsely decorated room. He nodded toward the big-screen TV. "How's the reception?"

"Not bad," Kyle replied, aware that something was strange about this conversation, but unable to decide exactly what was wrong. "I catch most of the games."

"I guess that's good—in lieu of a real life."

"Don't start with me, McDooley." Kyle crossed the room and sank into his favorite chair—only then realizing that he hadn't limped at all. He lifted a hand to his face, fingertips tracing his smooth left jaw. Unscarred. Why had he thought it should feel different?

"You think I'm going to tiptoe around your sensitive feelings the way everyone else has been doing the past few months?" Tommy grunted. "Get real, Reeves."

"Look, I've had a tough time, okay?" he snapped, though at the moment he couldn't remember what had been so bad. "And I'm getting tired of everyone implying that I've been moping around feeling sorry for myself."

"Fine. So stop doing it."

"That's easy enough for you to say. You're—"

What? *He frowned in confusion, trying to complete the sentence, but unable to come up with the right word.*

Tommy looked at him with a smile that might have held a touch of pity. "I want you to have more than this, Kyle."

"I don't know what you're talking about." Kyle glanced around the room, noticing that the place looked somewhat emptier than usual, but still nice enough. "I've got everything I need here."

"Everything you need, maybe—what about everything you want?*"*

"Like—?"

"Like someone to share it with. Someone to hold in the night. Someone to grow old with."

Kyle felt his cheeks warm. He and Tommy never talked about sentimental stuff like this. "You're the one who's thinking about getting married. Not me."

"I did *want to be married, you know. To have kids, a nice home, a relationship like my folks have. Even when I did stupid things that threatened my relationship with Connie, I never doubted what I wanted for the long run. It's what I want for you, too, buddy."*

"I suppose you've got someone all picked out for me?"

Tommy's grin seemed to brighten the room. "Dude, I've done everything but throw her into your arms, already."

Kyle crossed his arms over his chest and sank lower into his chair. "I don't know who you're talking about."

"Kyle, my friend, you're an idiot at times, but you've never been stupid. Do us both a favor and stop acting that way now. And, by the way, if I find out you're holding back out of some sort of misguided survivor's guilt—you know, denying yourself because you don't think you deserve the things I never got to enjoy—that's seriously going to piss me off. You knew me better than anyone else on earth, Reeves. Is that really what I would have wanted for you?"

"No," Kyle admitted dully. "That's the last thing you'd have wanted."

His friend nodded in satisfaction. "Damn straight."

"Tom, I—" There were so many things he wanted to say, but the words seemed to be jammed in his throat.

"I know." Tommy smiled again, more gently this time. "I know, buddy."

Kyle swallowed hard.

Tommy turned his head, as if he'd just heard something. "I've got to go. Take care of my folks for me, Kyle. And let yourself be happy, okay? If not for yourself, then do it for me."

"No, wait." Suddenly panicky, Kyle started to rise, one hand half extended in his friend's direction. "Don't go. Damn it, wait, Tom. I'm not—we haven't—Tommy!"

"Kyle? Kyle, wake up."

He opened his eyes with a gasp. He lay on his back in the guest bedroom at the Walker ranch, one arm outstretched. Molly leaned over him, her cool hand on his bare shoulder. Just as the moonlight filtering in through the thin curtains revealed her worried expression, he was afraid it let her see the moisture he felt on his cheeks.

Embarrassed, he turned his face away from her. "What is it?"

"I thought I heard voices in here. I knocked on your door, but you didn't hear me, so I looked in. I think you were having a bad dream."

"It wasn't a bad dream," he muttered, and he was telling the truth. The hard part had been waking up to the realization that Tommy had never really been there at all. That he was dead—a sentence Kyle completed all too easily this time.

"You were dreaming about your friend, weren't you? I heard you calling his name."

"Yeah. I guess I was."

"Do you want to talk about it?"

He let out a long, weary sigh. "No."

Accepting his answer, Molly straightened. The empty feeling the dream had left in him seemed to intensify when she took her hand away from his shoulder. "I'll let you get back to sleep, then."

"Yeah. Get some rest. I'm fine, Molly."

"Of course you are." She turned and moved toward the doorway, where she paused before stepping out. "Kyle? About those things I said to you earlier—I'm sorry. I shouldn't have talked to you that way. I had no right."

He started to tell her she wasn't the only one who'd given him a similar lecture lately. But because it would be too hard to explain, he said simply, "Don't worry about it. Hell, you might even have been right about most of it."

The night-light in the hallway behind her made the white nightgown she wore look sheer and ethereal. With her fiery hair tumbling around her shoulders, her face a pale oval in the dim light, she looked as unreal and as untouchable as the talking memory in his dream. "I don't have to go right now, you know. If you want me to stay."

He knew exactly what she was so sweetly offering—and every nerve ending in his body screamed out for him to take her up on it. His voice was hoarse when he managed to say, instead, "I don't think that would be a very good idea right now. Good night, Molly."

He watched her chin rise in a proud little gesture that made his chest ache. "Good night, Kyle."

She closed his door with a snap that spoke of injured

pride. And Kyle would have almost sworn he heard a man groan in sheer frustration from a far corner of the room.

Maybe it was simply an echo of his own voice, he decided, giving up any pretense at sleep as he lay there waiting for dawn.

Friday was a warm and sunny day, perfect for all the outdoor final preparations for the party. Molly, Shane, Kelly, Memo, Graciela and Kyle worked all day in the yard, setting up rented picnic tables and folding chairs, stringing paper lanterns, filling big pots with dirt and plants and arranging them around the new outdoor kitchen.

It was an early-out day for the local school district, so there was plenty of help after Memo brought the boys home. Even Lucy and Annie got into the act, trying to help, but generally getting underfoot.

The phone rang all day—various aunts, uncles and cousins confirming details, other guests announcing their arrivals at local motels and asking last-minute questions about the plans for the next day. Molly and Kelly took turns fielding calls, politely refusing offers to come help for fear that too many people would be counterproductive.

They took a break late that afternoon for a treat of ice-cream bars and sodas. Molly, Kelly, Annie, Lucy and Graciela sat at one of the two tile-topped café tables set up in the outdoor kitchen, while the guys sprawled around one of the rented picnic tables.

Molly glanced at Kyle, who sat some distance away from her, involved in a conversation with Jacob. Kyle had been helping Shane all day, staying busy enough that there was no opportunity to talk privately with her.

She suspected that he was embarrassed that she had seen him at his most vulnerable the night before, still shaken from his dream, a sheen of moisture in his eyes. She had wanted so badly to offer comfort, but he'd made it clear that he wanted to be left alone.

She wondered wistfully if he would ever reach out to anyone to help him through the hard times, or if he would spend the rest of his life alone. Maybe he would meet someone who could get through to him someday—obviously she wasn't the right one. As much as it hurt to picture him with another woman, she hoped he would find someone to love. She couldn't bear the thought of him being alone with his unhappy memories.

"Something wrong, Molly?" Graciela asked in concern. "Is your leg hurting? I've been worried that you were overdoing it."

Molly quickly smoothed her expression and smiled at the plump, kind-eyed woman whose patient smiles and prosaic manner had gentled several angry young men. "I'm fine, thanks. Just…thinking about something else."

Feeling Kelly's gaze focused on her, she cleared her throat and nodded toward the big planters arranged so artfully around the tile floor. "Kelly, I love the plants you picked out. They look perfect out here."

Still looking thoughtful, Kelly went along with the conversational switch. "I like the easy-care factor of cacti and succulents, and the nursery owner assured me these are all hardy for this area. There should be blooms by next summer."

Molly held on to her smile determinedly. "I can't wait to see them," she said, though she couldn't help wondering if she would still be living here next summer. Would she have found another place by then—or had

Kyle been right when he'd accused her of being afraid to strike out on her own? All those years she'd fussed about everyone making decisions for her—had she really allowed them to do so because she was secretly afraid of making choices for herself?

Darn Kyle for making her doubt herself, she thought with a sigh and an impatient shake of her head. For taking away some of the joy in the simple, mostly carefree existence she'd been living. For making her want things he couldn't—or didn't want to—offer.

Her cousin B.J. called after the break. Wiping her dirty hands on a towel, Molly sat in a folding chair to take the call, noting that the shadows were getting longer as late afternoon bled slowly into early evening.

"Is there anything I can do to help there?" B.J. asked, as so many others had.

"No, we've got it all under control. Just be here tomorrow. And don't forget you volunteered to bring a couple of bags of hamburger buns."

"I haven't forgotten. Is there anything else?" They chatted a few more minutes, and it was impossible for Molly not to notice how happy the newlywed B.J. sounded.

Lucky B.J., Molly thought, unable to suppress the tiniest pang of envy. Through her job at D'Alessandro Investigations, B.J. had been dispatched almost five months earlier to track down another elusive former foster boy—Daniel Andreas—to invite him to the party. She had found the undercover federal agent, all right—and during the ensuing adventure she and Daniel had fallen in love.

Daniel had followed B.J. back to Dallas, where they'd married in a quiet, simple ceremony. Daniel had joined the Dallas police department as a homicide detective. To keep the party plans secret, they'd had to make up a cover story for Cassie and Jared about how they'd hooked back up.

B.J. could be confident that the man she had brought home with her wouldn't be leaving as soon as the party was over, Molly thought with a sigh as she completed the call.

A sudden outburst from the far corner of the yard, close to the path that led to Shane's house made her whip her head around. What she saw made her grab for her cane, her heart suddenly beginning to pound.

A man with a reddish-brown ponytail and a mean expression had a grip on Jacob's arm. The man was a few years older than Shane, several inches shorter and a good thirty pounds heavier, most of the extra weight concentrated around his waist. He wore a denim shirt with the sleeves torn off, grubby jeans and heavy motorcycle boots. Jacob looked terrified as the man—his father—shouted at him and tried to drag him away.

Glancing quickly around the yard, Molly saw that Graciela was already herding Lucy, Annie and the other boys into the dormitory, though Elias looked as though he wanted to stay and help Jacob. Kelly had her cell phone already pressed to her ear—undoubtedly calling the police—while Shane and Memo, looking determined to rescue the boy, flanked Hayes and Jacob.

As for Kyle—blinking in confusion, Molly looked for him. He seemed to have simply faded into the background, disappearing from view.

Turning back to the confrontation in the corner of the yard, she saw something she had overlooked before—and the sight almost stopped her racing heart. Hayes was holding a knife in his right hand as he kept a cruel grip on this son's thin arm with his left.

Shane and Memo were also looking at that knife. Shane was talking, and while Molly couldn't hear his words, she heard the soothing, reasonable tone he was using as he tried to defuse the dangerous situation. It didn't seem to be helping. Hayes appeared completely immune to Shane's usual charisma.

She didn't know what she could do to help. She wavered in indecision, her knuckles white around the simple black cane, her other hand slightly extended in a subconscious appeal for the boy's safety. She strained to hear sirens or any other sign that help was on the way, but there was nothing.

Hayes shouted something at Shane and waved the knife. Molly choked back a scream, and Kelly talked more frantically into the phone. Her eyes locked on Jacob's pale, tear-streaked face, Molly found herself praying, wishing there was something she could do. Anything except standing here and watching helplessly as someone got hurt…

Kyle seemed to appear from out of the same nowhere he'd vanished into only moments earlier. Somehow he'd gotten behind Hayes, and he moved with a fierce, furious speed that made Molly gasp. It seemed that one moment he was leaping forward, and the next Hayes was on the ground and the knife was in Kyle's hand.

It would be a great mistake for anyone to underestimate Kyle on the basis of a few scars and a slight limp, Molly realized dazedly. There was no doubt that this man was still a warrior, battered though he might be.

Shane and Memo reacted instantly to the change in the situation. Shane threw himself on Hayes while Memo pulled Jacob to safety. The faint whine of a siren sounded in the distance, growing steadily louder as it approached.

Seeing Kyle's expression as he moved toward Hayes, Molly suddenly hurried forward, her cane thumping loudly against the ground. The danger was most definitely not over, she decided.

She caught Kyle's arm just as he seemed ready to reach for Hayes, whom Shane had pulled to his feet. "Shane has him," she said quickly. "It's okay."

Hayes had been struggling against Shane's grip, but Molly's voice made him glare her way. His eyes locked on Kyle's face, and the fight seemed to fade out of him. He wasn't drunk enough to mistake the dangerous look on Kyle's face—or the way Kyle held the big knife poised and ready.

"Look, I just want my boy," he blustered, shrinking back a bit from Kyle. "It ain't right to keep him away from his father."

Kyle spoke in a quiet, clipped tone that made Hayes go a shade paler. "You ever lay another hand on that boy, and I will personally make sure you never hurt anyone again. That clear enough for you, Hayes?"

A spark of temper lit the older man's bleary eyes. "Who the hell are you? What gives you any right to—"

"Kyle, no!" Molly clung more tightly to his arm as he surged forward again, nearly dragging her with him. "The police will take care of him."

He didn't even glance at her, his impassive gaze never leaving Hayes's face. "I can take care of him more permanently."

Shane looked at Molly from behind Hayes, his expression both relieved and bemused. "I think we'll let the cops handle it this time, Kyle," he murmured. "But thanks for the offer. If this guy ever shows up here again, we'll gladly take you up on it."

Hayes sputtered in drunken outrage. "This man threatened to kill me," he shouted at the two officers who rushed around the side of the house, prepared for trouble. "And this other one is conspiring with him."

Kyle offered the knife hilt-first to the closest officer, his expression unruffled, his voice even when he said, "We took this away from him."

Officer Rick Bulger—who'd spent a few months on the ranch while his parents had recuperated from a near-fatal car accident ten years earlier—looked questioningly at Shane. "This the same guy you've had trouble with before, Shane?" he asked, nodding toward Hayes.

"Yes, he is. This is Gene Hayes. He tried to kidnap his son, even though there's a court order forbidding him to come near the boy. And, as you can see, he came armed."

"Didn't you hear me?" Hayes yelled, even more furious now that it was obvious that Shane knew the officer. "That other guy threatened to kill me. Everyone here heard him."

"All I heard was my friend Kyle politely asking you to stop frightening the kids," Shane replied, his mouth twisting into the first sign of a smile since Hayes had appeared. "How about you, sis?"

"That's exactly what I heard," Molly seconded, still keeping a precautionary grasp on Kyle's arm.

Rick looked from her hand to Kyle's eyes, then nodded. "Okay, then. Doug, escort Mr. Hayes to the cruiser while I take a statement from these folks. I won't be long."

"I'd be happy to," Rick's partner drawled, reaching

for Hayes's arm. "Come along, Mr. Hayes. We're going to take a ride."

Hayes was still bellowing when he was led away, though he was no longer resisting the arrest. Maybe because Officer Doug was roughly the size of a minivan, Molly thought, finally beginning to relax a little.

Rick opened his notebook. "Now," he said to Shane, "you said your friend here asked Hayes to hand over the knife?"

"I took it from him," Kyle replied. "And I had to knock him down to do it, which will explain the bruise on his jaw."

Rick looked at Kyle again, then nodded. "Shane?"

Shane began to summarize what had happened. Finally feeling secure enough to release Kyle, Molly did so reluctantly, turning to check on Jacob, who was now surrounded by Kelly, Graciela and the other three boys, all of whom had been watching from the dormitory windows.

Molly noticed that the boys were now looking at Kyle with something akin to awe, and she knew he had only unwittingly reinforced their image of him as a hero.

She couldn't blame them, since she felt much the same way about him.

Chapter Fourteen

Kyle sat on the side of his bed, weariness draped heavily over his slumped shoulders. He couldn't remember being this tired in a very long time. The adrenaline rush of bringing down Gene Hayes had drained away, taking every ounce of his energy with it.

Everyone had treated him like a friggin' hero after Hayes was hauled away. He'd hated that. He'd done what was necessary, nothing more. Given the chance, he'd have returned Hayes's knife to him, point-first. Judging by the way Molly had clung to his arm, she had been well aware of that ugly fact. Which might have explained why she'd spent the rest of the day carefully avoiding looking at him.

Someone tapped on his bedroom door. Since he and Molly were the only ones in the house, it wasn't hard to guess who it was. "What is it?"

Her voice was slightly muffled by the door between them. "May I come in?"

He sighed. If he'd thought it would do any good, he'd have told her no. But since he figured she'd just keep knocking until he changed his mind, he merely said, "Yeah. Come in."

She entered wearing a soft green bathrobe over a white nightgown, and carrying a bottle of over-the-counter pain relievers and a glass of water. She wasn't using the cane, and she was walking very carefully on her braced right foot. "I thought you might need these. I noticed you were moving stiffly after dinner."

His leg was hurting from his toes to roughly the vicinity of his left ear, but he'd done his best to hide it. Guess he hadn't been very successful at it. Pushing pride aside, he nodded and held out his hand. "Thanks."

She sat on the bed beside him, her hands flattened on either side of her, her braced ankle stuck out in front of her. "Eventful day, wasn't it?"

"Yeah. Tomorrow's going to be another one."

She refused to be distracted. "Are you hurting badly?"

"I'm okay," he said after washing down a couple of the pills. "Just a little stiff."

"You moved so quickly. If you hadn't gotten that knife away from Hayes…"

"The police were on their way, thanks to Kelly's quick thinking. Hayes was too drunk to have gotten far—but not drunk enough to actually be stupid enough to use that knife on anyone. It was mostly bluff. I just called him on it."

"You're determined not to take credit for rescuing Jacob, aren't you?"

"I'm not a hero, Molly."

She touched his hand. "I know. But you're still a very special man."

"Damn it."

Her fingers laced around his. "What does that mean?"

He looked at their hands, then up at her face. "Fill in the blanks."

She lifted her free hand to his cheek, her green eyes so luminous he could almost feel the warmth of them. "You look tired."

"I am."

Her fingertips slid along his jaw, lightly tracing his scar. "Anything I can do…to help you relax?"

"Molly—" he warned, wishing his voice hadn't gone quite so hoarse.

"We only have one more night, Kyle," she whispered, her hand still soft against his face. "Do you really want to spend it in separate rooms?"

He reached for her, tugging her roughly into his arms. "No," he grated against her mouth.

No matter what this would cost him, he didn't want to spend this night alone.

He laid her against the pillows, his hands on her face, his mouth moving against hers. As she had before, she responded to his every touch with an eager delight that went straight to his ego. She could almost make him believe that he *was* a hero, he thought in bemusement. That he was whole and strong, someone who deserved the admiration of a woman like Molly.

Even as he helped her out of her clothes, he reminded himself that after this one last night, everything would go back to the way it had been before. She would forget about him soon enough, distracted by her family and her plans to find a new job and a new apartment. There would be plenty of men lined up to try to catch her attention.

As for himself—he would go back to being the broken, brooding loner she had accused him of being. But just for tonight, he needed to make a memory to take back with him when he left.

Maybe in the future he could dream about Molly and the brief time he'd spent with her, rather than being laughed at and lectured in his sleep by a ghost.

The silver anniversary party was a spectacular success. All the months of scheming and planning, all the worry and work were well worth it when Molly saw her mother's face as so many of the people she loved shouted, "Surprise!"

There was no doubt that Cassie and Jared were flabbergasted. Cassie shed a few tears, and even Jared was caught uncharacteristically off guard. They spent the rest of the afternoon admiring their new kitchen, chiding their family for going to so much trouble on their behalf and spending as much one-on-one time as possible with everyone who'd made the effort to share this day with them.

"You pulled it off, Molly. You really pulled it off." Shane shook his head in a mixture of admiration and disbelief. "I have to admit there were times when I had my doubts."

She beamed up at him, remembering the day so many months ago when she'd popped into the barn to tell him about the brilliant idea she'd had for her parents' anniversary celebration. "I couldn't have done it without you. Thank you, Shane."

He leaned over to kiss her cheek. "My pleasure. Look at them, will you? They're holding court."

Leaning against her brother's arm, she turned to look at her parents, who sat in the kitchen, chatting with the guests who were all but lined up to speak to them. "They're having a great time, aren't they? It's so good to see everyone here. It's funny to see so many of the guys with families of their own now, isn't it?"

Shane looked far across the yard to where Mark Wallace, his wife, Miranda, and the four young children they were raising together were looking at one of the gentle horses Memo had brought around for the children to ride. Other former foster boys mingled around the yard, sharing memories of their time on the ranch, catching up with the people they had known back then, introducing their wives and kids to the place that had meant so much to them in different ways. "It feels good to know we had something to do with so many of them turning out so well."

"That's what I wanted this day to be, you know. A reminder to Mom and Dad of how important they've been to so many people."

"Looks like Kyle and Daniel are catching up. They only knew each other for a couple of weeks before Daniel moved on, but they both said they remember each other."

Following his nod, Molly studied the two men sitting at a table, drinking lemonade and chatting as dozens of others milled around them, laughing and talking, children running and playing, teenagers lounging nonchalantly in clusters. As hard as this event must have been for Kyle, he'd done a good job of hiding his nervousness, she mused. As he had in the past, he tended to stay on the outskirts of the festivities, but he seemed comfortable enough when anyone initiated a conversation with him.

Her parents had been thrilled to see him, along with the other foster boys they hadn't seen in so long. Cassie had thrown her arms around Kyle, and Jared had shaken his hand warmly and thumped his shoulder in a masculine substitute for a hug. Kyle had seemed pleased, and rather touchingly surprised, that they remembered him so well and were still so obviously fond of him.

Molly had seen Jared and Kyle engaged in a long, apparently somber conversation at one point. She suspected they had talked of Kyle's wartime experience, and the painful recuperation he'd been through since. If anyone could draw Kyle out about that difficult time, it would be her father, she figured, her chest aching with emotion.

As for herself, she'd had little time to talk to either Kyle or her parents since the party began. She'd been too busy making sure everyone had enough to eat, that the large tubs of ice were refilled with canned drinks, that everyone was included in the conversations and festivities.

Her parents had demanded to know why she was wearing a leg brace and using a cane, of course, but she'd assured them—with the support of Dr. Joe D'Alessandro—that her injury was healing nicely. She promised to tell them all about it later—and she was resigned to the lecture that would surely follow her explanation of how it had happened.

"Look at Jacob." Shane nodded toward the boy who sat at the same table as Kyle and Daniel, listening to their conversation. "He hasn't strayed far from Kyle all day. He's going to hate saying goodbye to his new hero tomorrow."

That was a sentiment Molly could understand all too well. But she only said, "He'll be okay. Now that he's been reassured he's safe here, maybe he'll learn to be more trusting of you and Dad and Memo."

"I hope you're right. Because Kyle *is* leaving, Molly. He's made that very clear."

She looked at him in surprise, wondering why he made it sound as if she were in need of the reminder, rather than Jacob. "I know that."

Shane was looking back down at her with a sympathetic expression. "How do you feel about it?"

"I hate it as much as Jacob does. More," she answered candidly. "But, like Jacob, I'll get over it. You know how I am when any of our boys leaves us—I cry, and then I go on."

Shane looked at her skeptically. "That easy, huh?"

"It's never easy," she murmured.

"But this time, maybe a little harder than usual?"

So maybe she hadn't done quite as good a job of hiding her feelings about Kyle as she had hoped. Resting her head on Shane's supportive shoulder, she sighed as she looked at Kyle again. "Maybe a *lot* harder this time," she murmured.

After all, it would be the first time someone took her heart with him when he went away.

"That was so much fun. I can't believe you went to so much trouble. And the outdoor kitchen—well, it's just spectacular. Exactly what I've been wanting," Cassie raved late that evening as she unpacked bags. "I simply can't believe everyone did this."

Sitting on her parents' big bed, Molly smiled tiredly. "Everyone sort of figured the outdoor kitchen was a gift to the entire family, since we usually gather here for the big get-togethers. Michelle and Tony might have the bigger house in Dallas, but this is where everyone likes to come for the outdoor festivities in nice weather, since there's room for ball games and horseback riding and horseshoes, and no one has to worry about the kids breaking Michelle's family antiques."

"We love having everyone here. As often as possible."

"It's good to have you home, Mom."

Her once-fiery red hair now frosted attractively with gray, Cassie smiled lovingly at her daughter. "It's good to be home. As much fun as we had, we missed you all. Three weeks seemed like such a long time to be away from everyone."

"We missed you, too."

"It was so good to see everyone. All your cousins are growing up so fast."

Molly chuckled. "We had enough teenagers here to fill a couple of high school classrooms."

"Everyone seems healthy and happy at the moment. That's always a pleasure and a relief." She closed her suitcase and set it in the closet. "It was especially nice to see so many of our boys again, and to read the sweet notes from the ones who couldn't make it. They all look wonderful, don't they?"

"They do. Weren't Mark's little girls sweet? And his wife's twin nephews are adorable."

"Yes. I think they make a very nice family. I had Shane take pictures of everyone, of course."

"I noticed. Actually, there were several cameras in use all day. We'll have plenty of pictures to enjoy."

Cassie suddenly whirled, her expression dumbstruck. "It just occurred to me—is that how B.J. found Daniel again? Did she track him down to invite him to this party, the way you and Shane did Mark and Kyle?"

Molly laughed. "Yes. We led you to believe it was a coincidental meeting, but actually, she went looking for him."

"I knew there was something more to that story than she told us! It never quite added up."

"She'll tell you all the details sometime, but I nearly had a heart attack when she brought him home several months early."

"And you brought Kyle here. I still can't believe you drove all that way by yourself, but I'm so glad he was here with us. I've missed him so much."

"He missed you, too, Mom. He just wasn't sure about whether he would still fit in here after being away for so long. And he's had an especially hard time during the past year."

"I could see that in his eyes," Cassie murmured. "He told me that he was badly injured and that he lost a very close friend. But he seems to like his house in the Smokies."

Molly shook her head in bemusement that Cassie had drawn so much out of Kyle in a ten-minute conversation—and she had probably done so with such skill that he'd hardly realized he was revealing so much to her. Kyle was outside now with Jared and Shane; she would love to hear what they were talking about out there.

"He's made a good life for himself in Tennessee," she said, looking down at her hands. "A bit isolated, maybe, but he seems content, for the most part. He's certainly anxious to get back there."

Cassie gave her a searching look, as if she had heard something in her daughter's voice that concerned her. Before the conversation became any more awkward,

Molly stood, wincing a little when she balanced her weight on her right ankle.

She had overused that leg today, she admitted ruefully. Joe had admonished her several times to sit down more during the day and give it a rest, advice she had generally ignored. She was paying for that now.

"Is your leg hurting you, Molly?"

" A little. I guess I should go on to bed."

"You really should. Is there anything I can get for you? Do you need help to your room?"

"No, thanks. I've become an old pro at using the banister to help boost me up. I just need to give the ankle a few hours' rest. Tell Daddy good-night for me, okay?"

"I will." Cassie gave her a warm hug. "Thank you again for the lovely party."

Although she was glad her parents had enjoyed the surprise as much as she had hoped they would, Molly was aware of a hollow feeling inside her as she slowly climbed the stairs to her room. Maybe it was just the inevitable letdown after months of planning and anticipation, she thought. Or maybe just weariness. But she knew as her gaze fell on the empty bedroom at the end of the hallway what really depressed her.

Now that this day was behind them, there was no reason for Kyle to stay any longer. The party was over—in more ways than one.

Kyle and Shane had made arrangements to leave for the Dallas airport at ten o'clock Sunday morning. They had breakfast first with Cassie, Jared, Molly, Kelly and the girls.

Kyle didn't say much during the meal. Watching the animated interactions going on around him at the big dining room table, he remembered what it was like when he had lived here before. Always warmly welcomed into this generous, big-hearted family, but always secretly aware that he wasn't really one of them.

Molly, now, hers was a different story—he glanced across the table to where she sat laughing with her parents. She so obviously belonged here among the people who adored her. Who knew how to share their feelings, and to make sure she was happy and secure in their love. She had grown up surrounded by family, never lonely or ignored. She deserved nothing less now.

He had only a few minutes alone with her after breakfast to say goodbye. He'd gone up to the guest room to get his bag, and she was waiting in the hallway when he walked out.

"Do you have everything?" she asked, her voice rather strained.

"Yes."

She nodded and tucked a long strand of gold-red hair behind her ear, her expression pensive. "Shane's waiting for you out on the porch. The boys are there, too. They want to say goodbye."

"Are you coming down?"

"No." She attempted a smile, but couldn't quite pull it off. "I don't really want to watch you drive away."

"Molly…" He fell silent, the sizable lump in his throat choking off his voice. Just as well, he thought grimly. He didn't know what he would have said, anyway.

She stepped forward to give him one of her warm, so-natural hugs. "Take care of yourself, Kyle," she murmured into his shoulder.

"You, too," he said, resting his cheek just for a moment against her soft hair. Closing his eyes and savoring the feel of her in his arms, just for this one last time.

There were tears in her big, green eyes when he released her. He reminded himself that she always cried when one of "the boys" moved on—but it still hurt him to see them.

"I have to go back," he said jerkily, vaguely wondering who he was really trying to convince. "Jewel and Mack have come to depend on me. And, well…I belong there."

"I know," she whispered, swiping at her cheek with an unsteady hand.

He didn't add that she belonged here with her family. That was a given.

He couldn't take any more of this. Gripping his bag more tightly in his fist, he turned abruptly toward the stairway. "Goodbye, Molly."

She didn't respond. She just stood there, watching him limp away.

Downstairs, Cassie and Jared waited to see him off. It seemed wryly ironic that Jared stood by a bookshelf on which were grouped framed photographs of former foster sons. Kyle's senior portrait was among them. He had avoided looking at that photograph much while he was here. The memories tended to overwhelm him when he did.

Jared held out his weathered hand, his too-knowing navy-blue eyes searching Kyle's face. "It was good to see you, Kyle. Thanks for coming."

Kyle gripped Jared's hand, and realized somewhat disconcertedly that there was still a touch of hero-worship in the way he felt about Jared Walker. "It was good to see you, too, Jared."

"Give us a call sometime, okay?"

"I'll do that." And maybe he would. But then, again, he thought, remembering the tears in Molly's eyes, maybe he wouldn't.

He turned to Cassie then. Holding a large, sealed tin in one hand, she reached out to hug him with the other arm. Standing back then, she offered the tin. "I made a batch of cookies after breakfast," she told him with a slightly misty smile. "I remember how much you always liked them."

Damn. Shaken by the gesture, he nodded and said gruffly, "That was nice of you. Thanks."

Outside on the porch, the boys waited. One by one, Kyle shook hands with Colin, Elias and Emilio, then turned to Jacob. Jacob clung to his hand a bit longer than the others, his face twitching.

"You'll be okay," Kyle assured him quietly. "You're safe here. You should know that by now."

"Will you come back sometime?"

"I don't know," Kyle answered honestly. "But you'll be all right, Jacob. You're a decent kid, with a strong heart and a good brain. Don't screw up, okay?"

"I won't." Drawing a deep breath, Jacob took a step backward.

"Ready?" Shane asked, tossing Kyle's bag into his pickup.

Kyle shook Kelly's hand, then blinked in surprise when both the little girls threw their arms around his legs to hug him goodbye. He patted their heads awkwardly, told them to be good and then climbed into the passenger seat of Shane's truck.

As they drove away, he couldn't help but glance back toward the house, up to Molly's window. A movement of the curtains there let him know that, despite what she had said, she'd watched them drive away.

* * *

Molly sat curled in a big chair in her parents' den. A thick stack of photographs rested in her lap. One by one, she studied them, her gaze lingering on the smiling faces.

There was her aunt Lindsey, with her husband, Dr. Nick Grant, and their two teenagers, Jenny and Clay. Jared's twin brothers, Ryan and Joe Walker, stood with their wives, Taylor and Lauren. In the background of that photo, Joe and Lauren's twenty-two-year-old son Casey clowned around with Ryan and Taylor's twenty-one-year-old twins, Andrew and Aaron.

Layla and Kevin Samples beamed proudly at their grown offspring, Dawne, Keith and B.J. Daniel Andreas made a handsome addition to that family, Molly mused. Layla was already hoping for grandchildren—and beginning to nag Dawne and Keith to follow their younger sibling's marital example. Dawne claimed to be in no hurry to wed again after a youthful disaster of a marriage.

Another group snapshot showed Michelle and Tony D'Alessandro with their brood, Jason, Carly, Katie and Justin. Justin, at fourteen, was the youngest of Molly's first cousins. Carly's handsome fiancé was also in the shot, apparently making a place for himself within the family that had been so wary of him at first.

There were photos of Brynn and Joe D'Alessandro and their nine-year-old son, Miles Vincent, and of Joe's parents, Vinnie and Carla D'Alessandro, still fit and sharp in their eighties. And more snapshots of the now-grown former foster boys and their families, of food being eaten and horses being ridden, of hugs and smiles and a few happy tears.

Yet, in all those photographs, she found only two of Kyle, who seemed to have an uncanny ability to avoid the lens. In one, he stood between Cassie and Jared, self-conscious for the camera, but smiling a little, nevertheless. In the other, he sat in the background of a random crowd shot, listening gravely to something Jacob was saying to him.

Her heart aching, Molly slipped those two photos out of the pile, replacing the others in the envelope. Studying the picture of Kyle with her parents, she wondered how the pain could still be this intense even three weeks after the photographs had been taken.

She had thought—hoped, really, that her feelings for Kyle would prove to be no more than a passing infatuation, and would fade when he was no longer around every day. After all, they'd spent less than a week and a half together, hardly enough time to change her entire life, right?

Wrong. Nothing had been the same since Kyle left. Her former, rather smug contentment with her safe, predictable, sheltered existence had been diluted by the suspicions that she could have much more, if only she had the courage to pursue it.

She was living someone else's dream here, she acknowledged with a sigh. The ranch, and the group-home facilities—those were plans her parents and brother had made. She had pursued a degree in education because it had seemed useful for their plans—and though she enjoyed working with the boys, she still wasn't pursuing a course she had mapped for herself.

She had to ask herself now if her determination to live very close to her family was due to a real desire to see them every day—or to an insidious fear of moving away. Becoming fully responsible for her own decisions, her own mistakes.

She had so often used her aunt Lindsey as an excuse, reminding herself of how many impromptu gatherings Lindsey missed by living more than five hours away from the rest of her siblings. Yet now she could see that Lindsey had a good, happy life of her own in Little Rock. She loved her extended family very much, but she didn't have to be with them all the time to feel connected to them.

Of course, Lindsey had family in Little Rock, too, she reminded herself. She had been adopted as an infant by a couple with two sons, all of whom still lived in the Little Rock area. So it wasn't entirely accurate to say that Lindsey's situation was the same as Molly's would be if she…well, if she decided to move some distance from the ranch.

"Molly?" A door closed somewhere in the house as Cassie called out to her. "Are you here?"

Slipping the photos of Kyle into the pocket of the loose black cardigan she wore with a peacock-blue T-shirt and jeans, Molly rose to her feet. She no longer wore the brace, and her ankle was almost entirely back to normal—even if nothing else was. "I'm in here, Mom."

Cassie came in carrying several shopping bags. "I found the cutest Thanksgiving decorations for the dorm dining room. Little cornucopias and turkeys to set on the table, and some Thanksgiving napkins and placemats. They were on sale for a great price. I thought I'd set them out next week to get the boys into the spirit of the holidays."

Forcing a smile, even though she, herself, wasn't feeling very thankful just then, Molly said, "I can't wait to see them. I'll help you decorate the dorm whenever you're ready."

Cassie looked at her with a frown. "Are you sure your ankle isn't hurting you, sweetie? You just haven't been your usual self lately."

Which was exactly the problem, Molly thought, swallowing a sigh. "It's fine, Mom. Don't worry about it."

"Is there something you want to talk to me about?"

Cassie's eyes were entirely too perceptive. Molly suspected her mother knew something had gone on between her and Kyle, but she respected Molly's privacy. She probably assumed Molly would tell her about it when she was ready—but she was obviously getting a bit impatient for Molly to decide she was ready.

"Really, Mom, I'm okay," she said. "Let me see the things you bought."

For the first time in her life, Molly found herself unable to talk to her mother about a personal problem. Maybe it was because she was afraid that if she started to cry, she wouldn't be able to stop. Or maybe this was just something she needed to handle on her own.

Or maybe, she thought, it would just hurt too much to admit that not once had Kyle even asked her if she wanted to go back with him. Which made all her agonizing over her decision to stay close to her family a painfully moot point.

Chapter Fifteen

Two days later, Molly picked up the telephone in her room and punched in a series of numbers. She had waited as long as she could to make this call. Her eyes were focused on the photograph of Kyle and her parents as she listened to the ringing at the other end of the line.

It was answered on the third ring. "Hello?"

"Hi, Jewel. It's Molly Walker."

"Molly! How nice to hear from you. How are you, dear?"

"I'm fine, thank you. My ankle's almost completely healed."

"That's wonderful news."

"How are *you?* Last I heard, you were coming down with a cold."

"Oh, that only lasted a few days. I'm right as rain now."

"Good. And Mack?"

"Mean as a snake and twice as slippery," Jewel answered with a fond laugh that belied the joking insult. "He and Kyle are working on one of the rental cabins today. Putting new flooring in the bathroom, I think."

Molly drew a deep breath and asked, "How is Kyle?"

"He's working himself to a frazzle," Jewel answered frankly. "When he's not working on one of our places, he's fixing his own. I'm not sure he's sleeping very well—and I *know* he's lost a few pounds, even though I've been sending as much food as he would accept."

Was he pushing himself so hard because of her? Molly looked at the photograph again. Was it possible that he missed her even a fraction as much as she missed him? "Do you think he's okay? Physically, I mean."

"Physically—he's fine. Just needs some rest and some calories."

"And, um—emotionally?"

"I think maybe you'd better ask him that yourself, Molly," Jewel replied gently.

Molly started to reply that it was hard to ask him anything when she and Kyle were more than a sixteen-hour drive away from each other, and he had no phone. Instead, she changed the subject. "The reason I called was to thank you, Jewel. For your kindness and hospitality when I was hurt—and for your excellent advice about taking responsibility for my own actions."

"You're welcome. Is my advice helping?"

"I told my brother to put a sock in it today." Molly smiled at the memory of Shane's expression. "He was bossing me around about something this morning, and I let him know I don't need him to tell me what to do all the time."

"Good for you. How did he take it?"

"He got sort of mad at first—and then he acknowledged that I have the right to make my own decisions."

"It sounds as though you handled it quite nicely. Of course, you'll have to remind him a few more times before he really gets the message."

"I'm sure I will."

They chatted for a few more minutes, and then Molly concluded the conversation. Jewel made her promise to call again sometime before letting her disconnect.

"Just one more thing," Molly said before hanging up. "Would you mind not telling Kyle I called?"

"If that's what you want."

"I think it's best for now."

"Then I won't say anything."

Molly thanked her and replaced the receiver into its cradle. And then she picked up the photograph again, wishing she had the ability to read Kyle's mind through the snapshot and across the miles that separated them.

Kyle sat in his exercise room on the third Saturday afternoon in November, staring morosely at the equipment scattered around him. He wore sweatpants and a T-shirt with cross-trainers, and he was prepared to start working out—but he just couldn't seem to muster the energy.

Could be that he was thirsty, he decided, pushing himself to his feet. Usually he needed a drink *after* his workout, but what the heck. He needed to jump-start himself somehow. He'd have some juice. If he didn't start feeling more energetic soon, he might have to consider drinking caffeine again, he thought ironically.

He was halfway to the kitchen when someone knocked on his door. Probably Mack, he thought. They had said something about working on the cabin today.

But it wasn't Mack. Feeling his face freeze with surprise, he stared at the beautiful redhead on his doorstep. She wore a coat this time—a puffy, lime-green jacket that just skimmed the hips of her dark jeans. A fuchsia-colored shirt peeked out from beneath the jacket, and he noted in his first stunned glance that she wore boots. No sign of the brace she'd had on last time he'd seen her.

"Molly?" he said, finally finding his voice. "What are you…?"

He couldn't read her expression, though her emerald eyes seemed to be brimming with emotion. "May I come in?"

It was almost tempting to tell her no. He was afraid that if she came inside, he would never want to let her go again. Not to mention that he had spent the past five weeks trying futilely to exorcise her memory from his home. Now he was going to have to start that process all over again.

Instead, he stepped aside and said, "Yeah, sure. Come in."

He couldn't take his eyes off her as she crossed the room, shrugging out of her jacket and tossing it over a chair. She didn't even limp now, he noted, painfully aware of his own permanently halting gait when he followed her.

His hands clenched at his sides as he fought the urge to reach out for her. "What are you doing here? Do your parents know you've come?"

"I didn't need their permission the last time I came here, and I didn't ask for it this time. I'm an adult, remember?" She turned to face him, tossing her hair back over her shoulder. Except for her eyes, her face was smoothly composed, her posture relaxed. Only the faintest quiver in her voice betrayed her underlying nerves. "Do you remember that first time I came to your door?"

"Of course I remember." He could still see her standing on his doorstep for the first time, could still remember how he'd felt when he had seen her there. Even before he had known who she was, before he had known what it was like to touch her and hold her—even then, she had taken his breath away.

Her voice brought him back to the present. "You gave me five minutes to convince you to come back to Texas with me."

Rather embarrassed by the reminder of his inhospitality, he nodded shortly. "Yeah. I remember that, too."

"Consider this my way of repaying the favor." She glanced at her watch, then looked up at him again. "I'm giving you five minutes to convince me to stay in Tennessee."

Thoroughly confused, he shook his head. "I don't know what you're talking about."

"Then maybe I should put it in simple words so you'll be sure to understand." Her all-too-accurate mimicry of him made him wince. "I took you back to Texas with me, and you knew you couldn't be happy living there. Your heart, and the responsibilities you've taken on, are here. So, now's your chance, if you want it. Tell me why I should stay here with you."

He pushed a hand through his hair, annoyed to find that it wasn't quite steady. "This is crazy."

She nodded coolly, though he saw her swallow hard before she said, "If you aren't interested in having me stay, then there's no need to take this any further. All you have to do is say you're happy here alone, and that you would just as soon I'd go back to the ranch."

"Molly, you don't want to stay here. Your family, your job, your home—they're all in Texas. You would be miserable here."

She lifted an eyebrow. "You aren't very good at this, are you? I asked you to convince me to stay, or tell me you want me to go. I did not say I need you to make my decisions for me."

For some reason, he was beginning to get irritated. Maybe because it felt as if she was offering him just a glimpse of heaven—even though he couldn't believe he would be allowed to enter. "This is ridiculous."

She dropped her watch arm and nodded brusquely. "You're not interested. Fine. That's all I needed to know."

She reached for her coat. Kyle reached out quickly to grab her wrist. "Wait."

She looked at him with another tiny, telltale quiver in her lips. "Why?"

His tongue seemed to grow suddenly stiff and uncooperative. "Are you trying to tell me you *want* to stay?"

She shook her head stubbornly. "That's not the deal, Kyle. If you want me, you're going to have to take a few risks this time. You have to accept the possibility of rejection—or loss—or disappointment—or failure."

"You think I haven't dealt with all those things before?" he asked in disbelief.

Her voice gentled. "You've survived pain I can't even imagine, and it breaks my heart for you. But that's my point, Kyle. That's *life.* What you're doing here—keeping to yourself, staying uninvolved, protecting yourself from any more pain—that's not living. Just as my staying with my parents and letting my family make all my decisions for me wasn't really making the most of my life, either—as you pointed out, yourself."

He looked down at his hand, which encircled her slender wrist so easily. Drawing a deep breath, he said, "I can't go back to Texas with you. Jewel and Mack need me—they don't have anyone else now. And, frankly, I need them, too. Mack pretty much saved my life in Germany, when all I wanted to do was give up and join my lost friends. He and Jewel are as close as I've got to family now."

"I would never try to take you away from them. Having met them, I can understand why they mean so much to you. What you all mean to each other."

"And I know how much your family means to you."

"I adore them," she answered simply. "All of them. But they have their lives. I want my own."

"Here," he said skeptically. "With me?"

"That depends," she replied, refusing to budge. "Tell me why I *should* stay here with you."

"I don't believe this."

"You remember that advice Jewel gave me? It was for me to start making my own decisions. Examining all the facts and options for myself, and then making the choice that felt right for me. So that's what I'm doing, Kyle. I want you to give me some reasons, if you have any, why I should stay here with you. After I've heard your arguments, I'll decide for myself what's right for me."

She glanced pointedly at her watch. "You have two minutes."

Kyle was still staring at her as though she had lost her mind. To be perfectly honest, she was beginning to wonder about that herself.

It had seemed like a good idea at the time she'd gotten on a plane in Dallas. She had started questioning her decision when she had climbed into a rental car and pointed it toward Kyle's cabin. By the time she'd knocked on his door, she'd decided she was making a huge mistake—but since she was here, she'd figured she might as well go through with it.

She had needed to know once and for all if the reason Kyle had never asked her to come to Tennessee with him was because he hadn't believed she would agree—or because he simply hadn't wanted her.

She reminded herself that he hadn't said the words that would have sent her on her way, brokenhearted but satisfied that she'd done everything she could to give them a chance. Of course, he hadn't given her any reason to stay, either.

She cleared her throat. "Say something," she prodded.

"I don't know what to say," he confessed. "I'm still having trouble believing you're here."

"I'm here. And I'm waiting." She tapped her watch.

"You're waiting for me to give you a reason to stay here with me—hours away from everyone you know and love. Away from your parents, your brother, your nieces, your aunts, uncles, cousins, even your horse."

"Now you're catching on," she said in approval. "As you can imagine, it's going to take a powerful argument."

"I don't have one," he replied simply. "I can't imagine why you'd want to give up everything you have there to move here."

Her heart plummeted. Okay, she told herself. She had her answer. If Kyle had really fallen as hard for her as she had for him, he'd have at least made a token effort to keep her with him. He had to know she wouldn't have come all the way here if she hadn't wanted him to talk her into staying.

She reached for her coat again. This time, he let her pick it up and fold it over her arm. "Then I guess there's nothing more to say."

He let her get all the way to the door before he said, "I can give you a long list of reasons why you should go home. Why you deserve a hell of a lot more than anything I could offer you here."

Her hand was already on the doorknob. "I'm not interested in that list, thank you. I've pretty well figured those things out for myself."

"I couldn't list them all in just two minutes, anyway," he murmured, making no move to detain her. "There are probably a hundred reasons why you should go back to Texas. And only one reason why you should stay."

She froze, unable to look around at him, her heart starting to pound again. "That's the one I would like to hear," she whispered. "Why, Kyle?"

"Because I want you to. That's hardly a powerful enough argument to convince you."

She looked at him then, turning her head very slowly to study his somber expression. "That depends on why you want me to stay."

He started to speak, then sighed and shook his head. "I can't do this. Go back to Texas, Molly."

She sighed impatiently. "You're deciding what's best for me again?"

"Someone has to, damn it," he snapped, half turning away. "Before you end up making a reckless mistake that's going to get you hurt."

She let her coat fall to the floor, taking a determined step toward him. "You know what? I don't think it's me you're worried about getting hurt. I think this is all about you again."

That just seemed to irritate him more. "If that were true, I wouldn't trying to send you home when what I really want to do is keep you here."

"Why?" she challenged him, stepping in front of him so she could see his expression. "Why do you want me to stay?"

"Because I—"

"Why, Kyle?" she asked more quietly now.

His eyes were so tortured when she looked into them that her heart suddenly twisted. It wasn't that he didn't want to tell her, she realized suddenly. It was that he couldn't say the words. He simply didn't know how.

"Let me help you." She reached up to touch his cheek, her fingertips lingering lovingly on the scar that was merely a symbol of how much he had suffered and lost. "I think you want me to stay because you love me. You're afraid to admit it because loving someone makes you vulnerable again to being hurt. And you aren't sure you can survive being hurt again, the way you've been hurt so many times before."

He reached up to catch her hand, holding her fingers so tightly that she almost winced. His eyes were dark, his jaw so taut she saw a muscle jump spasmodically beneath his scar. "What makes you think you know how I feel?"

"Because I love you," she answered boldly. "And I think I got to know you pretty well in the days we spent together."

"We were together less than two weeks," he argued roughly. "That isn't enough time to fall in love."

"Oh." Disappointed, she let her hand fall. "I understand if it wasn't enough time for you. I suppose I was taking a lot for granted…"

"I think I fell in love with you when you stood out on my deck in the middle of a rainstorm and told me how beautiful it was to you," he said, his voice so hoarse it didn't even sound like his own. "The wind was blowing your hair, and your nose and cheeks were pink from the cold, and that same storm had stranded you up here on that mountain for the night, but you looked completely entranced—exactly the way I feel every time I look out my back door."

Joy exploded inside her. Breaking into a smile, she reached out for him.

Kyle quickly sidestepped her, shaking his head fiercely. "It's because I love you that I can't let you stay. You would never be happy here, away from your family. And I couldn't stand knowing that you would rather be there than here with me. Go back to Texas, Molly. Find someone who has more to offer you."

"Oh, put a sock in it, Kyle," she said, her smile fading into a scowl.

His expression might have amused her had she not been so annoyed with him. "What?"

"It's something Jewel told me to say whenever some smug, self-righteous, impossibly arrogant male starts making decisions for my sake because he doesn't think I'm mature enough to know my own mind," she informed him loftily. "If you want me to go, that's one thing. Have the courage to say so. But if you want me to stay, and you're sending me away out of some noble, self-sacrificing gesture for my own good, then you're going to find yourself with a fight on your hands."

He looked almost stunned, then—and she wasn't sure if it was due to the fact that she'd stood up to him, or if there was more to it. She suspected the latter when he muttered rather dazedly, "That sounds exactly like something Tommy would say."

"I think I would have liked Tommy."

He sighed. "I know you would have."

"I wish I'd had the chance to meet him. I wish you'd never had to lose your best friend that way. I wish you'd had a happier experience with your parents so you would have learned to be more trusting, and to be more confident that you deserved to be happy. But this is the hand we've been dealt, Kyle. Are you going to fold—or are you going to stay in the game and take a chance at finally coming out a winner?"

She met his eyes without flinching as he stared at her. "And if I do ask you to stay—and then you change your mind?"

"I love this area. It looks like a wonderful place to live, to raise a family. I like your friends, the McDooleys, and I would enjoy getting to know them as well as you do. I'm sure I can find a teaching job within a reasonable commute. Any time I need to see my family, all I would have to do is get into a car or hop on a plane, the way I did this morning. In the meantime, there are telephones and e-mail to let me stay in touch with them. I'm already aware of all those facts, Kyle. So now I want to hear the final argument about whether I should stay or go. Give me a good reason to stay, and I'll tell you if it's enough to convince me."

He lifted an eyebrow. "I've already admitted that I love you."

Her heart jumped in response to hearing the words again, but she continued to look at him steadily. "I know, and I can't tell you how pleased I am."

He planted his hands on his slender hips. "Still not enough?"

She shook her head, thinking that if she stayed the first thing she was going to do was to make him start eating more. He seemed to have lost weight again since he'd left Texas.

"How about if I ask you to marry me? To make a home with me here in the mountains?"

Her smile felt radiant, but still she held back. "You're getting a lot closer."

He reached out to place his hands on her shoulders, and his own expression was entirely serious when he said, "Would it be enough for me to tell you that I need you the way I never thought I would need anyone? That I can't imagine spending the rest of my life here without you? And that I'm willing to get down on my knees and beg, if that's what it would take to convince you?"

"That's what I wanted to hear," she whispered, gazing up at him through a sudden film of tears. "I needed to know that I wasn't the only one willing to risk everything—my heart, my pride, my dignity—anything necessary to give us a chance to be together."

"You aren't the only one," he assured her, tugging her into his arms. "I'm done being noble, Molly. Stay here with me. I promise I'll do everything I can to make you happy."

"We'll make each other happy," she promised against his lips. "Whatever might come, however long we might have together, we'll make the most of it, because we'll know how lucky we are to have found each other."

As Kyle's lips settled firmly over hers, sealing the promises they had made to each other, Molly had the oddest feeling that the house itself was watching them with an approval that bordered on intense satisfaction.

Very strange, she thought, losing herself in Kyle's kiss. Apparently, just kissing him made her half-delirious.

They were going to have a most interesting—and most amazingly happy—life together, she thought in eager anticipation, snuggling more closely against him.

They both deserved nothing less.

* * * * *

Silhouette®

SPECIAL EDITION™

THE BABY DEAL

by VICTORIA PADE

After a one-night stand in a tropical paradise, playboy Andrew Hanson never expects to see Delia McCray again. Three months later Andrew learns that Delia is pregnant—with his child! Can the youngest heir to the Hanson media empire find true happiness in fatherhood?

Bound by fate, a shattered family renews their ties— and finds a legacy of love.

DON'T MISS THIS COMPELLING STORY.

Available March 2006
wherever Silhouette Books are sold.

Visit Silhouette Books at www.eHarlequin.com SSETBD

SHE'S THE ONE

March 2006

After her credit card company called about suspected identity theft, Susan Pickering needed police lieutenant Brian Murphy's help. Was Susan's rebellious sister the culprit? As the questions mounted, one thing was certain—identity theft aside, the lieutenant made Susan feel like a whole new woman.

Visit Silhouette Books at www.eHarlequin.com SSESTO

MIRA®

Three brand-new stories about love—past and present

Debbie Macomber
Katherine Stone
Lois Faye Dyer

Grandmothers know best... especially these three grandmothers, all soldiers' brides. Their generation lived through war and peace, good times and bad, love and loss.

***5-B Poppy Lane* by Debbie Macomber**
All her life, Ruth Shelton has loved visiting her grandmother in Cedar Cove, Washington. Now Ruth comes to ask advice about her own romance with a soldier—and discovers a secret in her grandmother's past.

***The Apple Orchard* by Katherine Stone**
Clara MacKenzie's granddaughter Elizabeth arrives at her Oregon farm, needing comfort. That's exactly what Clara offers—and so does a childhood friend named Nick Lawton. But Nick wants to offer Elizabeth more than comfort. More than friendship...

***Liberty Hall* by Lois Faye Dyer**
When Professor Chloe Abbott finds herself caught up in a troublesome mystery, she turns to her grandmother. She needs Winifred's expertise as a wartime code breaker. She doesn't need suggestions about her love life—all of which involve ex-Marine Jake Morrissey!

HEARTS DIVIDED

Available the first week of February 2006 wherever paperbacks are sold!

www.MIRABooks.com MMSD2212

eHARLEQUIN.com

The Ultimate Destination for Women's Fiction

For **FREE online reading,** visit
www.eHarlequin.com now and enjoy:

Online Reads
Read **Daily** and **Weekly** chapters from our Internet-exclusive stories by your favorite authors.

Interactive Novels
Cast your vote to help decide how these stories unfold…then stay tuned!

Quick Reads
For shorter romantic reads, try our collection of Poems, Toasts, & More!

Online Read Library
Miss one of our online reads? Come here to catch up!

Reading Groups
Discuss, share and rave with other community members!

For great reading online,
visit www.eHarlequin.com today!

INTONL04R

If you enjoyed what you just read,
then we've got an offer you can't resist!

Take 2 bestselling love stories FREE!

Plus get a FREE surprise gift!

Clip this page and mail it to Silhouette Reader Service™

IN U.S.A.
3010 Walden Ave.
P.O. Box 1867
Buffalo, N.Y. 14240-1867

IN CANADA
P.O. Box 609
Fort Erie, Ontario
L2A 5X3

YES! Please send me 2 free Silhouette Special Edition® novels and my free surprise gift. After receiving them, if I don't wish to receive anymore, I can return the shipping statement marked cancel. If I don't cancel, I will receive 6 brand-new novels every month, before they're available in stores! In the U.S.A., bill me at the bargain price of $4.24 plus 25¢ shipping and handling per book and applicable sales tax, if any*. In Canada, bill me at the bargain price of $4.99 plus 25¢ shipping and handling per book and applicable taxes**. That's the complete price and a savings of at least 10% off the cover prices—what a great deal! I understand that accepting the 2 free books and gift places me under no obligation ever to buy any books. I can always return a shipment and cancel at any time. Even if I never buy another book from Silhouette, the 2 free books and gift are mine to keep forever.

235 SDN DZ9D
335 SDN DZ9E

Name (PLEASE PRINT)

Address Apt.#

City State/Prov. Zip/Postal Code

Not valid to current Silhouette Special Edition® subscribers.

Want to try two free books from another series?
Call 1-800-873-8635 or visit www.morefreebooks.com.

* Terms and prices subject to change without notice. Sales tax applicable in N.Y.
** Canadian residents will be charged applicable provincial taxes and GST.
All orders subject to approval. Offer limited to one per household.
® are registered trademarks owned and used by the trademark owner and or its licensee.

SPED04R

©2004 Harlequin Enterprises Limited

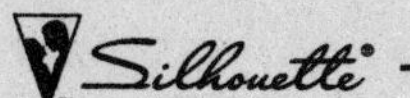

SPECIAL EDITION™

The McClouds of MONTANA

FAMILY FEUDS, BETRAYAL AND PASSION ALL PLAY A PART IN

LUKE'S PROPOSAL

by LOIS FAYE DYER

March 2006

Bad blood between the McClouds
and Kerrigans went back to the 1920s.
But when Rachel Kerrigan sought
Lucas McCloud's help to save her
family's ranch, he thought of their
fleeting high school kiss and agreed.
Now big changes were afoot in
Big Sky Country....

Visit Silhouette Books at www.eHarlequin.com

SSELP

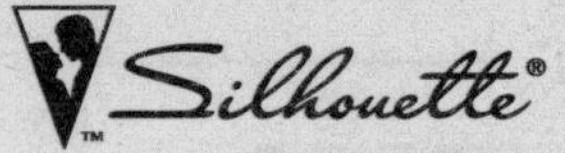

SPECIAL EDITION®

COMING NEXT MONTH

#1741 THE BRAVO FAMILY WAY—Christine Rimmer
Bravo Family Ties
Casino owner Fletcher Bravo wanted Cleo Bliss to open her on-site preschools at his resorts, and when they met face-to-face, he wanted Cleo Bliss—*period.* But the last thing this former showgirl needed was a brash, high-living CEO in her life. Would seeing Fletcher's soft spot for his adorable daughter open Cleo's heart to the Bravo family way?

#1742 THE BABY DEAL—Victoria Pade
Family Business
For Delia McRay, hooking up with younger Chicago playboy Andrew Hanson on a Tahitian beach was a fantasy come true. But what happened on the island, didn't stay on the island—for when Hanson Media met with Delia's company months later to land her account, there was a pregnant pause…as Andrew took in the result of their paradise fling.

#1743 CALL ME COWBOY—Judy Duarte
When children's book editor Priscilla Richards uncovered evidence that her father had long ago changed her name, she hired cocksure P.I. "Cowboy" Whittaker to find out why. Soon they discovered the painful truth that her father wasn't the man he claimed to be—and Cowboy rode to the rescue of this prim-and-proper woman's broken heart.

#1744 SHE'S THE ONE—Patricia Kay
Callie's Corner Café
After her credit card company called about suspected identity theft, Susan Pickering turned to police lieutenant Brian Murphy for help. Was Susan's rebellious sister the culprit? Hadn't she turned her life around? As the questions mounted, one thing was certain—identity theft aside, the lieutenant made Susan feel like a whole new woman.

#1745 LUKE'S PROPOSAL—Lois Faye Dyer
The McClouds of Montana
Bad blood between the McClouds and Kerrigans went back to the 1920s. But when Rachel Kerrigan sought Lucas McCloud's help to save her family's ranch, he thought of their fleeting high school kiss and agreed. In return, she made a promise she couldn't keep. Would her deception renew age-old hatreds…or would a different passion prevail?

#1746 A BACHELOR AT THE WEDDING—Kate Little
The oldest—and singlest—of five sisters in a zany Italian family, Stephanie Rossi had ditched her boring fiancé, and was too grounded and professional to let her heartthrob boss, Matt Harding, step into the breach. But attending her sister's wedding with the rich hotelier seemed harmless—or was Stephanie setting herself up to be swept off her feet?

SSECNM0206